DOUBLE EXPOSURE

Also by Stephen Collins

Eye Contact

DOUBLE EXPOSURE

A NOVEL

▲

STEPHEN COLLINS

WILLIAM MORROW AND COMPANY, INC.
NEW YORK

It is the policy of William Morrow and Company, Inc., and its imprints and affiliates,
recognizing the importance of preserving what has been written, to print the books we
publish on acid-free paper, and we exert our best efforts to that end.

Library of Congress Cataloging-in-Publication Data

Collins, Stephen, 1947–
Double exposure : a novel / Stephen Collins.—1st ed.
p.   cm.
ISBN 0-688-15893-5
I. Title.
PS3553.047632D6   1998
813'.54—dc21   97-42983
CIP

Printed in the United States of America

First Edition

1   2   3   4   5   6   7   8   9   10

BOOK DESIGN BY BERNARD KLEIN

www.williammorrow.com

For Madeleine and Cyrus Collins, parents extraordinaire

Acknowledgments

A second novel seems quantum leaps more difficult than a first. Huge thanks to Alice Gerstman, Sheila Russo, Fran Grossman, Pamela Stonebrooke, and Cy Collins for readings and helpful comments. Wriston Jones's ideas and suggestions were most welcome, and Janice Harbaugh not only read and gave fine notes, but offered immeasurably valuable encouragement throughout. My friends the Weaver Street Irregulars cheered me on like people at the sidelines of a marathon course holding out water for tiring runners. I thank my agent, Harvey Klinger, for his keen brainstorming on aspects of story, his ability to read a late draft as though it were the first, and for being true to his word. Stefanie Singer did more than I dreamed an assistant could, reading, ferreting out typos, and being a walking thesaurus. She was the sharpest of sounding boards for innumerable ideas during the final draft, helping me finish when I was beginning to despair.

Thanks to NYPD Detective Thomas Sullivan and former detective Mike Sheehan for advice on police procedure, to David and Kathy Bianculli for hospitality background, and innumerable insights into the life of a critic. To Reverend Anne Richards for her thoughts, to Roddy McDowell for his way with a camera and for generously sharing a title.

At Morrow, Beccy Goodhart gave dozens of helpful notes and Maria Antifonario solved many a problem. I thank my editor, Betty Kelly, for her enthusiasm, appreciation, taste, and great ideas.

I'm grateful to my daughter, Kate, ever patient during the often inconvenient times I disappeared to write. My wife, Faye Grant, was, as always, my treasured, private, at-home editor. I'm blessed that she tells me the truth even when it's not what I want to hear, and that her instincts for fixing prose are uncanny. For a host of reasons, the chief being her multifaceted support, I couldn't have undertaken this, much less finished, without her.

A STRIKING redhead in a short black skirt and sparkly yellow see-through blouse sat alone at a dark booth in a tiny, almost-empty bar on the corner of Third Avenue and Eighty-ninth Street, her eyes glued to a TV set suspended over rows of bottles. A glass of ice water and a flickering candle sat on her otherwise bare, stained table.

"We're back with our panel of TV experts," announced the news program's silver-haired host, "to talk about the winners and losers of this year's prime-time network season. Let's start with Joe McBride, from the *New York Dispatch*. Joe, can the networks survive the continuing onslaught of cable, VCRs, and the Internet?"

The redhead took a swig of ice water and pulled the candle closer.

"Yeah, let's talk about onslaughts," she whispered.

With one hand still on the glass, she slowly, deliberately moved her other palm directly over the candle, two inches from the flame, and held it there. A passing waiter slowed his gait as he took this in.

"Jesus," gulped the waiter, horrified. "Is that . . . a trick?"

The woman looked up into the waiter's eyes but didn't answer.

"Please," urged the waiter anxiously, breaking a sweat. "Stop."

"I can take it," the woman said matter-of-factly, leaving her hand above the flame. "I'm used to pain."

The waiter made a quick retreat from the booth, and the woman held fast a few more seconds before pulling away from the candle. After examining the damage, she picked up the glass of ice water, poured it over a blister that was erupting on the flesh of her palm, and rose to leave, glancing over to the bar as the TV switched to a closeup of Joe McBride.

The waiter returned, holding out an ice pack. "This'll help," he offered.

Deliberately, the redhead reached down and slowly brought her thumb and index finger together to snuff out the candle's flame.

"Sorry," she said to the staring waiter as she opened her purse. "I just couldn't resist."

She tossed a dollar onto the table and walked calmly out the door.

Working her way through the overstuffed walk-in closet of apartment 9B, the dark-haired young woman let her towel drop to the floor as she reached to touch the extra-sheer yellow blouse that hung on the rack. She ran her fingers slowly beneath the sparkly yellow material, which was so transparent she could see her fingerprints beneath it. She was dying to try it on, but stopped herself and pushed the hanger away.

"Thou shalt not covet thy sister's things," she told herself quietly as she reached instead for an oversized navy sweatshirt, black bicycle shorts, and a frayed New York Yankees hat.

There was a sharp sound in the foyer.

"Dean?" she called hesitantly. The sound came again.

After a few seconds, she realized it was only the clanking of a radiator. In early April there was still plenty of wet, chilly New York weather to come, and she resented that the building was apparently cutting off her heat again.

Rising, she caught sight of herself in an oval mirror on the bedroom wall and brightened a little as she glanced down at her breasts. She'd told the doctor to make them look just like Cindy Crawford's, and damned if he hadn't pulled it off. "You're going to hell, Amy Goode," she told herself almost cheerfully, "in the proverbial handbasket."

She finished dressing for her run, grabbed a laundry bag, and headed out her kitchen's service door. As she waited for the freight elevator, she idly fingered a crucifix around her neck. The doors opened and she was greeted by Ramón, the super, a small, stout, balding man in his late forties who smelled of ammonia.

"Good morning, señorita," he said respectfully as he taped a notice onto the elevator wall. The sight of her always brightened Ramón's day. He tried not to smile over-eagerly as he pulled her laundry bag into the elevator.

"Gracias, Ramón. Buenos días," she answered brightly.

"You always speak the Spanish so nice," said Ramón admiringly. "No sound like American. Is good."

"Shucks," she said, smiling and swatting him playfully. "How's Sammy?"

"*Much* better, miss," said Ramón, nodding his head. "He appreciates your card very well. So has my wife."

"Tell Sammy I asked about him."

"I do that, miss," answered Ramón with a slight bow of his head. "Very kind." He had always managed to keep his crush on her to himself.

She looked over his shoulder and read the sign as he smoothed another piece of tape onto it.

23 East Ninetieth Street Association
Today (Friday) from 1:30 on, a new resident will be moving in.
Access to the front and service elevators will be limited for a
few hours. Please bear with us.

"You know this TV writer man who move in?" asked Ramón. "Señor McBride?"

"I know *of* him," she said, nodding. "One-thirty, huh?"

"Sí," said Ramón. "I hope is not inconvenient."

"Of course not. Give Sammy a hug, you hear?" she said as he held the door for her. "And tell Mila I'll bring some soup later this week." Ramón, his wife, Mila, and their sickly eight-year-old Sammy, lived in the tiny ground-floor superintendent's apartment.

"Gracias. Adiós," said Ramón, beaming after her.

She started a load of white and one of colored, shoved what seemed like too many quarters into the slots, and, after using the little bathroom off Ramón's office, threw her laundry bag into a dented locker Ramón let her use, part of a row of gray lockers left from the days when the building employed a larger staff. Leaving through the basement exit and walking briskly down Madison Avenue, she spotted the morning papers on a rack outside a tiny tobacco shop. She found the tabloid *New York Dispatch,* picked one up, and flipped to the TV section, stopping at the byline of Joe McBride, who was reviewing two made-for-TV movies. Noticing that the clerk inside the store was facing away from her, she folded the paper, tucked it under her arm, turned, and walked off.

"Sorry," she said under her breath to the unknowing clerk. "I don't pay to read Joe McBride."

CHAPTER 2

Seconds before his alarm would have gone off, Joe McBride opened his eyes, rolled over, parted the rusty venetian blinds of the town-house basement bedroom, and squinted up toward the street. It was raining cats and dogs. For a few seconds he enjoyed the sound of plump raindrops falling into a puddle by the front stoop outside. Then a different sort of reality took over, as it had yesterday at this time — and his heart sank as hard as it had twenty-four hours ago.

Without warning, his fiancée had broken off their engagement two days before. A crackerjack business-affairs attorney for Paramount Pictures, Mary Beth had suddenly given Joe the word, then made a quick, dramatic exit from their duplex for a five-day business trip to L.A.

It re-ran in Joe's mind like late-breaking accident footage on the ten o'clock news. He still couldn't believe it. She'd been quiet since their alarm had gone off, but she was seldom talkative in the early morning. She'd put on gray flannel slacks, a tailored white shirt with no bra, and a black cashmere vest. Joe told her he thought she

looked too good to be leaving on a trip. Mary Beth smiled pleasantly enough, but a minute later, as she zipped up her garment bag,
with no discernible signs that it was coming, she'd blurted out,
"I'm . . . involved, I think, with someone from work. . . ."

Joe had been lying on the king-size bed of their rented Chelsea
duplex admiring the wedding invitations that had arrived the day
before from Tiffany. "You *think?*" he repeated as though she
must be joking. Her expression said otherwise. He looked at her.
She turned away. "What are you *talking* about?" he asked, feeling
as if he were in free fall. "Who?"

"I'm not . . . ready to say," Mary Beth answered as tears fell
from her hazel eyes. "I don't know if it's real, Joe. Do you really
care?"

The question left him speechless.

"You're so wrapped up chasing deadlines," she went on. "It's
like you never finish. My life doesn't stop for yours, Joe. Something's *happening* and I have to see it through." She looked sad,
but there was a clarity in her eyes that scared him. She moved
closer to the bed. "I love you, baby," she said softly, "but I just
don't think I can marry you and I'm not ready to move into a
new place together. I thought I was. I really did. But . . . I saw
those invitations last night and, God help me, I freaked out. I
guess maybe I don't know myself as well as I thought I did."

Having gotten it all out, she began to weep uncontrollably.

"I'm so . . . sorry," she sobbed, making for the front door as
Joe tried to breathe. "I know it's unforgivable, but . . ." She
fought off a new round of tears, dabbing lightly around her eyes
to staunch the flow of mascara. "Oh, baby, I have a plane to
catch. And I can't miss it. There's so much more to say. Please
don't hate me."

She spun out the door and made for a waiting limo on Twentieth Street before Joe, whose engagement ring she still bore, could
blink. "Have the movers take my things to the new place," she

called back to him, tears still flowing as she ducked into the Town Car. "I can always — I don't know — get them picked up from there." The driver sped east toward Eighth Avenue as Joe stood, bombarded by salsa music exploding from a heavily dented lime-green Camaro that was having its tires rotated by a pair of soon-to-be-former neighbors.

Now, in the drizzly dawn of Friday, two days after Mary Beth's exit, a sleep-deprived and desolate Joe tried to focus on the day ahead: moving day in Manhattan, the least mover-friendly place on earth.

He had to oversee the packing of the moving van, get to his new building uptown in time to meet the cable guy to set up his five TVs, make sure the phone guy arrived to install the phone, fax, and modem lines, and finish by eight so he could watch the premiere of a sitcom he'd been assigned to review. As head TV critic for the *New York Dispatch,* he was on deadline six nights a week, with no exceptions for moving day.

The sitcom, he'd heard through the grapevine, stunk. In his foul mood, Joe was almost looking forward to it. He had a reputation for fairness, but he saved his worst for bad sitcoms. The five TVs were for simultaneous taping or viewing, when deadlines and head-to-head scheduling of shows forced him to run three or four sets at a time.

There was a ringing in his head, a by-product of some old te-quila swigged last night while packing and trying unsuccessfully to banish thoughts of Mary Beth. Everything reminded him of her. He shook his head to clear it. The landlord had insisted he vacate the apartment by noon — another deadline.

The ringing continued at intervals too perfect for a hangover and Joe finally reached down and grabbed the receiver of the turquoise Princess phone that lay on the floor by the bed.

"Hootenanny Dog and Catbird Hospital," he answered, his throat still froggy, as he dragged on a pair of filthy khakis.

"You're there!" bellowed the anguished voice of Phil Korkes, his agent. "Thank God!"

"It's not even seven-thirty," said Joe, disbelieving.

"Listen. Brutus Clay changed his plans. He can't see you Monday. He's meeting the finalists *today*."

"*What?* I'm moving today," croaked Joe. "Are you kidding? It's out of the question."

There was a boisterous knock at the door followed by the repeated buzzing of his doorbell. Joe craned his neck toward the window and saw Dino, the moving foreman, spitting into a planter and shifting his weight impatiently on the front stoop.

"Noon. Today," ordered Phil Korkes. "Silvercup Studios in Queens. If you want the job, be there. The movers will understand."

When an Australian entrepreneur named Brutus Clay had announced a search for a TV critic with national recognition to host a weekly half-hour show for a new cable station, Joe had scoffed. But with Mary Beth no longer kicking in her share of the new mortgage, he'd shifted gears. Twelve years at the *Dispatch*, occasional appearances on NPR, and forays into syndication qualified Joe as one of the finalists.

"Who's gonna watch a TV station devoted to critics?" Joe asked bitterly.

The new station was called The Critics Channel, or TCC for short.

Phil didn't reply. Joe looked around at the mountain of boxes in the bedroom, muttering, "Since when do critics have agents? The world is coming to an end, I swear."

"You should have been a drama critic," laughed Phil. "You love to dramatize. You think Siskel and Ebert don't have agents?"

The doorbell buzzed again.

"I *was* a drama critic," Joe reminded him. For six months he'd been the third stringer at the *Times*. But Frank Rich had been number one back then, and Ben Brantley had just come on. As Joe began to see he wasn't being groomed for the top job, a generous offer came in from the *Dispatch,* so he left theater for TV, which he'd always unabashedly loved — though the grind of writing about it every day was starting to wear him down.

The Critics Channel, if it took off, might free him from the endless deadlines, the twice-yearly junkets to L.A. where networks and producers announced their lineup of shows and paraded newly signed, breathlessly excited stars — too few of whom had anything to say — in ten days of nonstop interviews Joe had to conduct.

The movers started pounding on the door.

"Just a minute!" Joe yelled, cradling the phone in his neck and buckling his belt. "Who are the other finalists, Phil?"

"Well, I hear TCC wants Caryn James from the *Times,* but she won't stoop — I mean, you know, *take* — an on-air job. And they're interested in David Bianculli from the *News.* But don't think about that . . ."

"I have to go, Phil," said Joe. "Thanks for making my day a living hell."

"You told me you need the money. Be there at noon."

He did need the money. His five-year-old daughter lived in Westchester with his ex-wife, Gayle. Mollie's private kindergarten tab alone was ten thousand dollars.

Joe called the super at his new building to remind him that he and the movers would be there at 1:30. He opened the door for Dino, whose pants seemed in permanent danger of falling down over his nonexistent hips and whose three associates looked like castaways from Captain Hook's ship. Joe pointed to the boxes, excused himself, went into the bathroom, pulled off the khakis, and took an unsatisfyingly quick shower. He dressed in his good navy Boss suit for the meeting at The Critics Channel just as Sandy Moss — whom *Rolling Stone* had recently dubbed "luscious and effervescent" — wrapped up an interview a block away and hurried across Twentieth Street, unknowingly heading straight for Joe.

CHAPTER 3

A SLIM woman with short platinum-blond hair and a black trench coat got out of the elevator at 23 East Ninetieth on the ninth floor. Her expertly applied heroin-chic makeup, accentuating fair skin, brown eyes, and full lips, could easily have caused her to be mistaken for a model. She headed toward apartment 9B and fiddled in a tiny faux Vuitton bag for her key. Ramón, who had just finished his weekly vacuuming of the hallway's aging maroon carpeting, called to her.

"Your sister not home, Miss Loree."

"Oh, yeah?" said the woman in a throaty voice with a tinge of Long Island. "Thanks."

"She do laundry and go for running, I thinking," Ramón explained.

"Of course," she said drily, turning her key and unlocking the door. "She loves her exercise." She gave Ramón a little wave and let herself in, closing the door quickly.

She made her way down the long, narrow hallway toward the

bedroom, unaware of the long-haired young man sitting quietly on the couch.

"You must be Loree," he said, breaking the silence as she walked by.

"Oh my God!" she shrieked, backing away and covering her mouth as she took in his hollow, penetrating eyes.

"Don't take the Lord's name in vain," he ordered calmly.

"Who . . . who are you?"

"Relax. I'm a friend of Amy's."

"Really?" she shot back angrily. "How do I know that?"

"I'm Dean."

She looked him over, composing herself. "Ah. The famous Dean. Well, pardon my blasphemy, but you scared the pants off me," she said, shaking her head. "God almighty."

He glared in disapproval.

"Whoops," she added unapologetically. "Did it again, didn't I?"

Dean frowned and looked away.

"Well," she said with a sniff, "this miserable sinner has to change. 'Scuse me." She moved toward the bedroom.

"Another . . . girl's night out?" he asked sardonically as she went by.

She stopped, enjoying the extent to which she had his attention. "What's it to you?"

"Amy told me about you," he said, eyeing her spiky white hair with distaste. "I've seen pictures, too. I liked you better as a redhead." He looked her up and down.

No shrinking violet, she returned the favor, scanning his flowing shoulder-length brown hair, black jeans, matching jacket, T-shirt, and wispy goatee. She liked what she saw — the slight curl to his mouth, his almost too-pretty face, the deep cheekbones — but kept it to herself.

"Amy told you all about me, huh?" she asked, slipping out of her long trench coat and revealing a tight black angora sweater.

She fidgeted for a cigarette and placed one to her lips. "Pop quiz: Which of us doesn't like smartass fundamentalists?"

"It would have to be you," answered Dean coolly. " 'Cause she likes me *a lot,* ya hear what I'm sayin'? Can I bum one of those?"

"You shouldn't smoke," she answered curtly, lighting up. "It stunts your sex drive. You've been seeing my sister for a couple of months and you think you know about *me*?" Exhaling some smoke in his direction, she added, "Lemme clear this up. You don't." She started again for the bedroom.

Dean shifted his weight. "I know that tomorrow morning, after your weekly night of slumming, you'll take the Long Island Rail Road back to Garden City, shower, and make your cuckold husband a meat loaf sandwich for lunch."

"Ham and cheese," she said flatly, moving into the bedroom and leaving the door ajar so he could see in if he chose to. "But I'm impressed you used 'cuckold' correctly in a sentence."

She whisked through the crowded rack, looking for a yellow see-through blouse. She'd bought it on impulse two weeks ago and stashed it in the closet with some of her other city outfits. She was starting to feel like it might be fun to mess with Dean.

Finding it, she moved a little out of his view, pulled off her sweater and bra, and put her arms through the sheer yellow sleeves, dropping the fancy wood store hanger to the floor as she buttoned quickly. The brakes of a bus screeched so loudly outside she couldn't believe she was nine stories up.

"I keep telling Amy she should get double-glazed windows. How can you sleep in this room?" she called out, making conversation to see if Dean was listening.

He didn't answer.

"When I'm here, I always crash on the couch. It's quieter," she added, but Dean continued to ignore her.

The Blouse, buttoned high and clinging perfectly, felt smooth and fine, like a second skin. She turned to check herself in the oval mirror.

With the shiny chartreuse pants she was already wearing, the outfit certainly made a statement. She dug out some spiky alligator shoes and pulled them on, too, tossing her lime-green jellies aside. Studying her reflection clinically, she posed another question loudly enough for Dean to hear.

"Too much?"

"Did you say something?" Dean called from the living room.

"I could use a second opinion," she answered as she stepped to the doorway and framed herself in it, facing Dean. "What do you think?"

He looked up, meeting her eyes. She took a drag of her cigarette. His face registered nothing.

"Loree," he said slowly, "you don't wanna know what I think."

"Gee, thanks," she replied, her eyes brightening as she smiled tightly.

"Your sister would look better in it, frankly," he added. "But only a whore would wear something like that in the first place." He jerked his head to one side, making a little cracking sound in his neck. "You know, since you asked."

"I did, didn't I?" she said. "Silly me. Tell Amy I won't be back this weekend." She threw the black trench coat over her shoulders and walked out the front door, letting it slam loudly.

HUDDLED in the rain under a tiny, broken umbrella fifteen minutes after the movers had arrived, Joe was overseeing the packing of the truck when Sandy Moss invaded his peripheral vision. She was almost a block away, but the cocky lilt of her walk was as unmistakable as her big, expensively coiffed hair.

A drowsy-eyed former Texas A&M homecoming queen, Sandy was five minutes into her fifteen minutes of celebrity as the flavor-of-the-month veejay from VH1. Joe had met her years before in an office when he'd gone to meet a casting agent for an article on up-and-coming talent. Possessed of the sort of shiny blond mane Joe thought existed only on Aaron Spelling shows, Sandy had walked into the place in a dazzlingly politically incorrect floor-length fur that might've made Joe re-think his stand on animal rights if he'd had one at the time.

They'd run into each other from time to time and the attraction was always palpable. Each time, too, in what Joe had come to think of as her signature gesture, Sandy would slip him her number — despite the fact that on two of those occasions she was married. Flattered, but married too, Joe had always thrown her number away. Sandy seemed fully aware of — and without qualms about — her ability to make testosterone levels jump at will. A quick study with a keen mind, she'd emerged from last week's short *Rolling Stone* interview seeming hip and showbiz savvy, succeeding in keeping just enough distance between herself and the word *bimbo*. She went about everything in her life with an unapologetic sensuality, including, as she was now, dodging puddles on Twentieth Street while Joe stood guard at the rear of the van.

It was partly Joe's blessing and partly his curse that most women found him attractive. At thirty-nine, he had clear, younger-looking blue-green eyes and a fair, mostly unwrinkled complexion. He'd gone to public school, but the way he parted his light brown hair on the side, his dimpled chin, wire-rim glasses, khakis and work shirts caused many to assume he'd gone to prep school. He didn't think of himself as handsome, and his Clark Kent–like, distracted air only deepened his charm. Smart, sure of his talent to put things into words, he was on less firm ground in relationships, which he thought should be easier to maintain than he'd always found them to be. Joe had married Gayle at thirty in the hopeless hope that marriage would create a happily-ever-after that would end his attraction to other women as well as theirs for him. Not that he was a Don Juan — he wasn't that aggressive — but he found aggressive women hard to resist.

He thought about letting Sandy pass without making contact. The day was already promising enough stress. The devil on his shoulder whispered that Sandy might be just the tonic for his troubled, jilted psyche. His angel countered with a reminder that Sandy was nearsighted, and that all Joe had to do was let her walk by.

He decided to clam up, but Sandy stopped a few steps after passing and turned back, facing him.

"Do I know you?" she asked, squinting quizzically, her VH1

umbrella protecting a yellow summer dress so short it seemed mathematically impossible.

"It's Joe," he offered. It had been a couple of years, and he was more spiffed up than usual.

"Well, so it *is*," Sandy drawled, with a slow grin, obviously glad to see him. "Hi, stranger. I was just *talking* about you! I can't believe it." She eyed the van and took a step toward Joe. "Are you . . . in the moving trade these days?"

He laughed. "Kind of, yeah. You want to do a little heavy lifting?"

"Oh, Joseph," she said, sounding pleased, her perfect teeth gleaming. "I thought you'd never ask."

It occurred to Joe that if there were still charm schools in Texas, Sandy must have matriculated. She was unstoppably winning.

"Why the suit?" she asked. "It looks terrific, by the way."

"Thanks," he said. "I've got a meeting later."

"For . . . ?"

"A job at the new C Channel."

"Oh, yeah, TCC — I heard about that," said Sandy as she wiped a speck of mud from one of her boots. "Suede," she muttered, shaking her head. "I don't know *what*-all I was thinking this morning." She looked back at Joe, who was trying to ignore the flash of uppermost thigh she'd just revealed. "I don't think a Brutus Clay–financed Critics Channel has a prayer, Joe. Don't you have loftier things to do?"

"I don't know," he said, masking his defensiveness. "I . . . thought it was worth a look."

"A look?" she shot back in a shift of tone. "I hear they're on their last round of interviews. I hear it's between you and Bianculli and somebody else."

Joe blanched. "Well," he said, caught off-guard and trying to look as though he enjoyed it. "Sounds like you've turned into a reporter, you sneaky thing."

"Why, thank you," she said, her eyes glowing. The rain, which had been easing, stopped completely, and a patch of sun broke through. Sandy collapsed her umbrella. "I just did an interview with Blair Brown," she said, shaking some hair from her eyes with a toss of her head. "She's so great."

Joe nodded. He'd spotted the actress around the neighborhood but kept his distance, as he did with all actors whose work he'd written about. He had a policy never to review people he knew personally.

Sandy shifted her weight and cocked her head at Joe. "How's Betty Sue?" she asked.

"Mary Beth. She's . . . fine, fine," he answered, taking the coward's way out.

"And your little boy?" Sandy drawled.

"Girl," Joe corrected. "Fine. She's, you know, with her mother."

"It stopped raining, Joe," Sandy whispered with a glance at his umbrella, which was still over his head. He pushed a button and it collapsed with a snap, taking a small piece of skin from his index finger. He pretended that nothing had happened so as to maintain a semblance of cool.

"You and I have amazingly bad timing," she went on, shaking her head and looking at him with a wouldn't-you-know-it expression. "My divorce was just finalized."

"Oh — I'm sorry," he replied, keeping an eye on two movers who seemed to be juggling his computer monitors onto the truck. "Guys! Hey! Those're worth more than I am." Poker-faced, the movers made a show of sliding the hefty screens delicately up and into the rear of the van.

"I'm thrilled to be free," said Sandy brightly. "Marriage number two was worse than the first."

"Ah," Joe said, fumbling, "well." He was, he realized, technically available. He glanced down, taking in the impossible shortness of her dress, her long, tanned thighs, calves dew-dropped from the rain, her almost annoyingly sexy suede cowboy boots.

Mary Beth would have called her a fashion victim, but it was a man/woman thing: The look was not without appeal.

"Can I meet Mary Beth?" asked Sandy, peering toward the open door of the brownstone.

"She's in L.A. on business."

"Smart gal," said Sandy. "Leaving the move to you. I like her!" Joe tried to laugh. Mary Beth, he figured, was by now huddled with the Viacom brass, no doubt looking hot in her best Armani, sipping three kinds of designer water in some plush meeting room at the Bel Air Hotel. "Well," said Sandy, "I'll let you get to it." She handed him her umbrella, opened her purse, took out a small pad and pen, and started writing. "Moving is hell," she murmured. "Why don't you call over the weekend? I'll bring you chicken soup or Chinese or . . . something. I'm very good at unpacking boxes." Keeping her record intact, she scribbled her number, ripped off the paper and palmed it to Joe, who stuffed it into a pocket and handed back her umbrella.

"Y'all take care of yourself, now," said Sandy. She started away, flipping her umbrella in such a way that Joe figured she must have been a twirler back in Texas. She stopped and turned back to him. "Call me," she suggested as though strictly on the up-and-up. "I won't bite — unless explicitly ordered to do so." She pivoted and walked on. Joe stepped back to the waiting movers.

"I wouldn't mind gettin' bit by the likes of that," Dino muttered, spitting on the sidewalk. Joe laughed nervously, his hand fingering the slip of paper with Sandy's number. He started to crumple it to toss into a nearby Dumpster.

But this time he didn't.

CHAPTER 5

FINISHING her stretches as she prepared for her run, she checked her watch. It was 11:30. In two hours Joe McBride was due to move in and she wanted to see him in the flesh. I'll have a cup of coffee, she thought, and read his reviews.

Then she stopped, remembering: the puzzle.

She smacked her forehead in disgust, turned, and headed back to her building.

Inside her apartment, she tiptoed by Dean, who'd fallen asleep on the couch, opened the puzzle box, and quickly spread its black-and-white pieces onto the glass-topped coffee table, worried now that it wouldn't be finished in time.

"Wake up," she called. "We forgot the puzzle."

"Hi," said Dean, brightening at the sight of her as he opened his eyes. "Did you run?"

"Not yet," she said, finding a corner piece and placing it on the table. "I'll go later."

"Okay," he said, yawning. She was less skittish when she exercised regularly. "What's so important about a puzzle?" he asked, picking up a piece halfheartedly.

"I just want Loree to see it finished, that's all. To see the look on her face."

"She stopped by."

She exhaled sharply, displeased. "I knew it."

"And I think you're crazy," Dean went on soothingly. "You're so much . . . I don't know . . . prettier."

She worked the puzzle for a moment before speaking. "Did she . . . ?" She stopped.

Don't, she told herself.

"What?"

"Did she . . . hit on you?" she asked compulsively, afraid to hear the answer.

"No," he assured her, half lying. "She waltzed in, changed her clothes, and shot out of here. Said she wouldn't be back this weekend."

She walked into the bedroom and saw a wooden hanger on the floor by the closet. She knew it was the one that had held The Blouse. The alligator shoes were gone, too. She took a breath, collected herself, and moved back into the living room. She knew as well as she knew her name that Dean had seen Loree in The Blouse.

He looked up into her eyes as if he understood what she was thinking. "She's got nothing on you," he said.

She smiled. Sweet, she thought, studying the lips that had performed such wonders the past few weeks.

"How do you know me so well?" she asked.

"You're pretty transparent," Dean answered simply. "You've been worried about me meeting her. Don't deny it. I mean, sure — she's something. But let's face it — she's, like, the devil." His face hardened. "She's an adulterer, she's a — "

"She's my sister," she said, cutting him off. "Let's have no more judgment on her. You passed the test."

"I want *you*," he declared, opening his arms to her. She moved to him and nestled her head on his shoulder.

"Bless you," she said.

The rain started and stopped again but the humidity was climbing relentlessly. Joe checked his ancient Timex. It was 11:30, time to leave for his interview at The C Channel. He went inside for a last once-over. It looked as though a hand grenade had gone off recently. He scanned the rubble, glad to leave behind Mollie's battered, outgrown Playskool kitchen stove, an assortment of unmatched socks, a bent fireplace poker, and a broken Cuisinart. One of Dino's henchmen disinterestedly tossed an assortment of Mary Beth's knickknacks into a box.

"I've got an appointment," Joe announced. "You guys still have plenty to do and it'll take you a while to get the van to the Upper East Side. If I time it right, I should be able to meet you at the new place at one-thirty. Okay?" He gave them a big, hopeful smile.

"What's to keep us from driving away with all your stuff?" Dino asked in a friendly way.

Joe peeled a much-needed twenty out of his weary wallet and glumly handed it to Dino. "I'm sure you'll take good care of me," he said unsurely, bending down and picking up a favorite lost picture of Mollie that had resurfaced when the bureau had been moved.

Joe handed the picture of Mollie to Dino, who wrapped it in newspaper and tossed it into an open box with some software manuals, a bottle of Windex, and two extension cords. Too distracted to correct Dino's filing system, Joe wiped the perspiration from his forehead, went out, and hailed a taxi, feeling that his life was, in its well-scheduled way, utterly out of control.

The cab stalled at 11:55 in the middle of the only open lane of the Fifty-ninth Street Bridge. Joe's C Channel appointment was for noon.

*　*　*

Dean was in the kitchen running water for coffee. As she worked the puzzle she began to feel frantic, unable to get even a corner started.

"McBride!" she cried out, swiping the pieces to the floor.

"What?" Dean called, shutting off the faucet.

"Nothing," she said, recovering, looking down at the mess. "It's nothing, never mind." She ran her fingers through her hair and took a deep breath. "Remember what the sisters used to say," she whispered to herself. " 'Don't give up five minutes before the miracle.' Concentrate. You can do this."

She got to her knees, genuflected, gathered up the pieces, and started the puzzle again.

Joe looked at his watch. It was 11:57. Hundreds of following cars blared their horns as though their collective honking might restart his Iraqi driver's reeking and obviously unmaintained cab. The appointment with Brutus Clay and The C Channel was in jeopardy and since this was not an acceptable option to Joe, he did what he usually did under such circumstances. He became hysterical. The driver, whose hack license revealed a name devoid of vowels, got out and attempted a perfunctory look under his foul hood while Joe peered ahead, made useless grunting noises, and pounded his fist on the cab's unupholstered ceiling.

Gayle had divorced him for "mental cruelty," much of which, she always claimed, occurred when they were trying to get somewhere on time together. His neuroses flew to the surface when he feared he might be late. He'd tried biofeedback and been hypnotized, but the only thing that calmed him was thinking of his daughter, so he closed his eyes while Cszmd, his driver, groped under the hood. It had been two weekends since Mollie's last visit, before the breakup with Mary Beth, who'd gone to her office that day to give Joe and Mollie some time alone.

"Let's watch TV," Mollie said when they got to Joe's place.

"Does Mom let you watch a lot of TV?" Joe asked, trying not to sound as if he cared.

"Mommy says *you* watch too much TV," returned Mollie, throwing her mittens on the floor and pushing the on-off button of Joe's largest Sony with her big toe.

"I do," Joe admitted. "But I get paid for it."

Mollie grabbed the clicker. "Let's see what's on Showtime," she said.

She expertly tuned the cable box to channel 37, where a mostly naked young couple kissed hungrily, the actress's breasts pressed into the guy's perfect pecs. After a stunned delay of a few seconds, Joe snatched the remote from her.

"I've seen this," he said, changing the station with feigned non-chalance. "It's really boring." On the Disney Channel a *Gummi Bears* re-run was mercifully in progress. Mollie didn't protest.

"Does Mommy let you watch Showtime?"

"Sometimes I sneak a peek," she said. "When she and Brian are watching."

"Brian?" he asked, still managing to sound disinterested.

"Yeah," said Mollie, reclining on her side and feeding herself pretzel Goldfish the way Cleopatra might feed herself grapes. "He brings me presents."

"What kind of presents?" Joe ventured after a minute or so.

"A Barney," she said, making a face of big-girl disapproval. "I'm *so* over Barney."

Thoughts of Mollie were interrupted by a fresh attack of honking from the legion of frustrated drivers behind him. Joe looked out the dirty window and spotted a little nook ahead, a slight widening of the lane about twenty feet beyond that promised enough room to fit the cab so that traffic might pass. He tried to lower the window, but it stuck less than halfway down. He turned his head sideways, managing to squeeze most of his face through.

"Put it in neutral!" he yelled to Cszmd, who lowered the hood a little and looked at Joe.

"No English!" he declared proudly, disappearing again, pulling wires and senselessly probing the workings of the overheated engine. Joe climbed over into the driver's seat, took off the emergency brake and pulled the gearshift to "N." The car lurched slightly forward, enough to scare Cszmd, who slammed the hood shut as if it were the final flourish of some great symphony for orchestra and engine cover. He fixed Joe with fury in his eyes. There was, Joe felt sure, a strain of madness in Cszmd's family. Keeping one hand on the wheel, Joe opened the door and started walk-pushing the car toward the little shoulder ahead.

"What you do?" Cszmd screamed as though Joe had stolen his young. He moved to the other side of the car and watched as Joe navigated the cab into the little space. A family in a Escort wagon behind them applauded. Joe began to perspire through his blue summer suit. He wondered how Brutus Clay would feel about on-air hosts with sweat stains.

The instant the cab was out of the way, cars that had been stuck behind them began to squeeze through. The Escort went jubilantly by, its inhabitants yelling, "Thanks!" as they rolled on toward Long Island City. Cszmd approached Joe with his hand out.

"Six-eighty on meter," he said with a suddenly solicitous smile.

"Does the phrase 'Blow it out your ass' mean anything to you?" Joe asked as he turned and began jogging toward Silvercup Studios, a half mile away.

After a few wrong turns down treeless boulevards of derelict warehouses, he arrived, dripping like a marathon runner, at the main entrance to Silvercup, which had housed a bakery before being converted to a TV and film studio. It was already 12:19. Joe rushed to the main desk.

"Brutus Clay, please," he said with importance. The receptionist, a uniformed security guard, seemed irritated that someone was keeping him from his newspaper, which Joe noted with useless pride was the *Dispatch*.

"Brutus Clay?" the guard asked, as though Joe had said something stupid. "They's no Brutus Clay here."

"With The C Channel," Joe added as though to clear it up.

"C Channel?" the guard grunted, shuffling through some well-worn lists on his desk. "What's that? You mean The Food Channel?"

"No," Joe said, resisting the impulse to point out that 'food' doesn't begin with a 'C.'

"That's not F/X, is it?" the guard asked. "Or The Talk Channel?"

"C Channel," Joe repeated, now wondering if he was in the right place. "The Critics Channel."

The guard punched four numbers on one of his phones and waited.

"LaToya — we got a Critics Channel here?" he asked. "Oh, yeah? Really?" He hung up and dialed again, simultaneously turning a register book in Joe's direction and offering his pen. "Sign in. Take the elevator to three. Someone'll meet you."

At the third floor a breathless, bespectacled young Asian man with a shiny shaved head appeared from around a corner, a clipboard in one hand and his other extended. Calm, graceful, yet full of energy, he was dressed in crisp green chinos and a starched pink button-down shirt.

"Mr. McBrider?" he asked.

Joe nodded. "McBride," he corrected.

The man consulted his clipboard. "We have 'McBrider,' " he said uncertainly.

"McBride, McBrider, McBridest," Joe said, amazed that he could attempt a useless joke while sweating too much to make a good impression on anybody.

"Sorry," said the young man as though he hadn't heard Joe. "I'm new here. Everybody is. I'm David Teng."

"And what do you do, David?" Joe asked as they moved down a long corridor.

"I'm Mr. Clay's assistant, head of talent, and program manager," he answered. Joe looked surprised. "We're starting small," David explained, grinning. "But we'll be available in eight million households the first week we're on the air. Which is very soon. Right this way. Mr. Clay is waiting. He hates that."

He led Joe though an utterly nondescript, absolutely undecorated, freshly painted corridor. It smacked of nothing. It made no impression, but twisted and turned past a host of industrial red metal doors with aluminum knobs. There were no windows anywhere. David Teng paused outside a door. A Rolodex card Scotch-taped to it read BRUTUS CLAY.

David opened the door, admitting Joe to a large office with a gray metal desk, one chair, and not another trace of furniture or decor. A small man stood with his back to them. With a pencil, the man was drawing a large rectangle on the wall behind the desk.

"I want a window here, Teng," said the man, who didn't turn around, and whose nasal, high-pitched voice seemed at war with his Australian accent.

"That's a bearing wall, Mr. Clay. I don't think we can do that," replied David Teng.

"Then have the art department *draw* me a window — with a nice view of Manhattan. Where *is* the art department?" He put a few flourishes on the imaginary panes.

"Well, sir," said David, his whole head blushing. "For the time being, I'm the art department."

"Nonsense," said Clay. "Who's building our sets? We have sets. I've seen them." With a few confidently placed strokes, he'd penciled in a nice impression of the New York skyline.

"I have Mr. McBrider — McBride! — I'm sorry. Mr. *McBride* to see you."

"Why didn't you say so?" demanded Brutus Clay, who turned

to face Joe. He was barely five feet tall, looked more like a dentist than a producer, and couldn't have been much past thirty. He wore an expensive green three-button Italian suit and incongruous alligator cowboy boots of a magenta tinge with brass studs on the toes — at which Joe didn't realize he was staring.

"They're eighteen-karat gold, since you're wondering," Brutus Clay said amiably. "That'll be it for now, Teng."

Joe was thinking that he'd probably wasted his time.

"On the contrary, Mr. McBride," said Clay without Joe's uttering a word. "This is exactly where you should be. You'd have to be an idiot not to be thinking you're in the wrong place, and I didn't get rich hiring idiots. I like a man who sweats! Now tell me: What do you think about TCC?"

Reminding himself of Mollie's tuition and the new mortgage that was in his name alone, Joe cleared his throat.

"Well, Mr. Clay — "

"Call me Mad Dog," Brutus said pleasantly.

Joe's eyes widened. "Oh. A . . . nickname?"

"I always wanted to see what it would be like to be called 'Mad Dog,' " Clay explained amiably. "Give it a shot, if you will."

Joe couldn't help himself. He laughed. Not a rude laugh, but a sort of release, which Clay didn't seem to mind in the least.

"Okay . . . Mad Dog," Joe ventured.

"Love it!" Clay said, beaming. Then he stopped himself and turned serious. "Go on, go on."

"What do I think about The C Channel?" Joe repeated, playing for time.

"Exactemente!" said Clay, whose every word seemed surrounded by exclamation points. He was the most enthusiastic man Joe had ever met.

"Well, sir . . . Mad Dog," Joe began. "May I call you 'Sir Mad Dog'?"

"Why not!"

"Well, Sir Mad Dog," Joe continued, fighting off another

chuckle, then giving in to it. "I think it's simple. If viewers can expect a good time, they'll tune in."

"Exactissimo!" said Clay as though Joe had solved a centuries-old riddle. "You think you can give them a half hour they can't get anywhere else? A half hour that *you'd* watch? Because if you can, I'm prepared to put you on the payroll and you'll be on the air in less than two weeks. What do you say?"

Joe hesitated.

"Who *am* I, you're wondering?" Clay went on. He caught Joe's look of surprise. "Of course you are! I'm a kid from Melbourne who came into a lot of money — and I want to win a bet."

"A bet?" Joe asked.

"I wagered my father ten million Yankee dollars that I could get Americans to buy anything. We were sitting around drinking too much of our fine beer one night, and we started joking about bad entrepreneurial ideas. I came up with flat-chested Barbies, he countered with a magazine for drug addicts, I suggested something called 'Electric Sand' — I won't bother explaining — and then we tossed around cable TV ideas. I said the American public will accept anything — anything! — in the way of a cable TV channel. He suggested the Demolition Channel, where guests compete to see who can demolish the most expensive things — which I thought was actually quite a sellable idea. In fact we're looking into a theme park where people can plunk down money, take a nice sledgehammer and break some really high-ticket luxury items — cars, big TV's — all the things they covet but can't have in real life. But I'm getting ahead of myself. When I came up with TCC — 'all critics, all the time' — Dad said, 'You're on.' I wish he'd said, 'Mad Dog, you're on,' but Dad would never play along like you, which is probably why fate has thrown us together, and why you're going to accept my offer of $75,000 for the first thirteen weeks of hosting *Everybody's a Critic*. It may have started as a joke, Mr. McBride, but let me assure you I'm absolutely serious about it now."

Joe was still catching up, which Clay took for reticence.

"Eighty thousand. That's my final offer or I go with the guy from the *Daily News*. Bianculli. I hear he wants this."

It was 12:42 and Joe had barely enough time — assuming he could find a cab that didn't break down — to reach his new apartment and meet the phone man.

Clay turned and began to fill in his wall drawing. "You'll be doing what I'm doing now, McBride — making something out of nothing. It doesn't have to be cheap or vulgar, though I certainly don't mind a bit of that. I know you have a reputation to maintain in the print world, but you're not one of those critics who looks down his nose at entertainment, are you?"

"Not at all," Joe replied.

"We're a tiny operation. You'll have a skeletal crew, simple sets, and jealous peers may crucify you for jumping to the other side of the lens."

"Mr. Clay," Joe said. "I think I should run this by my agent."

"By all means! Would you like some privacy?" Clay started to move out of the room. "Just dial nine," he said at the door. "I want your decision in five minutes." And he was gone.

Joe picked up the phone and dialed Phil Korkes, who was at lunch. He hung up and turned it over in his mind. Clay was eccentric but on the level, and had even inadvertently jacked up Joe's price.

David Teng walked into the office.

"Mr. Clay sends apologies. He was called away. Forgive me, but he told me to . . . demand your answer." Looking sheepish, David held up his watch and added, "You have thirty seconds."

Joe let a few seconds tick by, as though David's day might be bolstered by a little suspense.

"Tell Mr. Clay . . . the answer is yes."

"In that case," said David, breaking into a relieved smile, "welcome! Mr. Clay said you should be here at eleven sharp Monday morning. Please excuse me. We have to fly to the coast and back this weekend." He shook Joe's hand, bowed his head almost imperceptibly, and took his leave.

Joe dashed down the corridor to the elevator and rushed out of the building. It was raining hard and he realized he'd left his umbrella in Czsmd's cab. While he looked up and down the wet, empty street, a chauffeur got out of a preposterously long white parked limo and tipped his cap.

"Mr. McBride?" he ventured.

"That's me," Joe said.

"Where to?" the chauffeur asked, holding the back door open as if he didn't mind getting soaked.

"There must be . . . another Mr. McBride," Joe insisted.

"The critic?" the driver inquired. Joe nodded. "Mr. Clay said to take you wherever you need to go."

Joe got in gratefully. There was a small TV and a host of empty crystal decanters.

"Mr. Clay said to tell you not to get used to this," continued the driver as they sped toward Manhattan. "It's a one-time-only thing. Where to?"

An attack of heartsickness over Mary Beth struck, dampening Joe's excitement about the new job. At least, he thought, I still have a chance to meet the telephone man on time.

"Twenty-three East Ninetieth Street," he said, flipping on the TV, which didn't work.

"I didn't say it's over," she explained to the disbelieving Dean, who stood at her doorway as though he'd never leave. "That's not what I said at all."

"But — this is, like, completely out of the blue."

"I just . . . I don't know," she stammered, fingering her crucifix nervously. "I need some time to think."

"You didn't need to think last night," he countered bitterly.

"Oh," she said sadly, shaking her head. "Last night was wonderful. It's always wonderful, Dean." The fire in his eyes only made it worse, but she pressed on. "I'm sorry. You're . . . a beautiful man, Dean. And it's hard for me to say this, but I'm just not sure about . . ."

She faltered.

"About what?" he asked helplessly.

"You frighten me," she said simply. He looked bewildered. "*We* frighten me. You do drugs sometimes, don't you?"

He started to protest.

"I *know* you do, Dean," she pressed on. "I sometimes counsel people against drugs and it would be hypocritical of me not to tell you this: I can't have drugs in my life. I can't. There. I said it." She was shaking and he looked stunned. "I want to settle down, *remember,* and raise a family," she added. "I'm sorry. I have no right to tell you how to live your life."

"I'll quit," he said simply. "I love you. What else do I have to do?"

"It's not necessarily a question of *doing* anything, but for starters, you could get what I asked you for. What you promised."

"Okay, okay, I'll work on that," he said. "If it means that much to you."

She brightened a little and it made him feel suddenly on top of the world. "That would show me a lot," she said, smiling warmly. "I think I'd feel safer."

"Why? Is that guy stalking you again?"

"I think he was following me the other day."

"Why didn't you say something?" he asked.

"I didn't want you to worry. Maybe it's nothing. I don't know. But I think you're right. I need to protect myself and I'd just feel safer if . . ."

"Done," he said, reaching for her hand.

"No. Don't," she scolded, pushing him away, stirred, as always, by his touch. "I'm sorry. I need you to give me a little space. This has all happened so quickly. We've barely been apart the past few weeks. I need some time for *me*. Can you give me that?" He looked heartsick. "I'm sorry, Dean, but I really need it."

He took a deep breath as if to collect strength. "God brought us together for a reason," he said as he opened the door. "I can give you anything. Even solitude."

"Wait," she said. She went to the door, stroked his face, and joined hands with him, looking up into his eyes. "Dear Father," she prayed, "bless us in what we do." She stood on tiptoes, gave him a little kiss on the side of the mouth, and gently pushed him out the door.

She heard the elevator, peered through the peekhole to be sure he was gone, and looked back at the barely-begun puzzle.

Oh well, she rationalized, maybe it's better left undone.

She took the elevator down and pushed through the two front doors, catching a glimpse of Dean as he ambled east. She felt a mixture of sadness and relief. He adores me, she reminded herself. I don't have to have it figured out today.

It was 1:10. A number five bus blew by with an ad for the *Dispatch* on its side featuring a smiling Joe McBride. She wondered if he was as cute in real life. Not minding the rain, she turned west toward the park and finally broke into her workout jog with the certainty that she was twenty minutes away from taking fate into her own hands.

CHAPTER 7

TWENTY-THREE East Ninetieth Street was a ten-story, eighty-year-old brick building between Madison and Fifth Avenues with granite Doric columns on either side of an imposing wrought-iron-and-glass front door. Its apartments were still exorbitantly priced by any commonsense standards, but the fact that it no longer had a doorman had made it affordable for Joe. At 1:30, Dino and the boys were trying to find a place to park the van at Madison and Ninetieth. The intermittent rain was back and there was no sign of the phone man. Joe swatted some wetness from his shirt, pushed the outer door open, and worked his key into the second of the building's two locked front doors. He glanced at the clean marble lobby, which sported a few well-intentioned quasi-antiques in an attempt to lend it some of the grandeur it had enjoyed in the days when a white-gloved concierge had greeted all visitors. A woman drifted in behind him. Joe's attention was on the movers, but some sort of wired-in, automatic radar registered "attractive." He turned sideways and let her pass by, then called back to Dino, "Buzz the intercom when you're ready. I'm in ten D."

He turned and followed the woman across the black rubber runner that protected the marble floor of the lobby from rainy shoes, arriving at the elevator a few paces behind her. She pushed the up button. When the elevator didn't come right away, Joe pushed the button too — twice, hard, unable to restrain himself, as if the pressure of his thumb might make the elevator come faster.

"I don't know why I did that," Joe said awkwardly. She smiled. Nice lips, he thought.

Immediately attracted, he cautioned himself against rebounding too soon from Mary Beth, then chided himself for presuming that anything might happen with a woman who hadn't even spoken to him. His pulse, defying common sense, beat a little faster. And she wasn't even looking at him.

She'd apparently been running. She wore black stretch running shorts and a soggy navy sweatshirt pulled down over her hips that made it difficult to get a reading of her body. Her sweatshirt read ST. SEBASTIAN in gray block letters across the front and she wore a small gold crucifix around her neck. Her light brown hair was tied up under a New York Yankees hat, with a rain-drenched ponytail popping through the hat's rear opening. She was into her thirties, and there was a complicatedly attractive edge to her, something hemmed in and restrained, almost severe, as though through inner discipline she'd harnessed her animal energies. Brown eyes, high cheekbones, those lips. She was perspiring but looked healthy and flushed, he thought, like the girl next door after a morning of study and exercise. They got into the elevator. She pressed 9, he pressed 10.

"I guess we're neighbors," he offered as they began a slow climb.

Don't be a jerk, he warned himself.

"You're moving in?" she answered, friendly enough. "Great."

"Ten D." He nodded.

"Oh, I'm sorry." She covered her face and laughed as though embarrassed for him. With a disarming smile, she added, "You're on the wrong elevator."

He *is* cute, she couldn't help thinking.

Joe blinked.

"This elevator only serves the A and B apartments," she explained.

"Oh — right," he said sheepishly. "I forgot. There's a different one for the C and D apartments, isn't there?"

She nodded and pressed L for him. "Did you buy your place?" she asked.

"Well, yes," he answered. "Doesn't everybody own in this building?"

"Everybody but me," she said. "I'm the last of the renters. The co-op board doesn't like it, but frankly," she added almost cheerfully, "I can't afford to leave. And with prices around here, I can't afford to buy my place."

"I know what you mean," offered Joe, who wasn't sure he could afford his place either.

"Well," she went on as the elevator slowed, "when you get back down to the lobby, *your* elevator is right across from this one." She was grinning. "I'd say you can't miss it, but apparently you can. You walked right by it."

The doors opened at 9.

"Thanks," he managed, still feeling foolish. "I'm Joe McBride." He shrugged and raised his eyebrows, trying to think of what to say. "Let's go Yanks!"

She looked blank.

"Your hat," he explained.

"Is this a Yankee hat?" she asked, taking off the cap and looking at it as though she'd never seen it before. Light brown hair fell flatteringly around her face. Every move she made seemed to compliment her. "I know absolutely nothing about football."

"The Yankees are — "

"I'm kidding," she said, shaking her head. "I know the Yankees are a baseball team, but that's about it. I just like the hat. Anyway, I'm Amy Goode." He nodded. She smiled and added, "That's 'Goode' with an 'e.' "

"Well then," he said, "we have something in common. My name has an 'e' at the end, too." He inwardly screamed at himself to shut up as she nodded politely.

They shook hands. Her fingers were long and graceful and her grip was firm. Holding the elevator door open, she seemed almost genteel, like an aristocrat somewhat down on her luck.

"If you have your service door key," she said, "I can save you a trip down to the lobby." Joe looked confused. "You can get to your apartment through mine," she explained. "Out my back door, up a flight, and into *your* back door."

Joe remembered that the four service entrances on each floor shared a common area around the back stairway and utility elevator.

"Thanks," he said, following her. "That's very kind."

"My place is a mess," she cautioned, opening her door and motioning him in. She started to pull off her wet sweatshirt, revealing a few inches of taut flesh above her waist as Joe tried unsuccessfully not to look. Then, as if remembering she wasn't alone, she quietly said, "Whoops," and pulled the sweatshirt back down, but not quite over her hips, leaving it bunched at the waist. Joe experienced the next few seconds in a kind of slow motion as he followed her down the hallway. The bicycle shorts clung without a wrinkle, showing off the trim roundness of her hips. He wondered if she was aware that her backside was so exposed. Part of him wanted to warn her, but not a big enough part.

As she led him through her apartment, he told himself to direct his gaze upward and *not* to try to make out, say, the seams of her underwear, but he was no more successful at this avoidance than most men in his position would have been. When his search for panty lines yielded nothing, he was equally a failure at not wondering what, if anything, she had on underneath, simultaneously feeling guilty for the pleasure of imagining her without underwear.

He tried to remind himself that he was a free man, but he noticed he didn't yet feel free. It had only been two days.

Inside her apartment, things were actually quite tidy. She led Joe down a long corridor, its walls crowded with framed biblical scenes of assorted shapes and sizes. They went by a living room and through a small kitchen with aging plywood cabinets and a tiny stove. Arriving at her service door, she opened it, stepped into the back hallway, and showed him the stairs.

"Up one flight," she said pointing, "and that's you, neighbor."

"Thanks," he whispered.

He scratched his head. Why, he wondered, am I whispering?

As she turned to close her door, Joe availed himself of one last rear view of her running pants. She looked back, catching him.

Neither spoke for a second.

"Welcome to the building," she said quietly, and closed the door.

CHAPTER 8

SEVERAL hours later, sitting at her kitchen window in 9B, she looked up and watched the goings on in 10D. She saw Joe opening his wallet, apparently handing money to the movers, and shaking hands with one. Joe didn't seem to be aware of her or the juxtaposition of their windows. She opened a cupboard and found an empty jar of clover honey.

"Damn," she said out loud. Accustomed as she was to milk and honey before bed, she grabbed her purse and headed for the elevator.

Downstairs, she crossed the lobby and saw a uniformed repairman working at the open metal door of the building's main telephone box, next to the mail slots. The man was engrossed in probing the box and didn't see her as she went by. When she came back a few minutes later with the honey, she walked over to him.

Don't, she warned herself.

Why not, she argued back.

"Hi," she said, friendly. "You installing the phone for ten D?"

"Ten-D. Yes, ma'am."

"Great. My husband must be so relieved."

"Well," he said, pausing and wiping his hands with a rag. "I won't get all five lines going tonight, but at least you're hooked up with two for the weekend. And anybody calling your old number will get a recording giving them the new one."

"It's a start," she shrugged.

He turned toward her and reached for a screwdriver. She pulled her sweatshirt up so that it rested on her waist. He pretended not to check her out. She started to walk away, then turned back, and smiled as she met his eyes. He blushed.

"By the way," she said, as though she had no idea he'd been looking at her. "Can you tell me what our new number is?"

In the middle of his first night in the apartment, Joe woke up hungry. He'd forgotten to have dinner, a frequent occurrence when he was on deadline. In the master bathroom, he turned on the tap for a drink of water but the odor of chlorine was so heavy he decided to skip it.

He tried to count his blessings. The phone guy had been late, but at least he'd made it. The apartment needed new wiring for Joe's multiple-line set-up, and there'd only been time for a cursory installation of two of the five lines he'd ordered, but the cable guy, miraculously, had appeared on schedule, and Joe had managed to set up one TV on top of a bunch of boxes in front of the raised corner fireplace in the living room. From a folding chair, he peered out the wide double windows, admiring his new, open view across Central Park, mesmerized by the sight of two joggers who were seemingly oblivious to the well-publicized dangers of the hour as they made their way around the reservoir's track. He allowed himself a moment's serenity as he admired the semigloss white-painted brick of his new hearth, the wide-planked hardwood floors, and the fine old crown moldings that graced every room. Though not in a mood to work, he'd managed a favorable notice of a lavish Dominick Dunne miniseries, panned the awful new sitcom *Too Many Dads,* and faxed both reviews to the *Dispatch.* The only writing he'd enjoyed that evening was something he'd added impulsively at the end, under the heading "P.S.":

> *Am I the only one in a slow rising panic about drinking water? Have you noticed that people who can afford to are buying it these days? Cities put out advisories "suggesting" that tap water be boiled before drinking. Supermarkets are stocked with Brita filters. I don't know about you, but my tap water smells like a municipal swimming pool in August. New York used to have the best drinking water in a nation of great water. What are we, Mexico? India?*
>
> *If you have any spare change, dear reader, invest in Poland Spring or Evian, or "water futures" if there is such a thing. Hoard H_2O. Or at least keep up your gas and electric payments so you can boil the stuff.*

Without pondering or rereading it, he'd shut down his computer and, too exhausted from Brutus Clay, Mary Beth, and the movers even to phone out for moo goo gai pan, he'd fallen asleep on a bare mattress in his box-cluttered bedroom with his soggy, sweat-stained suit still on.

Now, as he made his way hungrily through the dark, overheated apartment, past the bookcase-lined formal dining room and toward the kitchen, he peeled off his crusty shirt and dropped it to the floor, feeling like an idiotic soldier on a suicide mission. There was no food in the apartment. He knew this. Like pushing the elevator button again, though, he couldn't help but search.

Coming into the spanking-new, black-and-white tiled kitchen, yanking open the black Sub-Zero refrigerator's empty meat drawer and noting its scuzzy bottom, he realized something worse than the fact that there was no food. Somehow, in the craziness of the day, he'd forgotten his nightly bedtime call to Mollie. It was too late now.

In the year since they'd moved out of the city, he'd never missed a call. The disorientation of the new apartment, the mad dash to set up his computer, modem, and TV, and fighting deadlines in a new place had completely distracted him. Tears came to his eyes. In Mollie's words each night was an implicit yearning and forgiveness that sustained the threads of self-respect Joe clung to. He'd call in the morning and hope Gayle would let him talk to Mollie then. His promise never to forget to call had now joined others, such as "Mommy and Daddy will always be together," in the ranks of his well-intentioned failures.

He was roused from self-pity by the sudden emergence of a soft glow from another apartment in the building. His eyes found the light — a kitchen window down one flight and across a courtyard not thirty feet from where he stood. When a distinctly female silhouette walked into view, Joe shut the refrigerator door and stood in the darkness.

Her hair was up in a loose bun and she raised herself on tiptoe to take something from a high cabinet. She was ever so slightly backlit by the green-blue dancing rays of a TV in an adjoining room.

Joe couldn't make out the color of her hair. But when she turned, he recognized the memorable rear view of Amy Goode. The L-shape of the building gave his kitchen a clear view of hers. There was no window above or below Amy's, and hers was the only one facing his that was close enough to afford Joe this kind of New York–style passive spying on neighbors. He stood stock still, like an escaping convict pressed against a prison wall evading searchlights. She turned around 180 degrees and rinsed a mug at her sink.

Now he could see her left profile, and the curve of her upper torso was clear beneath her clingy, striped pajamas. He squinted and completed the reflexive checking out of her frame that had been thwarted earlier by her bulky sweatshirt. Her breasts, neither small nor large, struck Joe as just right, making him both more attentive and more uncomfortable.

From the sanctuary of his darkened kitchen, he watched as she prepared some sort of hot drink. Joe imagined that she was humming peacefully to herself.

After a few minutes of voyeuristic reverie, he reminded himself to go to bed, but when she opened the refrigerator and took out a carton of milk, the opening and closing of the fridge took her within a few feet of the window, and in the brief flash of icebox-light Joe admired her, top to toe.

Wide awake now, he decided to make a cup of tea, which was the only food substance in the apartment. He reached for the light switch, but paused, part embarrassed, part excited at the thought that his new neighbor might see him shirtless. He'd been working out again lately, at Mary Beth's urging. She'd always been superbly fit and wanted Joe to be, too. He'd declared war on love handles, joined the nearby Chelsea Gym, and could now hold his own with most men in their late thirties.

He decided to pretend he wasn't aware of her and make a search of the glassed, window-like cupboards. He was grateful there were no cigarettes around. Recently, he'd promised himself that if he didn't start smoking again, the Mets would win the National League pennant. It was a big responsibility.

The gods smiled, and from the bowels of a deep drawer he unearthed a virgin bag of Doritos, mercifully neglected by whoever had cleaned the apartment. The chips' expiration date was a week past, but Joe and his empty stomach were willing to overlook it. He hit a switch and track lights flooded on above him. Feeling immediately overexposed, he grabbed the round dimmer and swiveled it counter-clockwise, placing himself in what he hoped was a more flattering glow.

Across the way she stirred her milk distractedly.

In the almost-darkness, he opened the bag and crunched on a

handful, wondering if she'd noticed him yet. The chips didn't taste as good as the cigarette he craved, but he worked his way through half the bag anyway, forgetting to enjoy them.

She spooned something — honey? — out of a glass jar and into her cup, turned, and stirred a pot on the stove. Yes, he thought — milk and honey — she's wholesome, like the herbs thriving in her window box.

She took a long-handled ladle from her counter and dipped it into the milk. Stirring, she turned her head toward the window and looked up. Right into his eyes.

"Bingo," she thought to herself, holding his gaze and sipping the warm milk. She seemed to stare through him for a moment. Then, as if he weren't there, she went back to her stove.

Maybe she *didn't* see me, Joe thought. Maybe she's nearsighted.

She turned away, pulled the pot from the burner, and rinsed it at the sink. He popped another Dorito into his mouth — actually a cluster of two or three, stuck together in a way that Joe liked. She put down her mug and looked directly up again toward him. His pulse quickened. She was smiling — a faint, bewitching Mona Lisa smile.

"What do you like?" she asked in a whisper, her lips barely moving. "Do you like coy, or direct? I have a feeling you like to watch. Sure. It's what you do for a living."

With the fingers of one hand, she waved lightly, drew the curtains, and disappeared from view. Her light went out and her kitchen was totally black.

Joe waited for several minutes, walked back to his bedroom, then returned to the kitchen and looked down in her direction. She didn't come back.

He had no sense that he'd slept, but as he opened his eyes he was greeted with the same sad attack of loss that had become a routine part of his waking process since Mary Beth had bailed. It was light outside, so yes, he thought, I must have slept a little. He'd been awakened in the night by new sounds around him, twice thinking the phone was ringing. But he'd dreamed it. Mary Beth hadn't called. He felt tight, unrefreshed, and overwhelmed at the sight of boxes everywhere.

He grabbed the phone he'd had installed next to the bed and dialed Gayle's house in Hastings. He always hoped Mollie would answer.

"Hello," said Gayle.

"Hi. It's me."

"Oh. Hello." There was the expected distance, but he was grateful that there seemed to be no edge in her voice. "What happened to you last night?" she asked.

"I moved, and I was on deadline. I got all turned around. I guess I blew it."

"Yeah," Gayle said simply.

"Is she okay?"

"Well, she cried herself to sleep."

"Oh, God. Can I talk to her?"

"Joe, I thought we agreed . . ."

"I can't make it till tonight. Please, Gayle . . ."

"Oh, for heaven's sake, don't whine. All right. She's getting ready to go to a birthday party, so don't settle in. Just tell her you'll talk to her tomorrow . . ."

"Why not tonight?"

"Once a day, Joe. We agreed. Mollie!" she called sharply. "It's your father."

Joe heard Mollie fumble the receiver, drop it, then finally get it to her ear.

"Daddy? Is it bedtime?"

"No," he laughed, trying to make a joke of it.

"I didn't talk to you last night. Did I fall asleep?"

"No, sweetie. It was me. Daddy moved yesterday and" — he paused to figure the extent of his lie — "the phones weren't connected until after your bedtime."

"You moved?"

"Remember I told you that Mary Beth and I are going to be in a new place?" He winced. He'd wanted to get through this without mentioning Mary Beth. It would be too much to deal with over the phone.

"Do you like your new place? Is it nice, Daddy?"

"It's great," he said, feeling dishonest about everything. "You'll be sleeping here next weekend, only now you'll have your own room."

"I want to sleep in your bed."

"Oh, you're gonna love your room. You'll see," he said, wondering how on earth he'd get it ready in time.

"I cried last night when you didn't call."

"I'm so sorry, Mol. Sometimes daddies make mistakes. . . ."

"They do?"

"Sometimes."

Ordinarily he would have taken a few minutes to get them past this bump, but his time was up, and handling Mollie was much easier with Gayle on his good side. "Listen," he went on. "This is our call for today, so—" He took a breath. "I'll talk to you tomorrow . . ."

She began to cry.

"I need to talk to you at bedtime, Daddy. Please promise you won't miss again."

"I promise. We'll talk tomorrow night, and every night after that." He heard Gayle tell Mollie to hang up.

"Bye, Daddy. Sweet dreams. Don't let the moving bugs bite." She kissed the receiver. Through the muffled smacks, he knew she was ritually hugging it.

Gayle took the phone. "Listen, why don't you go ahead and call tonight? It obviously means a lot to her."

Joe swallowed. "Thanks," he said gratefully.

"Okay," she said, hanging up.

He forced himself out of bed and, determined to make good on his self-promised run, jumped into his workout shorts and a faded *X-Files* T-shirt he'd been given at a Fox press junket. He wasn't supposed to openly advocate for shows, but he figured he was on the record as liking *X-Files,* so why not wear the damn T-shirt? Pulling it over his head, he remembered that Mary Beth sometimes borrowed it to sleep in. He inhaled a taunting vestige of her scent that had somehow survived the one-two punch of Tide and Downy.

He had an impulse to go into the kitchen and check on Amy, but, feeling it might lead to a wasted morning, he bet himself that if he could hold out until after his run, Mary Beth would call.

He laced up his gray Adidas, dropped a key into the tiny pocket of his shorts, and headed for Central Park. It was gloriously perfect weather, the kind that makes it impossible to remember it was ever cold. Joe found a grassy spot and tried for a hundred sit-ups in agonizing sets of twenty-five, but a cramp in his side slowed him down, and he stopped at fifty.

He stretched and began to jog. The park was jammed with runners, strollers, and bicyclers. As he moved across 110th Street, a young Rollerblading woman with short-short cutoffs glided by and for a split second Joe thought it was Amy. As he started to call to her, she turned toward him and he realized it was someone else. He picked up speed for the last leg of his run, almost unbearably impatient to get back to his kitchen.

Leaving the park and cooling down, he walked briskly toward Madison Avenue, remembering his empty pantry. About to enter a pretentious gourmet market called Le Shoppe, he stopped at the curb and looked at his new building, his eyes traveling up to the gleaming, freshly-washed windows of his tenth floor living room.

A casement window below and to the left of his apartment opened, and he saw Amy pop her head out, looking toward the park. It was definitely her. From a distance, Joe thought she looked even better than she had yesterday. He willed her to look down in his direction so he could offer a casual wave, but all she did was take a hearty gulp of spring air and disappear back inside.

Joe practically stormed into Le Shoppe. The floor was covered with sawdust and the aroma of freshly-ground coffee mixed incongruously with bug spray. He'd never laid eyes on so much pesto sauce. Desperate for a cigarette, he reached instead for a baguette, a banana, some linguini, a can of lentil soup, a jar of marinara, a liter of Evian, and two capuccinos to go. He found himself muttering "Come on, come on," as a kindly old woman checked out ahead of him. He watched in horror as the clerk tossed a heavy can into the old woman's bag on top of some perfectly ripened, horrifically expensive Bartlett pears. When it was Joe's turn, the vacuous clerk, whose frighteningly long nails made it difficult to grasp anything, held up the lentil soup with one hand, intoning, "Price check," every few seconds until the inflated price was finally yelled to her by a harried manager. While totaling Joe's items, the clerk announced testily, "I'm goin' on my break now, Marie, I swear to God," as though she were rightfully threatening suicide. Joe rushed out before she had time to figure his change.

Entering his building, and certain that Amy was, at that very moment, in her kitchen, he was a man on a mission. He pushed the elevator button twice, unable, as usual, to restrain himself. His sense of humor had left him completely. Determined to enter the elevator at the earliest possible second, he shifted his weight from foot to foot like a sprinter going into a starting crouch.

The door opened and he used body English to urge a wizened,

wheelchaired tenant out so that he could get in. Joe's unspoken manner was brusque enough that the old man, moving as though he'd recently suffered a stroke, was immediately apologetic.

"Terribly sorry," said the man, mortified.

"No problem," Joe answered unconvincingly as he scurried aboard and pushed 10 hard with his thumb — twice, of course.

It was impossible to enter that particular elevator and push a button faster than Joe had just done it. He felt he'd surely broken the world record. The thought gave him a familiar satisfaction he knew was utterly neurotic. Joe habitually set meaningless tasks or goals to occupy his mind as he made his way from one place to another. He might decide, for instance, when crossing a street, that if he made it all the way to the opposite corner before the DON'T WALK sign began to flash, he'd win an award, or land a plum TV assignment. One summer afternoon, he'd convinced himself that if he finished a Popsicle before a drop of it ran down the stick and onto his fingers, his beloved Mets would win that day. He finished it without a drop running, and in a double header that afternoon with the Pirates, the Mets won both games. Joe took full credit.

He peered at the elevator's indicator light and muttered the number of each passing floor as though it were impossibly irritating not to be beamed, *Star Trek* style, to his kitchen.

"Six, seven, *eight,* for Christ's sake," he said, tapping his fingers on the elevator wall. "Come on, come on — nine — thank you very much." He spoke patronizingly, as if to a stupid child. "Yes, yes, ten, thank you. Now, *please . . .*"

He made it to 10. His key was poised. He shoved it into the sole lock on his front door, pushed into the apartment, and made a dash for the kitchen window.

She was there! — but turning and moving away, out of her kitchen and out of view.

Stunned, and furious for not getting upstairs sooner, Joe sat on a kitchen stool, chewing on the baguette and sipping a cappuccino. He told himself he didn't care, but he couldn't help stealing a look from time to time.

She didn't return.

She was standing in her room, admiring The Blouse again.

No! she told herself, heading back to the living room couch. It's too soon.

He threw away the bruised banana that had been gashed by the can the store clerk had slammed on it and forced himself into the living room to begin unpacking boxes. There was a fax from his longtime editor at the *Dispatch*, Ferdy Levin.

Had some favorable calls and faxes about your P.S. One said you should mind your own business. Need I remind you that we have yet another new publisher and Edgar is as persnickety as they come? But he was in a decent mood today and seemed to like the attention. Three different readers referred to you as a "voice of reason," but the mayor's office called, pissed as hell. They're afraid people will panic about water — needlessly they say. Two of the papers that syndicate you didn't want to run it, but I reminded them that you have that no-cut clause in your new contract.

Is not smoking getting to you? Are you on the patch?

Don't forget the piece about cameras in the courtroom. I need it.

Ferdy

Joe attacked boxes all day like a man possessed, managing to limit his looks out the kitchen window to one per hour, none of which yielded a sighting. At eight P.M. he called Mollie, and by eleven a few closets were filled and two more TVs and VCRs had been set up in the dining-room nook that was to be his office.

He checked out a terrific live Whoopi Goldberg special on HBO. Figuring that in a less distracted mood it would have made him laugh, he went through the motions of a rave and faxed it to the *Dispatch*. He dug up an interview he'd banked with Whoopi two months earlier and faxed it to two of his syndication papers, *The Philadelphia Inquirer* and the *Milwaukee Journal*, adding this on the fly:

P.S.
Cameras in the courtroom? Why stop there? How about a camera in everybody's pants?

He set up the answering machine, sat on the couch, and twiddled his thumbs, first in one direction and then the other, trying not to think of Mary Beth. She'd been the easiest of traveling companions, could keep up a conversation with anybody, always looked smashing, and was intimidated by no one. He wondered how many Viacom execs were pursuing her at that very moment. Men routinely made idiots of themselves over her, even in Joe's presence.

Hitting a new bottom, he dialed Mary Beth's room at the Bel Air.

"This is Mary Beth," said her voice on the hotel voice mail, "and I'll be tied up till all hours this weekend, *but* — I will be checking in, so if it's really important, you know what to do." Joe thought she sounded stressed and nervous, yet somehow sexy. During the squelching beep that followed, he realized he had nothing coherent to say and hung up.

He moved into the kitchen and stood at the sink rinsing dishes from his makeshift lunch. It was dark across the way. Amy's curtains were still shut. He forced himself to bed.

After an hour of wakefully replaying the rest of his relationship with Mary Beth, he got up and made himself finish a comparative review of Leno and Letterman for Monday's paper. Wired, he logged onto America Online, venturing into one of its chat rooms, the Flirt's Nook, where lonely cybersurfers were gathered in a virtual pickup bar, angling for computer sex. He "listened" to the chat, marveling at how poorly people spelled and how bluntly they expressed their appetites. He longed for sex — for pure, hungry, out-and-out abandon — but couldn't coax his free-floating lust from his brain, through his fingers, and onto the keyboard. He reflexively visualized Mary Beth, but in the brief fantasies of her that he allowed himself, her face kept morphing to Amy's.

After a few minutes, he logged off, took three of Mary Beth's herbal "sleep-inducement" pills, and got into his still-sheetless bed, but the herbs were no match for his adrenaline.

He went back to the kitchen, turned off the overhead lights, and stood in the moonlight, lost. Hoping it might relax him, he pulled a bath towel from a box in the foyer and took a warm shower. There being no shower curtain, he gyrated with care so as not to splash water all over the bathroom floor, dried off, wrapped the towel around his waist, and brushed his teeth again.

While brushing, he drifted back toward the kitchen. Maybe I should call a friend, he thought, when there was still no sign of Amy. His pal Buddy Monk was out of town, but, he told himself, Ferdy could talk me down. He picked up the phone and started to dial, but his loneliness had become almost romantic to him and, nursing it the way a drunk nurses a last drink before closing, he hung up. Shuffling back to the bathroom, he placed the tooth-brush in the ceramic holder on the sink, threw the towel over the curtain rod, got into bed naked, closed his eyes again, and ordered himself not to think about Mary Beth or Amy. He was alert, sad, and about as sleepy as a shark.

Giving up again, he walked back into the darkened kitchen. In the twenty-four hours since he'd gone in search of a midnight snack, his brain had programmed the route. He could have nav-igated it with his eyes shut.

There was no sign of her.

Unbeknownst to him, though, she was there, in the shadows of 9B, watching him as he made his entrances and exits. Frightened, conflicted, and as wide awake as Joe, she watched him glance —

and sometimes stare — down in her direction, standing there sometimes for two or three minutes at a time. It nourished her.

Not bad, she thought. He's thinking about me.

She wanted to make a move, but reminded herself not to rush.

Maybe I'll just throw him a crumb, she thought, moving in the dark toward the small TV in the far corner of her kitchen.

Upstairs, feeling humiliated, defeated, and weak, Joe resolved once and for all to give up his absurd, barren vigil. But just as he turned toward his bedroom, the glow of her TV light re-emerged below.

His common sense screamed at him to go to bed, but not loudly enough to distract him from the dim, unmistakable outline of Amy, visible again in her kitchen.

D EAN sat on the unmade bed of his fourth-floor walk-up on 117th Street, the place he'd soon be moving away from forever, and stared at a line of bad coke he'd cut ten minutes before.

"Give me strength," he asked, folding his hands in prayer, then opening a tiny vial so he could pour the white powder back in. "The Lord *is* my shepherd," he said to the woman who wasn't there. "I can do this." He tried to gather up the coke with a tiny spoon, but his hands were too shaky.

"Pieces of *shit*! " he yelled at the powder, suddenly scattering fragments of the precious stuff. He looked at it, horrified, then reached to collect it with his finger, reflexively bringing some to his mouth, cleaning the finger with his tongue like a frog grabbing a fat mosquito.

He sucked on his teeth for a few seconds, then snatched a short plastic straw, lowered his nose to the table, and snorted the remaining powder like a Dustbuster. His eyes bulged. It was cut with talc or cornstarch. Disgusted, he stopped, remembering his promise, and swept the last stray dots of powder away.

"That's it," he announced, grinding the white dust into a filthy flokati rug and going to the window with his hands raised. "Forever! I'm clean. Praise Jesus!"

There wasn't much of a view, but he looked south in the direction of the suddenly confounding woman he adored. *Why* did she need to be alone, he wondered? What do women mean when they 'have to think'? Was it someone else?

Impossible, he told himself. Not the way she made love to him. Not after their talk the other night when her fingers were magically coaxing him back to another round of lovemaking.

"Truth or dare, Dean," she'd breathed into his ear, brash in a way she hadn't yet revealed to him.

He'd grinned, having no idea what was up. "Sure," he said, ready for anything.

"Okay. Here it is: I want you to tell me what you most want to do." She kissed his neck. "With me."

Dean blinked hard and looked away.

"Don't be shy," she said, sweetly. "You won't shock me."

"It . . . isn't right," Dean said, stammering but more excited than he could admit.

"Come on," she coaxed, kissing his ear. "We don't have to really *do* it. I just want to know your fantasy."

She sounded as though anything were okay, but his circuits were overloaded and he balked. She told herself to back off, but a few minutes later he was inside her and the words tumbled out.

"Come on, Dean. What would you like to do? With me. Other than what you're doing right now — which you do . . . so very well."

He turned away.

"Look at me!" she urged. He obeyed. "In your wildest dreams . . . what would you like us to do? Or have me do? If it could be *anything*. Come on, sweet man. I want to feel close to you."

"It's a sin," he whispered.

"We're already sinning, Dean. I don't remember you asking me to marry you," she laughed.

"It's not funny!" he said, pulling out quickly and turning away.

She reached for him carefully, caressing the back of his neck. "I'm sorry," she said tenderly. "Please come back." Slowly, he turned to face her again.

He wanted to comply, to go along with her, but feared revealing something that might scare her away. She'll think I'm slime, he thought.

"Nothing you say could be wrong to me, Dean," she said lovingly. "It's just words. We'd never actually do it. I just want to know you. I love you."

Still terrified and hoping to distract her, he pushed slowly into her, intensifying his efforts.

"That's delicious," she murmured, kissing him deeply then breaking away, leaving an inch between their lips as she gripped his slim waist and directed his slow, even thrusts. "Oh, my. Well, okay. If you're feeling shy . . . how 'bout if I tell you *my* fantasy?" she offered.

She seemed wholly available and vulnerable. It made him feel stronger. He nodded in agreement.

She took a deep breath and ran her fingernails lightly down his back. "Promise you won't run away when you hear this?"

"As if I could," he answered quietly.

"Kiss me," she begged suddenly and he did. After a few seconds, she opened her eyes and looked at his, which were closed, trusting as a baby. "Deeper," she said, pulling him by his hips till she felt him all the way inside her. "Okay, here goes." She inhaled deeply. "What I want is . . . I want to . . . ."

"Go ahead," he encouraged, almost impatient.

"I'd like to do exactly what we're doing now," she began. "But —promise you won't judge me — "

"Only the Lord can judge. . . ."

"I want us to make love . . . but maybe . . . with someone watching."

She waited, petrified. His face remained impassive but his thrusts became a little harder. Digging her nails into his lean, tight shoulders, she couldn't tell if he was angry or excited.

"Please say something," she said, worried that she'd put him off.

"Is that . . . really what you want?" he asked.

She was sure she'd blown it, but the recitation of her fantasy had also turned her on. She had to know more.

"I'm sorry, but . . . I think it would be wonderful, Dean, for someone to see how beautifully we do it."

His breathing became heavier and he finally spoke. "This someone who's watching," Dean said. "Would it be . . . male or a female?"

"Oh. Gosh. I don't know," she answered, brightening. "Absolutely your choice." She looked up into his eyes, now wide open and penetrating. "Which would you prefer?" she asked, as if anything were possible.

Moving rhythmically, his gaze darted from her eyes to her breasts to her lips.

"Well?" she ventured again. "Male or female?"

"We're just talking about someone watching — right?" Dean asked.

"If you say so," she answered carefully.

"A guy, then," he said quickly. "But he has to watch from a distance," he continued. "Because you're mine. . . ."

"Of course," she said as she turned him onto his back and straddled him, showing off her new breasts so as to focus his attention more, if such a thing were possible. "And he can't have me," she went on. "Only you can have me. He just gets to watch."

"Yeah. Well," said Dean hesitantly. "Maybe . . ."

58

"Maybe?" she asked carefully, her eyes widening. "Maybe what?"

"Maybe, I don't know, later, after I finish . . ." He paused.

"What?" she coaxed gently. "Come on." She felt the distant but clear onset of orgasm.

"You want to know what I want?" said Dean. She nodded, incredibly alert. "Remember," he warned. "You asked for it."

"Uh-huh, I did," she said, more brazen now.

"Well . . . maybe after we finish . . ."

"What?" she urged, writhing. "Come on. You're killing me."

"Maybe he can . . ." He sat up a little and buried his head in her chest.

"It's okay," she said softly, putting her arms around his neck and stroking his hair as he kissed her breasts. "It's only words," she reminded him. "Say it. I want you to."

"After we finish, maybe he can . . . I don't know . . . maybe *I'll* watch. . . ."

"Really?" she asked, her heart racing as she pulled his hands up and cupped them around her breasts. "Are you sure?"

He nodded.

"And could he . . . touch me?" she asked tenderly. "Like you are now?"

"If you're doing it for me — yes."

"And Dean?" she said, trying to contain herself. "One more thing. Can he . . . have me? Like you are?"

Dean closed his eyes. "Yes."

Her climax was nearing. "It would all be for you, Dean. I'm yours completely, forever." At the moment, she believed it.

His face darkened. "You wouldn't get all wrapped up and forget me?" he asked, worried.

"Never," she assured him, burrowing next to his ear.

"Promise?"

"No matter how it looked, it would all be just for you." She slowed down and sat before him. "If you *ever* wanted me to stop, I would."

"As long as I know you love me, anything is okay."

"I adore you," she said, losing her breath. "Your fantasy is my fantasy. I've waited my whole life for a man to make that okay."

"Well, then — it's okay."

She put a finger to his lips as he closed his eyes. "Someday, Dean, someday if it's absolutely the right time, and the right person is there, we'll . . . we'll just do it." The sound of her own voice and the words she was saying lassoed her orgasm, drawing it closer. "Would you like that, Dean?" He nodded. "Really? Would you?"

"We'd go to hell," he answered, fighting off the urge to grin.

"Yeah, but hey — it might be worth it," she added, laughing as she began a climax that, as he relived it now, seemed to have no end.

A sharp knocking on the reinforced-metal front door of his apartment brought Dean back from his recollection. Moving into the tiny foyer area, he peered through the peephole to give himself time for his excitement to subside.

Standing in the hallway was Lucas, Dean's contact from Operation Life in Florida.

A charter Operation Life member, Dean had grown weary of demonstrations and letter-writing campaigns and a year before had gone underground to try his hand at blowing up women's "health clinics." He'd heard Lucas Dellworth speak at an Op-Life meeting outside Miami and gone up to thank him after his speech, a passionate justification for "removing" abortion doctors. Lucas, to Dean's absolute amazement, had invited Dean out for a drink, during which time they discovered a shared fondness for heavy weapons as deep as their desire to "remove" abortionists. A former Navy SEAL, Lucas proved to be just the mentor Dean needed for an apprenticeship in explosives.

Lucas's interest in Dean was more than merely professional, but he'd never found the right moment to express his feelings, fearful that Dean wouldn't understand. Lucas, a romantic, told himself to persevere, and juggled his busy travel schedule in order to meet three times with Dean, providing follow-up by phone, always calling Dean from public booths in different cities.

Dean's first solo effort, a small clinic in Sarasota, had been disappointing. Only one room was destroyed and the targeted doctor had gotten out with second-degree burns and a broken arm. To make matters worse, Dean was horrified to find himself in a crisis of unexpected remorse. He plunged himself into the Bible, but one moment he'd read "an eye for an eye," which had led him to the bombing in the first place, and the next he'd revisit, "Vengeance is *mine*, sayeth the Lord," which made him feel he'd overstepped his bounds. Uneasy and guilt-ridden, he snooped around the clinic a few days after the bombing and stopped a nurse in the parking lot to ask after the injured doctor. The nurse, justifiably paranoid, phoned in a description of Dean to the police.

An all-too-decent composite picture began popping up on the local news, and in desperation Dean contacted Lucas, who was back in his cabin near Albany. Lucas managed to requisition some Op-Life emergency funds and set Dean up with a new passport, Social Security card, his present name, and a tiny tenement apartment in upper Manhattan, which, as Lucas pointed out, is an excellent place to disappear into. Dean couldn't officially work for Operation Life anymore — he'd come to accept that — but he had faith that something worthwhile would materialize for him. He explored the labyrinthian city, sampled churches (the strictest of which he found too progressive), and tried out new disguises, determined as he was never to be identified again.

He pulled the creaky door open and Lucas walked in, tall and quiet, his thinning black hair combed over and pasted down to disguise his encroaching baldness. His Gordon Liddy mustache, fleshless lips, and off-the-rack gray suit made him appear as stoic and solemn as ever. They gave each other something like a hug, slapping each other on the shoulders but otherwise not making contact.

"How ya doin' . . . *Dean*?" asked Lucas, trying on Dean's name.

"Coping," said Dean. "Ya hear what I'm sayin'? I miss the sun. I'm not complaining. I found me a friend, a woman — "

"Watch yourself," warned Lucas. "Women are grief."

Dean nodded. He'd never been quite sure about Lucas's sexual preference.

"This one's okay," Dean assured him, happy to notice that Lucas was toting a familiar weathered leather briefcase. "Is that . . . what I think it is?" he asked eagerly.

"Is the pope Catholic?" Lucas responded with a vicious grin.

Dean's brow furrowed. "I'm not Catholic," he said tightly. "But I take offense."

"Why?" laughed Lucas, placing the attaché case on a table next to Dean's door. "Catholics aren't real Christians."

"Not in the eyes of God," agreed Dean with a little shake of his head. "Sorry. I'm kinda jumpy today."

Lucas held his arm out and touched Dean on the shoulder. "How *are* you?" he asked.

"Didn't I just say?" answered Dean, confused.

"Of course you did," said Lucas, embarrassed. He cleared his throat. "Well, this should cheer you up," he added, flipping the briefcase's combination to 666, then snapping the locks open as Dean looked on. "I'd have brought you an AK, but you said you wanted something more discreet."

"Praise the Lord," said Dean, smiling and reaching to stroke a pearl-handled Beretta, a huge .357, and a beat-up .45. When he finally saw what he wanted, he looked back at Lucas, who was glowing.

"May I?" Dean asked.

"But of course," said Lucas proudly.

Dean pulled out an almost-new .38 and fingered its trigger. "Bless you, Lucas, this is positively prime."

"What'd you expect — I'd bring an old comrade junk? After what you've been through? No, no. And it gets better." He reached into one of the briefcase's side pockets, gingerly removed a silencer, and held it up like a rabbit he'd pulled from a hat. "Can you perhaps use one of *these*?" he asked with a thin smile.

Dean took the silencer from Lucas and screwed it onto the .38. "This is *so* righteous," he said looking at Lucas the way a kid looks at Santa. "This is just what I had in mind, and a little bit more."

"What'll you be using it for?" Lucas inquired, beaming. "Or is it better if I don't know?"

"I'll just be doing what I do," answered Dean quietly, taking out his wallet. "You know — doing His will."

"In that case," said Lucas grandly, waving Dean's wallet away, "it's on me. A good luck present."

In the dark of his kitchen, Joe, unsure if Amy could see him, thought about turning on the light to let her know he was there. But he was naked.

She came closer to her window, her hair up in that same attractively blowsy bun. He admired the outline of it, the easy, thrown-together look.

Just beyond his kitchen was a tiny bathroom that Mary Beth had earmarked as a powder room for guests. Remembering a towel left by the painters, he backed slowly into the john, found it, and draped it around his waist.

At the same time, Amy snuck a look up at his window. Oh, no, she thought — is he gone?

Seconds later, he turned on the bathroom light, spilling just enough light on himself to be visible to his neighbor. It was a test: She'd either close her curtains — or not.

She saw his light go on and watched carefully, still in the dark.

He stepped again toward the window. Wanting to make it look as if he had a reason to be there, he spotted a pile of dirty T-shirts and socks he'd left on the stacked washer-dryer, opened the washer's lid, and began tossing in clothes as if it were normal to be doing laundry at this hour.

Watching him from below, terrified but pressing through it, she reached for her phone and dialed.

"Yeah," answered Dean, trying not to sound as if he'd pounced on the phone.

"It's me," she said. "What're you doing?"

"Sleeping," he lied.

"Got a second?" she asked.

"Sure," he said, hanging, as he always did, on her every word.

As she spoke, she kept an eye on Joe, who was sprinkling detergent into a washing machine.

When they hung up, Dean sat without moving, a shiver shooting up from the base of his spine.

"Heaven or hell?" he asked himself. He looked slowly around his room and smiled. It was a no-brainer.

Trying to busy himself and appear nonchalant, Joe went to the fridge, removed a cappuccino, and put it into the microwave. He pushed Reheat, waited until the oven beeped, and removed the coffee, overheated and steaming, its froth deflated but the smell of cinnamon still strong. With one hand holding his towel in place, he took a sip. It had a kind of Dead Sea flavor, but he didn't much care.

Below, his neighbor moved to her refrigerator, opened its door, and took out milk as she had last night. It gave Joe another well-lit look at her. As she prepared her milk and honey, her pajamas clung to her so that, while there wasn't an inch of exposed flesh, the effect, in shadow, was almost as if she were nude. She moved to the window, but instead of looking in Joe's direction, she sipped her milk and gazed up at the stars. It made Joe crazy.

He moved closer to the window, unabashedly looking down, his forehead pounding. She reached for something behind her and her kitchen lights came up full. His fatigue disintegrated. Awake and alert, his failure with Mary Beth was temporarily blotted from consciousness.

After a few seconds, though, she backed out of her kitchen. Joe watched, disappointed, but thinking there was a chance she'd come back since she'd left the light on.

Sure enough, she came partially into view a few moments later — leading someone by the hand — a slim young man with long, curly hair. She laughed in delight and threw her arms around the guy, giving him a kiss so movie-perfect that Joe could practically see credits rolling over their embrace. Joe retired a step into shadow, afraid now that they might see him.

She broke the kiss and raised her eyes heavenward, taking a deep breath. With one arm extended to the side, she slowly turned in a circle — then round again, head thrown back, the long-haired man holding one of her hands like a dance partner. She closed her eyes, whirled to a stop, grabbed the windowsill for support, reached down with her back to Joe, took her pajama top in both hands, and pulled it over her head, tossing the top away and throwing her arms again around the young man. As she kissed him this time, she reached down, untucked his shirt and pulled it off, revealing a lean, tight, dancer's body. She kissed his chest and stomach, disappearing partly out of Joe's sight as she undid the buckle on her partner's black jeans and tugged them down, her head staying at his waist as her hand reached up and dallied with his chest. The long-haired man put his head back and closed his eyes.

Joe watched, unable to move.

"He sees us," she whispered to Dean.

"Oh, sweet Lord," said Dean. "I'm gonna burn for this."

She put her head against the window and he grabbed her, knocking over the tea mug she'd set on the sill earlier. The mug shattered and Dean lifted her off her feet and onto the sill to protect her from the porcelain shards. As he shifted his weight, he stepped on a long piece that tore into the fleshy part of his heel.

"It's a judgment on me!" he cried out, looking heavenward in a mix of pain and pleasure as she reached across his shoulder and hit the light switch and Joe, to his alarm, couldn't see them at all.

He stood, waiting one, two, five minutes for the light to return. When it didn't, he felt angry and sleazy and sick with himself.

He stared down into darkness, furious with Amy but mostly at himself, then made his way back to the bedroom, dissolving onto the bed.

He looked up at the ceiling breathing deeply, unable to locate his equilibrium. Getting up suddenly, he scoured the room for the khakis he'd worn the day before, dug his hand into a side pocket, and pulled out Sandy Moss's number.

Don't, he warned himself.

He grabbed the phone by his bed and dialed Sandy.

It rang twice before Joe hung up as impulsively as he'd dialed.

He got back on the bed and stared out the window, only to find that, perversely, all he could think of was Mary Beth.

The phone rang. He grabbed it. Yes! He had willed Mary Beth into calling.

"Hello?" he said impatiently, his voice low.

"It's your neighbor in nine B," said the woman he'd just spied from his kitchen. "I wonder if I could borrow a cup of sugar."

THE hair on the back of his neck stood up. "How'd you know my number?" he asked. "It was just connected . . . it's . . . it's un-listed."

"I did a terrible thing," she answered with good humor. "I hope you'll forgive me, but I, well, I conned it out of the phone man. I couldn't help myself. I . . . what can I say? I liked you when we met, and I thought it'd be easier than slipping notes under your door. Is that terrible? Do you forgive me? Press one for 'yes,' two for 'no,' or press the star key at any time if you want me to shut up because I definitely tend to talk too much."

Be careful what you wish for, Joe thought, furious with himself for being so excited. He cleared his throat for no reason. "What can I do for you?" he asked.

"How're you fixed for sugar?"

"White, dark, or powdered?" he said, trying to play along.

"Whatever," she replied.

"Are you . . . baking at this hour?" he ventured.

She laughed. "Hey — you do laundry at two A.M., I bake."

"So you . . . *did* see me?"

"Once or twice," she confessed. "Why? Did you see me?"

He paused for a few seconds. "Once or twice."

"Oh, dear," she said, mortified. "Should I be . . . horribly embarrassed?"

"No, no," he lied, stalling, not wanting to give away what he'd seen.

"So listen," she said, changing tone. "This is kind of crazy, I know, but . . . are you tired? 'Cause I can't seem to make myself go to sleep."

"I've been sleepier," he admitted.

"Well, hey. Come on down and visit," she offered, as if it were the most normal thing in the world under the circumstances. "Forget the sugar."

"I . . ." He stopped. He had no idea what to say. He wanted to hang up, but not nearly enough to do it.

"I'm alone," she said, as though he might be wondering. "I don't know, I sure would like it if you'd come down." She waited and he reminded himself that it *was* possible, after all, to visit with a woman, even at this hour, without it becoming sexual. He couldn't quite get a beat on her intentions. "I may never get this crazy again," she added. "I think it's the new moon."

"I really should go to sleep," Joe said.

"Probably a good idea," she agreed, matter-of-fact. "Forget I called. I'm not really like this."

Let everything go, he urged his bewildered brain, just for one night. He wasn't sure if it was revenge against Mary Beth or an anesthetic for the pain, but he couldn't hang up.

"Earth to Joe McBride," she called in a quiet singsong. "Are you . . . still there?"

"Yeah," he answered. "I'm less and less sure where 'there' is, but — yeah."

"Good," she said, relieved. "I'm starting to get a little embarrassed, but I'm working through it. Just knock on the back door. I mean, if you want."

"I don't know," he said. "Now?"

"Pretend it's the beginning of the evening," she suggested pleasantly. "I just took a quick shower. What can I say? Don't make a girl beg."

He laughed in spite of himself.

"You seem like someone who takes himself very seriously," she observed. "So do I, usually. I don't know what's going on. I don't want to think too much right now. But let me put it this way — if you're not here in about one minute, I'll come to my senses and pretend this never happened. In fact, maybe that's better. I'll just keep the curtains drawn from this day forward, and we'll — "

"Amy?" he said, sitting up. "It *is* Amy, isn't it?" he asked, as if her name hadn't been all over his mind since the moment they'd met.

She interrupted. "I'll wait by the back door — for about thirty seconds. Come as you are. After that, I'm locking up and going to bed."

"Listen, it's just that I . . ."

"'Bye, McBride. Or hello. Your call."

She hung up.

A cigarette, thought Joe, would give me time to think. But there were none in the apartment, he'd made sure of that. Still naked, he made a dash to one of the boxes in his room. Stumbling into a misplaced chair, he gashed his leg just below the knee. It was paralyzingly painful, but a host of endorphins were kicking in and he ignored the wound, tearing at the box's packing tape with his nails like so many knives, paper-cutting the tips of two fingers. He finally opened it, extracting an extra-long *ER* T-shirt from his vast collection. "Come as you are," she'd said, but he wasn't up to making the trip in the nude.

Moving to the kitchen and then to his back door, he unlocked the top lock and opened it a few inches, making sure there was no one around. The fluorescently lit service hallway, a bleak gray, held an entrenched odor of exterminator's fluid and Lysol.

Realizing he didn't have his key, he started to go back, but then, taking Amy at her word and figuring he might only have a few more seconds to get to her place, he pressed the button on the inside of his door latch so he could open it later. He knew that this left his place vulnerable to intruders, but gambled that none would find their way past the two locked street-level doors and up the fire stairs to the service entrance of a tenth-floor apartment at this hour.

He tiptoed like a cartoon character down to 9B, rapped hesitantly on the door, and flicked a bead of perspiration from his forehead.

Inside, she heard the knocking and stood for a moment, more excited than she thought she'd be, holding the pajama top in her hands, trying to decide in what state of undress to greet him.

To Joe, ten seconds felt like an hour. He waited, his heart beating as though he'd pumped a hundred sit-ups. Finally the door opened.

Clad in the bottoms of her pajamas and holding the top to cover herself, her bare shoulders still damp from her shower and her hair tousled about her high forehead, she looked at the T-shirt that covered him below the waist like a brief tunic.

"My daddy used to say that a skirt should be like a good speech," she said. "Short enough to be interesting, and long enough to cover the subject." She looked down at him, nodding. "Your T-shirt certainly . . . qualifies."

He blushed and bowed mock-politely. She opened the door wider to let him in.

Moonlight shone through the window. He turned his body sideways as she closed the door and they stood, inches from each other.

"Well," he said, "do we . . . shake hands?"

"I can't remember the proper etiquette," she answered, looking right at him, studying his face.

"I think there's something in Emily Post about late-night, service-door greetings," he whispered jokingly. "But damned if I remember it."

"How do you do?" she said finally, with an increasingly easy grin, extending her hand. He took it. Her handshake was firm.

On impulse he pulled her close. One of her arms went around his shoulder like a slow dance partner, while the other dropped to his side as the soft firmness of her chest cascaded against his. He brushed a strand of hair from her forehead, pulled her head back a little, and moved his face slowly closer to hers. Just as their lips were about to touch, they heard the clinking of keys in her front door.

"I don't *believe* it," she sputtered, darkening. "Just a second. Please. Don't move." She left the kitchen, her exit allowing him to admire the white, white skin of her back as she disappeared into the foyer. He arched his neck around to watch as she intercepted whomever had arrived. Figuring it was the guy he'd just seen with her in the window, Joe turned sideways, flattening himself against the kitchen wall, trying to make himself disappear, but managing to keep a piece of Amy and her visitor in his sights.

Amy whispered something that Joe couldn't make out. He moved a step closer to hear better.

"You have a *guest?*" answered a smoky Long Island female voice. "I guess you got luckier than me. Can I meet him?"

"No. Absolutely not," insisted Amy, trying unsuccessfully to keep her voice down. "How many times has the shoe been on the other foot, Loree? Just go to bed."

"It's too noisy in the bedroom," Joe heard Loree whine. "I want the couch!"

"Not tonight," insisted Amy.

"Well, I'll be," taunted the other. "Miss Goody-Goody steps out!"

Joe heard a dry laugh and watched as Amy pushed, ushering her guest into the bedroom. He caught a glimpse of spiky white-blond hair and a long black trench coat. As the bedroom door slammed shut, she called out from the other side and Joe realized she was drunk.

"Pardon my sister, Mr. Whoever-You-Are. She's so rude she wouldn't even . . . introduce us. Are you cute?" She laughed again as Amy shuffled back to where Joe was standing in the kitchen.

She still held the pajamas to her otherwise naked top.

"Maybe this isn't . . . such a great time," Joe said, thinking it had been too good to be true. "I can leave."

"She's so drunk she'll pass out with her clothes on," Amy said, meeting his eyes and holding them. "Stay. Please? I can't afford the therapy I'll need if you go." He smiled and before he could answer she took his hand and led him past the window. He saw the faint light of his own kitchen above.

"Daddy always said life is what happens while you're making plans," she observed. "Score one for the old man — Loree usually stays out all night. She said she wouldn't be back this weekend. I'm sorry." She stepped a few feet into the hallway she'd led him down yesterday. "I just want to make sure she goes to sleep." She turned her head toward the bedroom, and not hearing anything, led Joe into the living room.

"Let me show you my etchings, so to speak," she said.

There were no lights on but the moon lit the small room through windows facing north and west across the park. There was a weathered traditional fireplace with a mantle that sagged slightly in the middle surrounded by messily crowded bookcases, an old yellow-rosed chintz sofa, and an overstuffed chair with almost matching ottoman. Three well-placed fake Oriental rugs managed to cover most of the floor, and while everything was neat, the place was long overdue for a paint job. An open, black, flimsy Bible rested facedown on a glass-topped coffee table next to a barely-begun jigsaw puzzle.

"What's it going to be?" Joe whispered, seeing no pattern in the few black-and-white patches that were so far fitted together.

"I'm told it's a bruised, defiant woman," she answered, glancing at it almost affectionately. "That's all I know. It's a killer. There's no picture on the box and black-and-white puzzles are the toughest. There seem to be a lot of words on it." She shrugged. "It was a gift from my sister," she added, nodding toward a small folding silver frame in three sections that stood next to the puzzle.

"I *think* Loree went to bed," she whispered. She looked down at the pajama top she was still holding up to herself. "I feel like a complete idiot here, but never mind, never mind." She smiled in a defenseless way that Joe found captivating.

The middle photo showed Amy, her arm around an equally pretty woman with a sharply cut dark brown page-boy and straight bangs. The woman, who bore a strong resemblance to Amy, was made up like a runway model and dressed in leather pants and a low-cut beige angora sweater that contrasted sharply with the simple high-collared black dress Amy wore in the picture.

"Are you twins?" asked Joe.

"I've got about eight minutes on her," Amy laughed. "That's Loree. Which she now spells L-o-r-e-e, because God forbid she do anything the usual way."

"Oh," he said, taking this in. "And you're just . . . the picture of normalcy."

"Well, tonight," she mused, "is kind of a time-out." She smiled, still standing, still whispering. "Welcome to my time-out."

He moved in again, taking her free arm and placing it around his neck. As she clung to the pajama top with her other hand, he leaned slowly closer until there was no measurable distance between their lips. He paused, looking into her eyes, feeling her breath, its aroma instantly appealing. Her lips parted and melted into his, but it was nothing like a first kiss. It felt startlingly magnificent to them both, as though neither had ever been kissed before and were stumbling across the process now, inventing it, making it up as they went along.

As she pulled him tighter and started to reach under his T-shirt, they were distracted by a shuffling sound from the bedroom.

"Sweet dreams," called Loree as the light that spilled from under the bedroom door went out.

"She was pretty soused," whispered Amy, waving her hand in the bedroom's direction. "She'll conk out any second. Really." She held the back of his head and pulled it gently toward her face. "Do that again."

He kissed her, and it occurred to him to toss away her top and touch her breasts, but as he reached for her, there was a slight crash in the bedroom, as if a plastic cup had loudly dropped onto the floor.

"Whoops," called Loree. "Sorry. I'm not here."

Joe looked into Amy's eyes, almost laughing. She peered back, less amused.

"She do this kind of thing often?" he asked.

She backed away, moving quietly toward the bedroom.

"Loree has a life she can't stand in Great Neck and she comes in and crashes here after a 'girl's night out' with her friends. You'll meet her one of these weekends. And, be prepared — you'll probably fall in lust," she added with a sigh, putting her head to the bedroom door again, the pajama top still held over her breasts.

Joe glanced at the photo on the left of the little triptych. It was Amy and Loree in cap and gown.

"Your coloring is so different," he observed.

"Loree's not happy unless she's changing something about herself," she said, walking back toward Joe. "She's a platinum blonde now."

"You sound like you disapprove."

"Women don't take to Loree," she said flatly. "It may have something to do with the fact that she ritually steals their men."

Joe had a feeling that Loree had taken at least one from her sister.

"She smokes, too," Amy said, spotting a well-used ashtray and picking it up with disgust. "Let me get rid of this." She dashed into the kitchen with it, returning a few seconds later to find Joe staring at a painting above the fireplace, a portrait of a haloed, naked, long-haired man writhing from a host of arrows piercing his body, eyes rolling heavenward in pain.

"My boy Saint Sebastian," explained Amy, a few steps from Joe, her bare shoulders taking on a flattering trace of blue from the moonlight. "I'm kind of a sucker for the saints," she went on, directing his attention to the rest of her collection. "Maybe that's why I haven't been able to let go of my pajama top. Just shut me up if I talk too much. I tend to do that whenever I entertain gentleman callers half-dressed. That's Saint Kevin, Andrew, Paul, Thomas à Becket, and my personal favorite, Mary Magdalene."

Joe walked up behind her and ran his finger slowly down her back.

"I found Sebastian in England when I was studying," she continued, shivering slightly at his touch. "Always thought he was kind of sexy."

"Sexy?" Joe asked, admiring the slight curve of one breast that had eluded her cover. Everything about her looked better at close range.

"Something to do with all those arrows sticking in him," said Amy. "What can I say? I'm sick, I'm perverted."

"What did you study in Europe?" he asked, touching her shoulder and turning her around to face him.

"You *are* going to kiss me again, aren't you?" she asked as if she needed to know.

He nodded.

"Oh, good," she said. "Because, well — just, good." Joe moved a finger from her shoulder to her breast, not quite making contact, barely grazing her skin.

"I'm supposed to keep talking, is that it?" asked Amy.

He nodded again, gently pulling her pajama top from her fingers and letting it drop to the floor.

"Okay," she said, trying to catch her breath. "Let's see. I went to Union here in the city and did an exchange semester at a seminary in York." She inhaled sharply as his fingers slowly found and enveloped one breast from underneath. "Thought it might make me feel a little closer to God."

"Did it?" Joe asked, as his free hand reached for her other breast. The fact that another man had touched her that very night was only making his desire more unmanageable.

"Okay, okay," she said suddenly, pushing him away with both hands but keeping her eyes fixed on his. "Time to take off that T-shirt."

"Really?" he asked. "You think?"

"Simon *says* take off the T-shirt," she added sweetly.

He shifted his weight and slowly began to lift his shirt, hesitating for an instant as an uninvited, subliminal image of Mary Beth came to mind, then pulling it over his head and tossing it by her feet. Amy took a step toward him, pushed him down into the soft chair behind him, and, still standing, traced up his leg with her toe, grazing the cut that was still fresh from his stumble in the dark. He winced.

"What happened?" she asked, concerned. He looked down. An ugly greenish bruise had formed there. Only now did it occur to him how much it hurt. He brushed her foot away and reached to touch her, but she shook her head, denying permission, peeling her pajama bottoms down to the floor and stepping out of them.

He started to rise but she leaned over him and planted her hands on the arms of the chair, her lips now inches above his, her breasts suspended, close enough, it occurred to him, to lick. He moved his mouth toward them.

She slapped him lightly on the face. "Uh-uh," she said, brushing her breast against his cheek. "Your turn. Make small talk."

He exhaled and laughed, whispering, "Right. Okay. Did you . . . graduate from divinity school?"

"*Cum laude,*" she answered barely audibly, turning her head as if measuring the angle at which to set her lips against his. "It would have been *magna,* but my thesis caused a bit of an uproar."

"Let me guess," he ventured. *"Just a Sucker for the Saints?"*

"Smartass," she whispered, closing most of the distance between their lips. "If you must know," she said, her breath sweet, "it was called *The Search for the Divine in Everyday Secular Life.*" She moved a hand from the arm of the chair to his knee, lazily running a finger along his inner thigh, never quite making contact with her goal. "Is there a woman in your life?" she asked. "Not that I have a right to ask," she added, "but after being kissed like that, I suddenly want to know."

"There was recently," he answered, searching her face. "But no."

Swinging one leg over him and straddling the arms of the chair, she lowered herself until the soft hair between her legs grazed his abdomen. She inched her breasts toward his chest and her nipples touched his.

He raised his arms to bring them around her shoulders but she intercepted them and placed them firmly back down.

"What is it?" he asked with an edge.

"Say a little prayer for me," she whispered, barely loud enough for him to hear, rubbing her pelvis against his stomach. "Make one up."

He didn't say anything.

"Oh," she said, licking his neck, "you think prayer is incompatible with sex?" She slid herself down and worked her legs until she held the tip of him poised at the intersection of her thighs.

"Can we . . . stop talking?" he asked.

"I'm a talker, Joe." She reached under a throw pillow and came up with a foil-covered condom. *"Semper paratus,"* she murmured, unwrapping it. "Did you take Latin? It means — "

"Always prepared," he recited, laughing. The rubber glistened and she applied it herself, balling up the foil and tossing it on the floor. She knelt by his chair and moved her head to his waist. "You smell *so* good," she said, slowly running her tongue around the place where the condom ended and met his skin. In seconds he was ready. She got up, pushed him back slightly on the chair, and again began to lower herself onto him, this time taking him into her.

"Look, ma," she said, sliding down slowly, closing her eyes contentedly, "no hands." She leaned closer, inviting him to kiss her again. He raised his head to meet hers, their lips not quite touching. She put more weight on him and with a stifled cry pushed all the way down, giving him a kiss even more tender and intense than before.

He opened his eyes to find her studying him.

"If you ever open a kissing booth," she said, "I'll buy stock." The soft-hard muscles of her insides caressed him slowly as she moved up and down. "McBride?" she asked, looking down at her breasts and back up to him.

"Yeah?" he answered, barely audibly.

"Aren't you glad you moved?"

He kissed her again.

It was impossible not to compare these kisses with Mary Beth's, and the comparison rocked Joe, because in addition to sensual perfection, they were more intimate than it made any sense for them to be.

"This is weird," she said, coming up for air and nuzzling his neck. "I feel like I know you."

"Me, too."

"I'm not complaining," she added, holding him closer. "I just didn't expect it." She kissed him softly again. "I have a favor to beg," she declared, sitting above him and moving him in and out of her smoothly.

"You don't seem like the begging type," whispered Joe.

"How little you know me," she said, leaning down to kiss him again, taking his face into her hands. "I beg you. Watch me. Look into my . . . eyes . . . while I . . ."

She put her arms down and displayed herself, somehow vulnerable and narcissistic at once. As her orgasm flowed and reinvented itself, her face became relaxed and lovelier than he'd thought possible.

"I don't deserve to feel so close to you," she whispered into his ear as her climax finally waned. In the following silence she wrapped herself around him, kissed him again, and he fell, gladly, as if disappearing out of his life, down her throat, and into her breath.

12

THEY couldn't stop kissing, this time in absolute stillness — only their breath flowing between them, back and forth, something each was glad to give and receive from the other. Although deep inside her, he didn't move. Their arms, legs, lips, and tongues gave way to the kiss as though freeze-framed. Nothing stirred but their breath, the slight rising and falling of their chests. Joe felt she had nested inside him.

A look of worry crossed her face, then one of fierce concentration. She began to move again, taking his face in her hands and steadying it. "I shouldn't say this, okay?"

He closed his eyes, ready for anything and nothing.

"McBride, look at me."

He did. She moved to whisper in his ear.

"I could love you," she said so softly he thought he might have imagined it.

The words excited her and she began to climax again. This time it was fast and hard and he was about to join her, but held off until she was beyond her peak. Having discarded the condom after their first time and not wanting to compound this already complicated moment with procreation, he slid out and rubbed himself against her belly, slick with their sweat.

It lasted longer than he thought possible and his pleasure seemed to extend hers, though he was no longer inside her. She held him tightly and tried to pull him closer, which was impossible.

They lay facing in opposite directions and finally she propped her chin onto her elbows and peered into his eyes.

"What do we do now?" she asked like a lost child. "I mean, I had this plan. I wasn't going to feel anything. And now . . . oh, dear God. I'll shut up."

"It's okay," he said.

"Everybody has secrets," said Amy. "Tell me yours and I'll tell you mine." He smiled. "And I don't love you," she added. "I couldn't possibly." She closed her eyes, then opened them. "I'm sorry. Instruct the jury to ignore these last comments." She turned her head, embarrassed.

"May I, uh, approach the bench, your honor?" Joe asked.

She looked back at him with a grin. "Approach, Mr. McBride."

He adjusted his weight and felt the warm stickiness where their stomachs joined. He reached down, picked up his T-shirt, and wiped them both, his eyes avoiding hers as he looked out the window. The lights on the far side of the reservoir shimmered.

Sometimes, he realized, it happens; you have to tell the truth more quickly.

"I said I don't have a woman in my life," he made himself say. "Strictly speaking that's true. But up till three days ago I was engaged." He looked back at her.

For a moment she seemed to look right through him but she snapped out of it with a surprising and endearing impression of a stern judge. "Well, Mr. McBride, it's not a direct violation of the commandments, so I'll just sentence you to . . . eternal damnation." She kissed him, taking the T-shirt from him and lifting her hips to daub at a spot he'd missed, then tossing the T-shirt back on the floor and rolling onto her side, curling up with him. He put an arm around her and stroked her fabulously messed-up hair.

"I should ask you to leave now," she said. "I feel like I'm cheating."

"Why?" he asked.

"I guess it's time for *my* confession," she answered, taking a deep breath. "But then I have a little experience with confessions."

"Really?" Joe asked. "How so?"

"Well," said Amy, looking into his eyes. "I'm a cop."

She paused, letting it sink in.

"And you, sir," she continued, "are under arrest."

CHAPTER 13

Joe lay there, staring into her eyes. Before he could speak, she took pity.

"I'm kidding," she said quietly.

He exhaled. "You mean you're *not* a cop?"

"No. I'm a cop," she said easily. "I mean you're not under arrest."

"Oh," he laughed nervously.

"Though judging by the color that left your face, you seem to feel you have some reason to be taken into custody. Shall I hear your confession after all?" She slipped into a garden-variety Nazi impression. "Ve have vays of making people talk."

He laughed, trying to get used to the idea. "A cop?" he said. "Surely you jest."

"I should've told you," she admitted.

"Well, yes," agreed Joe. "But then, I didn't ask. Wow. Are you gonna cuff me?"

"Oh, you're goin' to the hoosegow, buddy," she said, giving

him a two-second version of one of her patented kisses. "I'm ta-kin' you in."

"Things I never thought I'd do," he mused, as though it were a category on *Jeopardy!* "Make love to a cop. Whatta you know?"

"Less than I thought," she answered quietly.

"A cop," he repeated, the information finally having cleared his brain. "Where do you work?"

"Ninety-ninth Precinct in Queens," she said, adding sarcasti-cally, "it's very glamorous. Out in Flushing Meadows."

"Near Shea Stadium?" he asked, perking up. "Home of my Mets?"

"You got it," she said. "If you like tennis and you bribe me, I can get you into the Open, too. Flushing is a cornucopia of sports delights."

"You were wearing a Yankee hat when I met you."

"I wear a lot of hats," said Amy with a shrug. She hesitated a split second as if to consider what she was about to say. "I work undercover."

Joe swallowed. "Full of surprises, aren't you?"

"I try. I try."

"What about the saints and divinity school?"

"My first love. But I didn't have the right stuff — the calling. I did get to use some of it in my latest cover, though, which was kind of a kick. I guess I can talk about it now. It's over." She looked at him as if to see if he could be trusted. "I was working as a pretend minister at a church up in Forest Hills. Long story. I shouldn't say any more."

"What've I gotten myself into?" he asked kiddingly. "Aren't undercover cops crazy? Like . . . pilots, or stunt people?"

"Yeah, I guess," she said, looking utterly sane. "It's edgy, sure. But I love it. I tried other things after I left divinity school. I was the world's most pathetic model for about two excruciating minutes, but I finally found my way to this, and it's really what I was meant to be doing. I get to be all sorts of people. Carry a gun one day, a cross the next. It's a scary, involving, pretty intense kind of acting sometimes. My minister cover was a terrifically sweet, shy lady. She became very real to me. I'm gonna miss her. It was almost, I don't know, peaceful."

"What kind of cases?" he asked, running a finger along her arm. "Can you say?"

"Drugs, mostly. I can't talk about it much. I've got two big trials and another . . . thing still pending. Some other time, maybe — if we ever have one."

"How do guys keep from falling in love with you?" asked Joe, reeling pleasantly. "You're a little overwhelming."

"They drop like flies," she laughed. "No, seriously, I'm, you know, maybe not the best person to fall in love with. I'm good at my job, but my love life is a mess." She shook her head and looked away. "Ask Dean."

"You have somebody, too?" he said, though he already knew. She nodded. "How long . . . have you been with him?" Joe asked, more curious than he would have admitted.

"Let's not go there," she replied, keeping some distance. "You're not the best person to fall for either. Someone who can waltz in here and make love to a stranger so beautifully . . ."

"I've never done anything like this before. . . ."

"Yeah, right," she said, teasing. "I'm glad I'm not in love with you. What do you do?"

"I'm a writer," he answered. "Kind of a columnist. Well, not really a columnist, though I suppose that's what I'd like to be when I grow up. I write TV reviews."

"A critic?"

"Well, yes," he said, shifting his weight.

"Huh," she said looking at him differently. "You don't . . . look like a critic."

"You probably mean that as a compliment," Joe offered with a half smile. "So thanks — I guess." She seemed to scrutinize his face for telltale signs of his trade.

"I lied," she said suddenly. He blanched. "I knew you were a critic. I just wanted to hear you talk about yourself." She kissed him lightly. "I'm sorry. The super told me you were moving in. I mean, your picture's on the number five bus. We're all very impressed around here."

"Isn't there a law," he said, disarmed by her candor and wanting the focus back on her, "that cops have to identify themselves to prospective lovers — you know, like a black belt warning a potential victim?"

"I should have read you your rights," agreed Amy, nodding and toying with the hair below his waist. "Not that you told me much about yourself. Are you still in love with her?"

"I suppose I am," he admitted.

"God bless her," she sighed. "And Dean." She lay next to him, looking up at the ceiling. "Aren't we a pair? You had me going from the time I saw you in the window. Before you saw me."

"No, no," he protested. "I saw you first."

She grinned. "I saw you *way* before we made eye contact," she said. "Yesterday afternoon. You were — how you say in your country — naked. Putting stuff into your cupboards. I loved that you had no idea I was watching. The last people who lived in your place were an old couple who kept their curtains closed. Then, whammo — an attractive man who looks good with no clothes on. Mayday! Mayday!"

She moved in for a quick kiss, then stopped.

"Okay. Now this is completely stupid," she said, "but I just have to ask: do you like *NYPD Blue*? Careful. This is a test."

"Well," he replied, enjoying it. "The actors are terrific, and the writing, too, but anybody can tell they shoot the show in L.A.," said Joe. "As a New Yorker, I hate that."

"A-plus," said Amy, patting his arm. "Well, Joe McBride. I'm kind of a *Post* girl at heart — hope you don't respect me any less — but I'm gonna start reading the *Dispatch*." She laughed. "Not that you necessarily respect me all that much, after the way I shamelessly Sadie Hawkinsed you."

"Do you have a bathroom?" he asked.

"Think you can manage without waking up Loree?" she said, pushing him gently and standing. He sat up.

"A model, a twin, and a cop?" he marveled. "Has anyone bought the rights to your life? You and your sister are a living, breathing TV series."

"Don't start," she said. "I was just a hand-and-leg model. I couldn't hack it. It was awful."

He whispered, imitating a breathy TV announcer, "She's a high-fashion model by day, a hardworking, man-killing under-cover policewoman by night. She's — *Model Cop!*" He did a scat-style improv of the show's theme song. Amy gave him a noo-gie, helped him up, and pushed him down the hall. She opened the bedroom door slowly, peered in to check on Loree, then looked back at Joe.

"She's dead to the world," Amy whispered, "but just in case, tiptoe, okay?" He nodded and she led him past the bed. Joe was curious to see if Loree could possibly be as alluring as her sister, but she was turned away from them on the bed, curled up with a pillow over most of her head.

"I don't know how anybody can sleep like that," whispered Amy. "But she always complains that the buses wake her up." She led him past a desk and computer and pointed to the bath-room door.

"The facilities," she announced in a stage whisper.

He went in, noticing two toothbrushes and a messy pile of makeup in a basket on a shelf by the sink. On a higher shelf lay Amy's ID, the flap open, revealing her badge. He rinsed his hands and walked out, still unclothed, moving carefully by Loree and closing the door without a sound.

Amy was leaning against the wall by the door waiting for him, her pajama top on.

"I was chilly," she explained, moving to him and taking him in a soft hug, pressing her whole self against him, making contact all the way to their knees. She reached up and massaged his neck in the exact place where a headache was distantly forming.

"The laying on of hands," she whispered.

Their intimacy jolted Joe, whose logical mind was re-entering and telling him that this episode would prove ill-advised and way too on-the-rebound. They stood, arms around each other, the embrace neutralizing the damp cool in the room.

"Hot milk?" she offered quietly.

"Do people really drink hot milk?" Joe asked.

"This people does," said Amy as she led him to the fridge, took out the milk, and poured some into the saucepan he'd watched her use through the window. "Good for the ol' nerves," she added, turning on one of the gas stove's burners. She waited for the tick-tick-tick of the flame, opened a cupboard, found the new jar of Golden Blossom, took two unmatching mugs from her dish rack, spooned in the honey, and stirred.

"By the way — are you a Joseph, a Joe, or a Joey?"

"My mother's the only one who ever got away with calling me Joey," he replied. "Joe or Joseph. Your call."

"There was a Saint Joseph, you know. Maybe I'll call you the Saint."

She poured milk into the mugs, handed him one, and looked up to his kitchen. "I can see you up there," she said, "playing with my head, making me crazy." She shook her head and took a sip. "Do you miss your fiancée?"

"I have no desire to answer that," he said, his headache growing.

"Sorry," said Amy, looking at him as though she'd never really seen him before. "I don't know much about you, and we just traded karma."

"We . . . what?"

"The Hindus say that when two people have intercourse, they exchange all their karma — everything we brought into this life and everything we've accrued on earth."

"Do you do things like this a lot?" he asked, beset by a stab of wholly unearned jealousy. She looked hurt. "I'm sorry," he said quickly, looking away. "That was completely out of line."

She stared at him for a few seconds. "Maybe we should kinda forget this happened," she suggested. The throbbing in his head worsened. "I mean, I wasn't even going to talk to you. I don't know what's going on. I'm . . . involved, and you're in love, for God's sake." She gave him a nudge toward the back door. "So . . . go in peace. I promise not to bother you."

He was conflicted enough not to know if he liked the sound of that or not. "What do you mean?" he asked.

"I mean that if and when we meet in the lobby, and you're with . . . whomever . . . or I'm with Dean, I absolutely won't mention how gorgeously you fucked me, Joe. Unless somebody asks. I'm a lousy liar."

"Listen — " he said.

"Get a sense of humor," she interrupted as they reached her door. "My partner and I just wrapped up a stakeout that's been going on for months. Tonight was me being out of control. Comes with the job, I guess. You spend a few nights thinking you might die — and then you don't. I have four versions of my fucking will around here. I'm always amending it. I'm sorry. It's . . . never mind." She shook her head to stop herself and tried to laugh. "Pay no attention to the blathering woman with the hot milk. I just didn't expect all these . . . feelings. Loree would've done it better. Watch out for her, by the way — okay? — 'cause you're a pretty nice guy. For a critic."

Joe had a sudden flash of certainty that his phone was ringing — that Mary Beth was trying to reach him.

"I guess I'll . . . see you," he said, turning the doorknob.

"I'm easy to find," she shrugged.

"Ninety-ninth Precinct?"

"Yeah. I'm sure you go to Queens all the time," she joked. Ironically, he thought, with the TCC job, he'd be there quite a bit.

"I asked them to put me behind a desk for a while," she added. "I need something really boring for a while, you know?" She patted his shoulder and gave him a push into the hall. "Corona Avenue and Forty-seventh Street, if you're on your way to the airport or something. It used to be a church, kind of neo-Gothic and imposing. Hard to miss."

She pulled him close, making her patented contact above and below. Still convinced the phone was ringing in his apartment, Joe was amazed to feel himself stiffen.

"See you in the window," she said, pushing him, naked, toward the stairs.

He dashed up to the place he didn't yet think of as home. The phone was silent, and there were no messages.

As he passed out on his unmade bed, he realized he hadn't gotten Amy's phone number and had left his T-shirt — Mary Beth's favorite — behind.

Oh well, he thought, drifting into a dream where he and Amy made out on the desk of a Gothic precinct office while a choir of cops with pillows over their heads serenaded them. Joe put his arms around her neck as she planted a series of small kisses on his chin. There was something about these lips that was different from Amy's, yet something about her smell that was wildly familiar. It was amazingly vivid — as though his hands and fingers were touching real skin. As the flurry of kisses continued, he grinned a shameless grin of pleasure and was about to say, "I could love you," when she spoke first.

"Wake up," she purred as her tongue teased his. "We need the sheets for the table."

It was an old joke between them, and he realized with horror that it was not Amy in a dream, but Mary Beth — in the flesh.

"I LOVE you, Joseph McBride," Mary Beth whispered in his ear. He started, terrified, as though a monster were in the room. "No — don't move!" she said urgently. "Don't say anything. Please. Just give me a minute. I know how upset and angry you must be. You have every right. But please, *please* listen to me, Joey."

He hated when she called him "Joey," but he was a deer in headlights. She pressed on before he had time to think.

"I've come to my senses," she said. "I'm here. The retreat ended early. I took the red-eye. I couldn't wait. I just pray that you can find a way in your heart to forgive me, Joe, because, well . . . I'm *here*."

Now that he'd collected himself enough to see more than the tears in her eyes, he noticed with dismay what would normally have aroused the daylights out of him. She'd removed her blouse and was dressed in a tantalizingly paltry black lace bra and the short, tight, dark blue skirt of her Cerruti suit. Her jacket, blouse, hose, and shoes lay in a little heap by the foot of the bed. The suit was one of her sexiest outfits, the bra his absolute favorite.

He couldn't help thinking she'd worn it on the plane. He'd only been awake a few seconds — it was hardly a moment for jealousy — but then no feeling seemed appropriate.

Judging by his grogginess and a migraine that was gathering steam, he figured he'd slept an hour or two at best. The digital alarm on his clock radio read 7:46. He tried to piece together how he might respond to Mary Beth if he hadn't just traded karma with a cop.

"Wait a minute," he said, waking fully, pushing her away, and finally locating his anger. "What the hell is going *on* here? You think you can just . . . *change your mind*?"

She stood and moved away, her eyes fixed on his as though he were a lion and she a tamer. "You're right. You're absolutely right," she said. "I was lost. I was . . . I don't know Joe, insane or something. The pressure from work and this retreat has been unrelenting and my hormones were raging before I left. I was just plain scared about everything." She broke down. "Please don't push me away. I love you. I've been going through so much, such changes, and then this weekend, it was so difficult, so challenging, my whole future was at stake. But it was also like, I don't know, a miracle. I suddenly got clear. Our facilitator knocked so much sense into me. I could *see* again. And all I could see was *you*, Joe. . . ."

Joe watched for signs of a performance.

"It was suddenly so crystal clear to me that I love you," she went on as though she'd discovered a cure for all the diseases of the world. "I couldn't just call. I'm sorry — I had to surprise you."

"You succeeded," he said, still trying to get any sort of grip.

She got to her knees. "I'm going to ask you in the name of . . . us. Can't we please, somehow, erase the last few days? *Please.* I need you so much." She began to weep at his feet.

In spite of the fact that he was glad to hear what she was

saying, he was still reeling from the mere fact that she was there at all.

"I'll make the last week up to you," she added, and to his horror, she got up and started to peel away the sheets.

He hadn't showered since his return from Amy's. He rolled out from under the covers and started across the room, leaving her alone on the bed.

"Where are you going?" she asked, bewildered.

"Just a minute," he said curtly, disappearing into the john. Instead of using the toilet, he flushed it to make noise, grabbed a washcloth, ran hot water on it, and quickly rinsed himself below the waist, grateful, as things were developing, that Amy didn't wear perfume. He still had no idea how he felt, but he was in motion nonetheless. He toweled off quickly, tried to straighten his Bozo-the-clown hair, took a swig of Scope, sloshed it around, spat it out, and looked at himself in the mirror.

He felt closer to Amy than he could control, as though he'd been dyed a faint shade of her. Mary Beth's presence, on the other hand, seemed invasive.

He opened the door. She was naked, stretched enticingly on her side with the shades down and a candle lit on the bedside table. She was tall with a long back, fine legs, and narrow hips — a boy's ass, she always said.

"Don't I look good?" asked Mary Beth, with one finger tracing her breasts seductively.

It had always been a kind of foreplay, her saying things like that, and it usually made Joe crazy.

"I love my breasts," she went on, matter of fact. "Ain't much meat on 'em, but what's there is choice."

"What are you doing?" he shot back. "You're amazing. You think I want sex? I think maybe you should leave."

"If you say so, I will. But first come here. Please, Joe," she said, patting a spot next to her on the bed and squirming in a way he would usually have found delectable. He moved closer and bent over to pick up her discarded clothes. "Forget those," she said. "They have to go to the cleaners anyway. Come here."

"I can't believe you think it's this easy," he said, shaking his head in amazement. "It's so patronizing."

He picked up the jacket and blouse and as he dropped them on a chair he noticed the corner of a business card peeking out the pocket of her jacket. He turned his back to her and pulled it out quickly. It read ROGER SHECTMAN, SENIOR EDITOR, SIMON & SCHUSTER. He flipped it over and saw a phone number scrawled in pen with (h) next to it. The throbbing in his forehead intensified.

"Who's Roger Shectman?" he asked, his voice low.

She seemed unfazed. "An editor. We do business together. I make deals with his authors' agents."

"Was he at the retreat?"

"Yes."

"On the plane, too?"

"Yes."

Images of Mary Beth and Roger locked in a washroom at thirty thousand feet invaded Joe's brain. He moved around an unpacked box to the window, parted the curtains, looked out at the emerging day, and wondered if Amy was asleep.

"I thought *I* was the jealous one around here," she said nervously, pulling the covers over herself and taking a deep breath. "The place looks fabulous, Joe. Really. I don't know how you did it. It feels like home. Like *our* home? Is that still possible? Can it still be our home?" She held her arms out desperately, tears in her eyes. "Come here — please."

He didn't turn to her but kept on looking out the window, flicking Roger Shectman's business card against his thigh. He felt relieved, exonerated, victorious — and simply glad to see her. But part of him wondered if the relationship could ever work again.

"Do you think I'd leave his card where you could find it if I was having a thing with Roger Shectman?" she asked when he didn't speak for a moment.

"I don't know what you'd do," he answered evenly. "About anything."

"He was hitting on every woman there," said Mary Beth, with a wave of her hand. "And since there weren't many of us, it left a lot of time for me."

Joe felt a reflexive jolt of possessiveness. "What were you doing wearing that outfit on the plane?" he demanded. Then he caught himself and covered his ears. "No. Never mind. I don't want to know — "

"I was in a hurry when the retreat ended," she interrupted. "I wanted to see you and I didn't pack well, so I just grabbed the suit. I did have another outfit, but I thought I'd need it for Ferdy's party tomorrow night."

"Ferdy? Oh, jeez, I forgot," he said. They'd accepted an invitation to one of the high-power dinner parties his editor often threw at his SoHo loft.

"Come *here,*" implored Mary Beth. "Please, Joe. Roger Shectman doesn't interest me in the least." Shaking, she opened her arms to him.

He moved tentatively to the bed and let her hold him, which he immediately regretted. It was totally disorienting. She smelled so comforting, so Mary Beth–like, her skin's oils mixing with familiar traces of Clarins lotions and the usual dash of No. 5.

"I'm yours," she said as she pulled him closer. "I'm so sorry."

Knowing that she mistook his reasons, Joe began to cry.

She rocked him slowly. "You have nothing and no one to be jealous about. This," she murmured, squeezing his arm, "is the last body I'm ever going to make love to."

"Oh, God," he whispered to himself. She took it as an expression of relief on his part, but it was actually involuntary bewilderment.

"Sshh," she said. "I'm here, I'm back." She held him by the

shoulders and looked searchingly into his eyes. "We don't have to make love. I'm too tired, if the truth be known. They barely let us sleep all weekend. I'm fried. Can we maybe just go to bed? I guess what I'm saying is — may I stay?"

He looked at the ring on her finger and thought of the expensive, engraved wedding invitations.

"Can you still sleep?" she asked gently as she snuggled next to him.

"I'll lie here with you," he said, sounding like a good sport, but not answering the question of whether she could stay. "Maybe I'll fall asleep."

"It's a little chilly in this place," she said, rubbing her shoulders. She popped out of the bed with her arms folded for warmth and peered into an open box. "I don't suppose you unpacked your *ER* T-shirt, did you?"

B ACK in his apartment, Dean sat in the tub scrubbing every inch of his body with an old loofah, his skin red and prunish from so much time in the water. He sat up in the tub, folded his hands, and prayed.

"Forgive me, Lord, for the ways of my flesh. Forgive me the shame of my pleasure. Drive away such desire and make us clean, Father. Show me it's not too late."

In her apartment, the woman Dean adored found the *ER* T-shirt on the floor by the couch, picked it up, walked into the bedroom, got into bed, and pulled the T-shirt to her face, taking in Joe's scent.

Pull yourself together, she told herself. So you liked it. And why not?

Joe tried to finesse the missing T-shirt problem, arguing that it would be like trying to find a needle in the haystack of un-packed boxes. Mary Beth rummaged around for something else to sleep in.

"You used to wear nightgowns when we first met," he said, propping himself up in bed on one elbow. "I kind of liked that."

"I just love your old T-shirts, and that's the only one you have with long sleeves. It smells like you and it's broken in perfectly. I meant to take it with me to L.A.," she said, her head disappearing into a tall open box. "Don't worry, I'll still trot out those trashy little items you like so much, but they're not really great for sleeping. More for foreplay." She tossed a few T-shirts out of the box, then stopped, coming up, of course, empty. "Every other T-shirt you own is in there. It's downright cold," she said, almost shivering.

"So wear whatever you wore in L.A."

"Duhh," she said cheerfully, opening her garment bag and finding some light blue pajamas in one of the zippered pockets.

She got into bed and fell asleep almost immediately.

Joe, ever prone to guilt, spent the day reminding himself that, at least technically, he hadn't been unfaithful — he'd thought all bets were off with Mary Beth. But whatever had gone on between him and Amy was percolating within him, creating a constant, wakeful alarm.

He replayed his visit downstairs, wondering if Amy would indeed prove to be discreet if and when he called to explain that things were back on with Mary Beth. He couldn't get his mind to settle down.

The next thing he knew, Mary Beth was kissing him again, rousing him from a nap.

"Wake up!" she said playfully. "It's bedtime."

"What?" he croaked.

"It's almost nine. I didn't think you'd want to sleep all night in your clothes." He'd thrown on a work shirt and khakis in the afternoon and unpacked a box while Mary Beth dozed. He'd gone into the kitchen but there'd been no sign of Amy.

"Have you forgiven me yet?" Mary Beth asked. Sheepishness

didn't come easily to her, but she was trying it on. Her distress gave him an excuse, badly needed, to act distant.

"I'm working on it," he said, telling the truth. "I'm gonna get some hot milk and take a shower. You want some?"

"Hot milk?" she repeated. "What are you, Rebecca of Sunny-brook Farm?"

"It's good for you," he said, invisibly leaping to Amy's defense.

"Tea, thanks," she answered, trying to make nice. "Earl Grey."

"Earl Grey has caffeine. It'll keep you up," he warned, starting toward the kitchen. "I'm going to call Mol," he added. "Then I'll make you some chamomile."

"Yes, sir, thank you, *sir!*" she said, good-naturedly snapping off a formal salute like a private who's just been dressed down by an officer. "Whatever kind of tea you think would be good for me, *sir!*"

Normally he would have used the phone in the bedroom, but he felt like talking to Mollie alone. And he desperately wanted to go into the kitchen. Just one look, he promised himself as he dialed Gayle's.

"Hootenanny Dog and Catbird Hospital," answered the tiny voice of Mollie. Joe laughed hard with a silly, but proud, fatherly delight.

"Is this Mr. Hootenanny?" he asked in a funny voice. "Or the missus?"

"This is little . . . Crystal Hootenanny," replied Mollie in the high-pitched tone she used when they played make-believe. Crystal was her favorite name of the moment. "Daddy?"

"Hi, Crystal," he said as though he hadn't a care in the world. Talking to Mollie usually made him half believe he didn't.

"All right, Daddy," she said getting down to business. "Let's pretend you're the daddy and I'm little Crystal and you're also the bad guy who wants to marry me, but my daddy saves me — and then we turn into bunnies on a picnic."

At the picnics they had in Central Park before Gayle's flight to the suburbs, they often pretended to be bunnies, readying the park for Easter. Mollie nattered on, but Joe didn't catch the next part. He was distracted by the sight of Amy in her kitchen wearing nothing but his *ER* T-shirt.

H E held the phone to his ear. Mollie was mercifully into an extended riff in the character of Crystal Bunny. Amy saw Joe and waved. He returned it quickly and guiltily, remembering, too, that she had his phone number. The letters *ER* read loud and clear across her unencumbered breasts. There was no mistaking that T-shirt.

Unable to move for several seconds, he finally took a few steps out of the kitchen, bending his head to see if Mary Beth might be coming. He prayed she wasn't.

The prayer wasn't granted.

He moved back toward the kitchen window to block it from Mary Beth's view, and sat on the sill.

"Well, Easter Bunny," Mollie continued on the phone, "is that *really* true?" Having blacked out for a few seconds, Joe had no idea what his daughter was talking about.

"I . . . think so," he tried, vamping. Mary Beth walked in and opened the fridge. He turned his head so he could check Amy, who was making her nightly hot milk.

"It's a wonder you didn't starve to death," observed Mary Beth, peering into the still-empty refrigerator. "I'll go shopping tomorrow after work," she added like a martyr. Mary Beth loathed the supermarket.

"I can go shopping tomorrow," Joe said, placing himself between Mary Beth and the window, maneuvering her toward the kitchen door. "Wanna talk to Mol?" he asked. "You can take it in the bedroom. Mollie, Mary Beth wants to say hi."

"I'll take it here," said Mary Beth, grabbing the phone while Joe countered to block her view of Amy. "Hiya, little person. I missed you. . . . You, too? . . . Uh-huh. Sure, I'm fine. . . . Okay. Night, night." She held the phone out to him laughing. "She wants to talk to the Easter Bunny. I'll make tea."

"No, no," he said, astoundingly calmly, adding into the phone, "Just a second, Crystal Bunny." He looked at Mary Beth lovingly. "You need a little TLC after what you've been through. Let me wait on you." She blinked, seemingly beguiled, and went back to the bedroom.

"Crystal Bunny," he said, with a look to the window. Amy had her back to him. "I'm afraid I have to sign off now."

"Daddy? Can we go on a picnic soon?" Mollie asked sadly. Joe wondered if she missed their picnics as much as he did.

"Sure," he said. "As soon as it's spring."

"It's spring now, silly," she reminded him.

"So it is. Sure. Next weekend, if the weather's good."

"Night, night, I love you," she said, smacking the receiver with big, sloppy kisses. "Oh — have you finished moving, Daddy?"

"I've got a lot of unpacking left, but the move is finished."

"Don't let the unpacking bugs bite, I love you," she said, and hung up.

He turned to the window. Amy saw him. He thought she looked sad. She mouthed something, but he couldn't make out the words.

He prepared the tea on a little tray and just as he flipped off his kitchen lights, the phone rang.

He leapt for it, managing not to drop the tray. "Yes?" he said.

"It's me," said his T-shirted neighbor. "What are you doing?"

"Oh, hi," he whispered, straining to sound casual. "Listen, I'm on deadline. Can I call you tomorrow?"

"Sure," she said. "I just haven't been able to stop thinking about you."

"Me, too," Joe admitted. Trying not to sound abrupt, he added, "We'll talk tomorrow, okay? Good night." He hung up before remembering that he still didn't have her number. A drop of flop sweat trickled down his arm. He steadied the tray and went to the bedroom.

Mary Beth had dimmed the lights and was waiting, stretched out on the bed, which she'd made. She was, Joe couldn't help but notice, extremely naked.

He made a deal with himself that if he could get through whatever was about to happen, his new TV show would be a megahit. He also remembered that he had a meeting in the morning with Brutus Clay.

Turning up the lights on the dimmer, he pretended he hadn't seen Mary Beth and was only there to serve tea.

"I haven't even told you about The C Channel," he said, setting the tray down.

She turned onto her stomach and pulled a sheet over her.

"Well?" she said.

"They want me."

"Great. But do you want them?" she asked. "I've heard mixed things about that guy — what's his name?"

"Brutus Clay?"

"Yeah."

"He's crazy," agreed Joe, "but it's hard not to like him. And the money's nothing to sneeze at considering the mortgage here. . . ."

"Not to mention the cost of a wedding," she said nudging him. She studied him, still waiting for some acknowledgment that they were back to normal, that the wedding was, in fact, on.

"So, anyway," Joe said, not going there. "I guess I'm going to be on TV."

"Then all the other critics can review *you,*" she cooed, stretching and arching her back. "Come here and let *me* review you."

He moved into her arms and everything from that moment became a spontaneous, unwanted comparison between his wife-to-be and Amy.

Mary Beth's lovemaking was usually aerobic and loud. As she kissed him hard and tore at his back with her manicured nails, he did his best to pretend it was giving him the kind of pleasure they were used to. But he couldn't stop comparing it to the smooth, silent sweetness he'd shared with Amy. With too many thoughts in his head and the distinct feeling that his oil was down a quart, he feared for his erection.

They grunted and panted. It would have looked good in a movie, Joe thought. He was able to channel bits of anger and confusion into something resembling passion and longing, but he couldn't fool himself. Whatever can be given and taken in sex had already been given to and taken from Amy. His heart, to say the very least, wasn't in it.

Suddenly she pulled away fiercely. "No," she said. "Oh, God . . . no! Something's wrong. I can't."

She got up, crossing to where she'd left her clothes.

Joe was mortified. He'd blown it. Now I have to tell her, he thought. Oh, well. It's inevitable.

He felt like a death row prisoner rolling up his sleeve for a lethal injection.

"I'm sorry," he began, unglued.

"It's not you," she said, hurriedly dressing.

He paused, staring.

"I'm an idiot. I can't do this, Joe. I thought I could, but I can't.

Something's happening with Roger Shectman. I don't know if I'm in love with him, I don't know anything right now, but . . ." She stopped and let out a huge sigh.

"*What?*" said Joe.

"I promised myself I wasn't going to have this conversation with you today," she said, pacing back and forth.

"Really," said Joe.

"Well . . . oh, God, let me back up." She put her hand out as though to keep him from speaking, closed her eyes, and took a breath. "Please don't say anything for a minute, okay?" Joe nodded. "Roger read something of mine, and . . ."

"Something of yours?" repeated Joe. "You've been . . . writing?"

"Please let me say this. I had an idea for a screenplay and I showed it to him. Just a few pages, really, but . . ."

"Why didn't you show *me?*" asked Joe.

"I was afraid. You're a writer — "

"And he's an *editor,* for crying out loud — "

"I . . . I can't have this talk with you right now. I knew it. I'm not prepared for it."

"Oh, and you think I *am?*" asked Joe incredulously.

"The *point* is," Mary Beth steamed on, "that this man — and he's not a jerk, Joe; as a matter of fact, he happens to be a big fan of yours — this man thinks I have real talent. Which he believes in. And, I don't know, I didn't major in English to end up in business affairs, Joe. I've told you that. . . ."

"So this marriage cancellation is . . . a career move?"

"Don't put it that way. I didn't say that."

"You didn't have to," he said, the wind fully knocked from his sails. "This is your moment, and I guess you're taking it."

"I'm not that ambitious, Joe," she argued.

"Apparently you are," he said, his head swirling. "Which I never understood until right now."

"Oh, baby," she said sadly, giving it up. "I'm so sorry."

Avoiding each other's eyes, neither of them moved.

"So. Did this guy put some money on the table?" Joe asked, more curious than jealous. "Did he offer you a job?"

"Oh, God . . ."

"You can tell me. Don't sugar-coat it. Just be honest. We've always been honest with each other, haven't we?"

Mary Beth nodded, her lips tight.

"I don't know how to tell you this," she began hesitantly, "without sounding like some kind of opportunistic . . ."

"Just say it," said Joe, accepting once and for all, with very mixed feelings, that he had lost her.

"He . . . sort of offered me a job, yes."

"A 'sort of' job?" prodded Joe, relieved not to be on the defensive but deeply hurt nonetheless.

"Please don't hate me," she went on. "I'm going to my mother's. Don't look at me. I can't take it. No matter what you think of me right now, I love you. But I've always prided myself on knowing exactly what I want and now I'm just totally inside out. So if you *do* hate me, don't say it right now because I'll just dissolve, Joe." She'd closed two suitcases which he now realized she hadn't unpacked. She dragged them toward the door, found her purse, and turned to him.

"Déjà vu," he muttered.

"What?" she said, as though looking for comfort.

"Nothing," Joe managed. They looked at each other for a moment. Joe saw in her suddenly undefended eyes the friend he'd fallen in love with, the woman who'd comforted him during his breakup with Gayle, the woman whose smart, New Yorky abruptness was prized by Mollie, the woman who'd been the outwardly perfect partner for him. And he saw quite clearly that in the throes of her confusion and ambition, she was almost a total stranger.

"Thanks," she said, pausing at the door.

"For . . . what?"

"For the last eighteen months. For those days in Aruba. For being such a great dad. It was . . . glorious."

Joe forced back a sudden surge of tears. "That's awfully past tense," he said.

"It's all I can manage right now," she answered with a sniff. "I'll call you," she said, and walked out.

That night, Dean opened the door that led to Joe's roof, walked out onto the gravel, and scanned what he thought of as the perimeter. He saw a water tank, the brick housing for the elevator machinery, and a wood-slatted fence separating a private penthouse sundeck from the rest of the roof.

He looked in every direction, not seeing what he wanted. Walking carefully around the water tower, though, he turned a narrow corner — and there it was.

The roof of the building next door was ten feet away — a chasm, to be sure — but its height was roughly level with the roof where he stood.

If I could lay a couple of four-by-eights across, he thought, it would make a dandy bridge. Just right for moving a body.

The other building had a roof door that Dean figured led inside. The next step, he thought, is for me to get into that building and rig the lock of that door.

He rode the elevator down, raced home, changed into the only suit he owned, gathered his hair in a ponytail, put on a black beret, checked himself in the mirror, and dashed over to Ninety-first Street.

Like Joe's building, there were two locked doors in front. Dean thought about picking the locks, but there were a lot of potential witnesses around. It was Sunday night and weekenders were returning from the Hamptons.

As always, Dean had a Plan B.

He bought a paper at the Korean market on the corner and sat on a bench across the street and down the block, keeping his eyes on the front of the building, where years of New York grime had turned once-white brick almost black. After twenty minutes, a heavyset woman in her late fifties pulled up in a green Taurus, her elderly husband riding shotgun. The woman got out and walked around to open his door. He made his way feebly toward the entrance as she struggled with their luggage. Dean moved to the door, too, fiddling with a set of keys as though he lived there.

"Oh — can I help you?" Dean offered.

"Why, thank you," said the old fellow. "Here, I'll get the door." Dean pocketed the keys and reached for their bags.

"I'm Hank Potter," said Dean. "Just moved in last month."

"Irene Small," said the woman gratefully as she joined them. "And that's Charlie. Welcome! And thanks. We used to have a doorman, but those days are gone."

Dean carried their luggage in.

"Thank you, Hank," said the woman as Dean and her husband got into the elevator. "I'm going to park the car, sweetie." Dean prayed, literally, that they didn't live on the top floor, where he wanted to get off.

The old man pushed 3, and Dean pressed 9, one floor below PH, not wanting to give away his destination.

"It's a nice old place, you'll like it, yup," said Charlie as he watched the floor indicator lights. "What apartment are you in?"

Dean broke a sweat. "Nine A," he guessed, hoping Charlie didn't know the building too well.

"The Jensens' place?" said Charlie wistfully. "I didn't realize they'd moved." The elevator slowed to a stop at three.

Dean felt sweat trickle from his armpit.

"Never liked the Jensens," said the old guy. "Good riddance!" Relieved, Dean took a breath. Charlie began to get out and Dean lifted the old man's suitcases into the hallway.

"Lock your doors," Charlie warned. "Security isn't what it used to be."

"Ain't it the truth?" agreed Dean, getting back in as the elevator door closed. "You take care now. God bless."

Dean knelt, crossed himself, rode to nine, and took the stairs up one flight to the top floor. In the small foyer was an apartment door marked PH opposite a passageway with a few steps. Taking the steps, he found the door to the roof.

It had a heavy dead bolt on the inside. Dean got out his Swiss Army knife and carefully loosened the screws on the bolt casing till he was sure that the door, even when bolted, could be forced open from the outside.

17

JOE lay on his bed, a migraine in full tilt, not having moved since Mary Beth's latest exit. He conked out with the lights on and slept fitfully in an all-night attempt at comfort. When he awoke for keeps just before dawn, he couldn't stop himself — he went immediately to the kitchen.

Her apartment was dark. He was disappointed but calmed.

His machine clicked on and he took a step toward it, hoping it might be Amy. To his surprise, it was his mother, who hadn't spoken to him for months.

She said simply, "Did you move or something? I got a recording giving me a new number. Call me, Joey. I want to read your palm."

He reached for the phone, but she'd already hung up.

His mother had been ill for years with a respiratory problem, holed up in her small house on a remote Wisconsin island in Lake Superior. She had forged a fierce connection with Gayle and made no bones about her opinion that the breakup had been Joe's fault. She hadn't spoken to Joe since he and Mary Beth had become engaged. It was half joke, half tradition in Joe's family that his mother, who claimed to be one-eighth Gypsy, could read palms. Her batting average as a soothsayer had always been incredibly low, although she had, she often reminded Joe, predicted the miracle Mets' World Series win in 1969, and, on a less happy note, had foreseen the cancer that had taken Joe's father. She'd also predicted that McGovern would beat Nixon, that the first astronaut to step on the moon would die on contact with the lunar surface, and that Wayne Newton would, in his dotage, be elected to Congress.

"It could happen," she'd always insisted. "Have you seen his act? He's very charismatic."

Such mixed results didn't stop her from indulging with gusto in palm-reading whenever she could find a taker.

After he heard the machine disconnect, Joe stared at the phone as if it were his mother. Was her call an olive branch?

He wandered into the shambles of his office and opened a three-day-old FedEx envelope that had arrived at his former apartment the morning of the move. A couple of cassettes of A&E's *Biography* were enclosed, one featuring Al Gore and the other on Steven Spielberg. He popped them in and found them both compulsively watchable, which he wrote in reviews he managed to fax off that morning. He wasn't sure if it was out of a need to pass the time or because his equilibrium was unraveling so quickly, but another P.S. flew from his fingertips:

> *There are grocery packers who put ripe fruit into bags and then toss in heavy cans that smash the fruit and ruin it, while hollering to each other about "going on break."*
> *I want them dead.*

He walked into the kitchen, looked out the window, and returned to his desk when there was no sign of Amy. Unable to sit still, he went down to the lobby and found her mailbox. Next to 9B was a little plastic tag that read GOODE/BATTOCHI. He rode the elevator back up, called 411, and requested a listing for Amy Goode. There was none. He tried "A. Goode" and was told the number was unlisted. He tried "Battochi" but there was no such name in Manhattan. He tried "Battochi" in Garden City, but it, too, was unlisted.

He showered and found clothes from several boxes. Mary Beth's things were everywhere. He tiptoed around them, mentally and physically, wondering when and how Mary Beth would come for them. Or would she call in a few days begging him to take her back again?

The phone rang. He pounced.

"Yes?" he said.

"It's Rhonda," answered the flat voice of Rhonda Spivak, an editor at the *Milwaukee Journal.* "Are you . . . all right?"

"Hi, Rhonda," he said, trotting out a decent social front. "I'm fine. Why?"

"That A&E review you faxed in this morning. It had so many typos I thought your daughter must've written it. It was, like, in Chinese."

Rhonda was prone to exaggeration, but Joe walked with the phone to his computer screen and pulled up the review. It was ludicrously obvious that he'd neglected to proofread it. He'd been so distracted by repeated forays into the kitchen that he'd sent in the first rough draft, and his first drafts were always a mess.

"Something must have gone wrong in the transmission," he bluffed, looking hard at the screen as though it might change something. Rhonda was a careful, old-school editor, meticulous and demanding. "You know," he went on, trying to sound perfectly normal, "I'm in this new place, and — "

"Is it great? Do you love it?" she asked with no curiosity at all.

"It's wonderful, thanks. But anyway," he went on, "I think it must've been a software glitch or something, Rhonda, because I'm looking at it right now and it's fine."

He put down the receiver, switched to the headset he normally wore when working, and madly began rewriting on the fly, striking the keys softly so Rhonda wouldn't hear.

"Well, fax it right over, can you, we're running it in the early edition."

"Sure, sure," he said, mind racing, fingers flying over the keys. "You mean — *right* away?"

"ASAP, sweetheart," said Rhonda who sounded more New York than Joe did.

"You got it," Joe said.

"Oh, and that thing about bag packers? Excusez-moi, but what does that have to do with the price of eggs?"

"Don't you agree?" Joe asked a little too pointedly.

"I actually do, yes. But you complain about violence on TV, and then — "

"I didn't say I wanted to *kill* them," Joe countered. "I said I wanted them dead. Isn't anybody allowed disagreeable feelings anymore?"

"Some people were just wondering what those feelings were doing on the TV page," said Rhonda carefully.

"Which people? I want names."

"Are you okay?"

"Bear with me, Rhonda. I have PMS."

"Don't talk PMS to an angry broad with PMS."

"Can I call you later?"

"I'm always here," she said, and hung up.

He sat in front of the screen, hastily patched together a rewrite, and, knowing he had only a few minutes to make the deadline, reread it, ran the spell checker, flipped on his modem, and faxed it again. On his other working line, the phone rang.

"McBride here," he said into the headset.

"Mr. McBride, hello. It's David Teng. Did you have a restful weekend?"

"Hi, David," he said, ignoring the question. "What's up?"

"Just a reminder that you're meeting with Mr. Clay at eleven to go over your ideas for *Everybody's a Critic*."

My ideas, thought Joe — what ideas? He hadn't had time to come up with any.

"We're on the air next week," David reminded him, "so we need to get the process going. We'll see you in a couple of hours."

He flipped on Channel One. It was sixty-eight degrees outside. He changed into gray flannels, a tattersall shirt, and his trusty black sports coat that went with everything. It seemed odd not to run his outfit by Mary Beth for approval. He grabbed his wallet and left the building in search of breakfast.

At a corner coffee shop called Jackson Hole he ordered scrambled eggs, but when they arrived, piled high and steaming, he found he had no appetite. He forced a piece of toast down and managed half a cup of coffee, but his intestines were on strike. Early for the meeting with Brutus Clay, he decided to walk down Fifth Avenue for a while before grabbing a cab to Queens.

On the corner of Ninetieth Street, he passed the neo-Gothic Church of the Heavenly Rest. It gave him an idea. He hopped a cab, and to Joe's astonishment, its driver, a woman, was of American — or at least English-speaking — ancestry, her license proclaiming her to be Sally McCue. Had Sally not been a hundred pounds or so above her fighting weight, Joe felt sure he would have found her attractive. She had such an open, pretty face that he found her attractive anyway.

It's a disease, he thought to himself. I find all women attractive.

"Morning!" she said with a genuine smile. Joe couldn't remember the last time a cabdriver had smiled at him.

"Hi," said Joe, closing the door and finding a seat belt that actually worked. "How well do you know Queens?"

"I'm a Brooklyn kinda gal," said Sally with a shrug. "But try me. I've been doin' this for a while."

"The corner of Corona Avenue and Forty-seventh Street," began Joe. "Is it anywhere near Silvercup Studios?"

"They're not exactly next-door neighbors," said Sally as she plowed down Fifth Avenue. "Ten, maybe fifteen minutes apart, depending on traffic." Joe nodded thoughtfully. "You gonna tell me where we're goin', or am I supposed to, like, divine your destination?"

"Sorry," said Joe looking at his watch. "Okay. Take me to Corona and Forty-seventh. There's a police precinct there."

"Turnin' yourself in?" asked Sally.

In his sleep-deprived state, it took Joe a second to realize she was kidding. Not wanting to chance the Queensborough Bridge again, he directed her through the Midtown Tunnel, and they arrived at Forty-seventh Street with about twenty minutes to spare before his meeting with Brutus Clay.

"There it is," said Sally, pointing ahead to the converted church that Amy had mentioned. "Ninety-ninth Precinct."

"Would you mind waiting for a few minutes?" Joe asked, knowing how cabbies usually hate to wait. "You can keep the meter running."

"Oh," said Sally with a smirk. "Like I'd wait with the meter *off*? And you're supposed to say you'll make it worth my while."

"I'll make it worth your while," repeated Joe as he got out. "Ten minutes, max."

He walked up the sidewalk past uniformed police coming and going on motorcycles, in squad cars, and on foot. It was as busy as a high school when the bell has just rung. Joe worked his way up the four front steps and through the double doors of what had once been a small, quaint, if poorly located, church. Its architecture struck Joe as too rich, too upscale, even in its run-down, converted state, for what appeared to have always been a working-class neighborhood.

Inside, it bore no resemblance to a church. The interior had been gutted long ago. It could have been anywhere. Joe walked toward the front desk.

An old Haitian janitor was sweeping, the scratch of his broom a counterpoint to the scuffling footsteps everywhere. Joe nodded at him and smiled. He felt ridiculously excited. His headache was gone.

The swarthy sergeant on duty barely looked up from a pile of papers he was rubber-stamping.

"Yeah?" he offered.

"I'm looking for Amy Goode," said Joe.

"She was just here," said the cop, stamping three pages in quick succession. "Jimmy!" he called to someone in a room behind him. "Is Amy still here?"

"Think so," said a distracted voice. "In the back."

Joe started toward the back of the building. "Is this official?" asked the sergeant, slowing Joe down.

"Not really," returned Joe. "I just need to talk to her for a minute."

"Down that hall, second door on your left. The old choir room. It still says that on the door. It's our smoking room."

As Joe walked, the lines and angles of the building's geometry adjusted pleasingly to his changing perspective. He came to the doorway the sergeant had indicated. It was slightly ajar.

Looking in, he saw two women, both smoking, neither in uniform, in heated conversation with a patrolman. One woman was in her forties, dark, with a bad complexion and an ill-fitting, bluish, polyester skirt with matching vest over a white blouse. The other was thickset and blond, her hair pulled back plainly, framing a handsome, stern face, dressed in baggy jeans and a maroon windbreaker. They looked at Joe and stopped talking.

"Can I help you?" asked the younger woman, annoyed at the interruption.

"Sorry to bother you," said Joe, automatically lowering his voice. "I'm looking for Amy Goode. I'm a friend. I . . . just wanted to say hello."

"Well, then," she said, standing up and extending her hand to Joe unenthusiastically. "Hello — friend. I'm Amy Goode."

18

THE floor was marble, so Joe knew it only seemed to be sinking. "Oh," he said, trying, as always, to appear at ease, even when his personal sky was falling. "How good to meet you. I mean — see you. Again. Good to *see* you."

"I'm sorry," said the real Amy Goode, frowning at herself. "I can't remember where it was we met." The patrolman and the other woman watched.

"Well," Joe answered, having no idea what to say and trying to gather what was left of his nerves. "We haven't actually met. I've just heard a lot about you, and . . ."

"From who?" she asked.

"Well," Joe stumbled on, improvising. "My next-door neighbor, actually. A few days ago I moved into a new building in Manhattan and I have this neighbor who's been . . . raving about you."

"Well, that's very flattering, I'm sure," she said. "Who's the neighbor?"

"I was afraid you'd ask me that," he said, laughing falsely. "It was someone I met in the hallway as I was moving in, and we struck up a conversation about the city and how the mayor and the police have really, you know, brought it back to its glory days, and she mentioned this story about how she'd once been lost in Queens and gone to the Ninety-ninth Precinct and how you helped her out — you probably don't even remember, but — this is so embarrassing . . . I'm sorry. I never even caught her name. You know how that is." She nodded. "So anyway, I'm a writer and I'm researching a story about undercover cops — do you mind the word 'cop'?"

"Not really."

"I've always wanted to ask a cop that. Anyway, I was walking by this morning and what do I see but the Ninety-ninth Precinct, and I just kind of put two and two together and thought I'd chat you up and see if you could help me out, you know — go over some of the details of my story and make sure they're accurate."

"This is a *movie* you're writing?" she asked. The two others looked more attentive.

"A novel, actually," said Joe. All three cops seemed disappointed.

"Well, listen, Mr. . . . ?"

"Dean," said Joe, wondering why on earth he'd chosen to lie. "Brutus Dean." He stuck out his hand and she shook it listlessly.

"Look, Mr. Dean," she continued. "We're kinda in the middle of something here. Why don't you leave me your number and I'll call you." She didn't sound too caught up in the excitement, and Joe, eager to make his getaway, scribbled a phony number.

He had managed to bluff — convincingly, he hoped — but considering he'd faxed a first draft to an editor this morning, and, what with his new lover's identity now in question, he was sure of absolutely nothing except that he felt like throwing up.

The officers seemed antsy to get back to their discussion, and Joe, relieved to be over the hump, glanced at his watch. His appointment at The C Channel was twelve minutes away. "Well," he said, as though he'd just completed a routine inspection of the premises, "I won't keep you. Nice to meet you."

"I'll call you," Amy Goode said as Joe turned.

"I look forward to it," Joe replied, mindlessly backing away. He rushed outside, grateful to find Sally double-parked at the corner.

During the refreshingly uneventful cab ride to Silvercup Studios, Joe tried to brainstorm ideas for The C Channel. It was hopeless. He felt like someone holding a deed to the Brooklyn Bridge who'd just run into the real owner. The extent of his bamboozlement left him in a kind of extended shock. He looked out the cab's windows and saw nothing but the face of his downstairs neighbor. He tasted her. He saw her brilliant white skin and recalled the intuition of her touch. He tried to imagine why she'd lied and who she was, and told himself he was the most gullible person and the biggest fool for love — or lust — on the face of the earth.

He did his best to clear his head for the meeting with Clay, and when he ambled into Silvercup, the guard who'd greeted him Friday was back on duty.

"Joe McBride," he muttered. "To see Brutus Clay."

"You're goin' to The C Channel, am I right?" the guard asked proudly.

"Yes, thanks," Joe said. He signed in and was waved toward the elevator.

"Who's gonna watch a bunch of *critics*?" the guard chuckled good-naturedly. "I think 'C' must stand for 'crazy.' " Joe moved like a sleepwalker to the elevator.

The doors opened on the third floor, and Joe was met by an extremely tall young woman with a radio headset over her thick pigtails. Built like a fullback, she was dressed in overalls, a sweatshirt, and combat boots. In his nightmarish haze, she looked to

Joe like one of Maurice Sendak's wild things, and he braced himself for her to roar a terrible roar. She seemed to know who Joe was, which was more than he did at the moment.

"I'm David Teng's assistant," she explained shyly. "Sumitra." Joe exhaled, relieved that she was friendly. Did she have a last name, he wondered, or was she, like Cher, simply Sumitra? Or was Sumitra, for that matter, her real name? Maybe her name was Amy Goode, too.

He mentally slapped himself back to reality as she led him to Brutus Clay's office, which now sported an impressive brass plaque proclaiming his name.

"Go right in," Sumitra said, waiting to be sure he did.

Clay was once again facing away from Joe when he opened the door, but that was the only thing about the office that hadn't changed. A beautiful window had been drawn based on Clay's sketch, and the boss was now apparently admiring the "view." The place was furnished lavishly from top to toe, with wall-to-wall carpeting of a deep, forest green. There were framed Currier and Ives prints on the walls and leather furniture surrounding a large, imposing desk with inkwells, feather quills, and blotters. Had Joe been capable of enjoying anything at that moment, he might have thought it looked charmingly turn-of-the-century.

"The Joe-meister! Excellentissimo! How are we?"

"Terrific," Joe said as though reciting a script and hoping he was convincing.

"Liar!" Brutus Clay shouted in an abrupt change of tone, pointing at Joe, who broke a sweat instantly. Clay saw Joe's discomfort and laughed. "What's the problem?" he asked more gently. "Out with it!"

"How . . . do you know there's a problem?"

"I've been re-reading Sherlock Holmes," Clay replied. "Clearly you haven't slept. It appears you've lost five pounds over the weekend. Your cheeks are pale and hollow. You didn't eat.

What's the problem?" he asked cheerfully. "Prospect of working for me got you down?"

"Not at all, not at all," Joe said, laughing it off unconvincingly. "It was just a tough weekend."

"Need some time off?" Clay asked.

Joe was afraid to say yes — though he wanted to — and afraid to say no, figuring Clay would somehow, Holmes-like, catch him in the lie.

"I can't give you any time off," Clay went on. "Wish I could. Can't. We're on the air next week. What've you got?"

"Well," Joe said, plunging in without a clue as to what he'd say, "taking your title, *Everybody's a Critic,* I thought the show might start with my own review of something, then cut to me, you know, interviewing people on the street, asking for their own, on-the-spot review of the same program — showing how many different opinions there can be. . . ."

"Go on," Clay said, gazing out his fake window.

"A lot of stations and newspapers try to make it seem that their critic's view is the be-all and end-all," said Joe, picking up a little steam. "Let's turn that upside down, remind our audience that it's okay — even healthy — to disagree with critics."

Clay drummed on his desk with a pencil. Joe went on.

"Maybe finish the show by putting somebody from the street behind my desk, and letting *that* person review something. Everybody's a critic — simple, but cheap." Emotionally hungover and terrified that it was written all over his face, Joe smiled wanly to show that he was finished.

"It sounds *inexpensive* — which I like — but that doesn't make it cheap," said Clay with a wink. "It needs tweaking. Let me think on it. You go home, for goodness sake, and get some sleep. I can't have my anchor looking so peaked. I'll talk to David, mull this over, and we'll meet again tomorrow."

Joe was grateful and relieved. "Same time?" he asked.

"Same time," said Clay, decisively. "What time *is* it?"

"I arrived at eleven," Joe said.

"Eleven, then. And let my chauffeur drive you back. Absolutely the last time, but you need to take it easy. Tomorrow we'll show you the sets and you can meet your producer. Do you like my office?" he asked at the door.

"It's . . . amazing," Joe answered.

"I'm not sure," he said. "Maybe it needs a bit less Sherlock Holmes and a little more Mad Dog."

Joe shrugged. Clay looked up at him.

"Love problems, eh?" Clay said, shaking his head as though Joe had brought up the subject. "The best and the worst. Rest up. It'll look brighter tomorrow."

Joe had that "how'd you know" look on his face.

"Your work is going well," Clay went on. "My research tells me you're not gay. Who else but a woman makes you lose sleep and not eat? Is there a Mrs. McBride?"

"Yes," Joe answered, "but we don't live together."

"Say no more," said Clay. "I mustn't pry." He closed the door and sent Joe on his way.

He fussed and fidgeted in the limo all the way home, muttering at traffic and backseat-driving Brutus Clay's chauffeur, who was so unflappable he didn't take offense. When Joe entered his apartment, he made a beeline for the answering machine and was rewarded with a long-awaited message from his downstairs neighbor.

"PLEASE come by tonight," she said on the machine. She sounded contrite. "I really need . . . to talk. I'll leave the back door open, and you can let yourself in."

This is a woman, Joe thought, who could surely foil a lie detector.

He erased it, wondering if Mary Beth might have called from an outside phone to retrieve messages. Joe tried to remember how to change the three-digit code needed to pick up messages from the machine. He knew the manual was packed away somewhere and tore into what he thought was the appropriate box. It was filled instead with dozens of Fotomat envelopes and little picture albums. He opened one at random, flipping to a snapshot of himself, Gayle, and Mary Beth, taken on the beach at Aruba by a stranger they'd stopped. Mary Beth, tanned, topless, her back to the camera, and, as Joe remembered, on her second mai-tai; Gayle, strained, as though she were trying to have a better time than she was, lovely in a black one-piece bathing suit that was far more alluring than he'd remembered.

Joe thought about what might have been if he and Gayle had gone to Aruba alone and not brought along Gayle's old college friend, Mary Beth Wise. It was in Aruba that the trouble had started. Joe had taken Gayle in hope that some time alone with her might net them their long wished-for pregnancy. Gayle, who'd been feeling neglected and, unbeknownst to Joe, was contemplating an affair at home, had suggested Mary Beth as a buffer. But Gayle came down with the flu almost on arrival, which threw Joe and Mary Beth together for the first few days. They'd spent hour after hour sunning on the beach, Mary Beth first going topless and eventually driving Joe insane by swimming and sunning in the nude. They snorkeled, talked, and ate meals alone. For two days, they didn't so much as hold hands or talk about their increasingly obvious attraction. On the third night, though, when Gayle's coughing had forced Joe from their bedroom, he'd found Mary Beth on their patio overlooking the ocean, dressed in a diaphanous short nightie that blew his circuits. They made out for two hours and finally succumbed to hurried, shame-filled intercourse. The next day, Gayle was better and Joe and Mary Beth behaved for the rest of their stay as though nothing had happened.

Ten months after Mollie's birth, when Joe was on a press junket in L.A., Gayle began her affair, admitting it to Joe a month later. He comforted himself with Mary Beth and they quickly found that the night in Aruba hadn't been a fluke. Joe and Gayle agreed to stay together for Mollie's sake, but the dual affairs continued for two years, and they finally separated. Gayle's affair eventually fizzled but Joe's didn't, and unable to stand that Joe was contemplating marriage to her old friend, Gayle left the city. Joe carefully and painstakingly encouraged Mollie's friendship with Mary Beth, and finally, with Mollie's blessing, Joe and Mary Beth had become engaged. Everything had been progressing toward a summer wedding until Mary Beth's bombshell.

Joe closed the little album and rifled through a few more boxes, unable to find the folder containing compulsively saved, never-used instruction manuals and guarantees. Meanwhile, if Mary Beth chose to, she could intercept his messages. Maybe she already had. Maybe she'd heard Amy — he still thought of her as Amy — inviting him over tonight.

He began to anticipate the humiliation of telling everyone that the wedding was off — though he wasn't a hundred percent sure it was, or even if he wanted it to be. The phone man showed up and installed the remaining three lines. Only after he finished, leaving a $700 installation bill, did Joe realize he wouldn't need two of the lines if Mary Beth wasn't coming back.

He managed to connect the rest of his TVs and fit them into the area off the living room that Mary Beth had designated for them, noticing he was still putting the apartment together so as to please her.

Ferdy Levin's party was at seven. Joe dressed, called Mollie, and, fortified by her words and phone kisses, headed downtown.

She stood by the entry of his tiny studio apartment with the front door open.

"Why did you come here?" asked Dean.

"I missed you," she said as though she meant it. "One more kiss."

"Are you kidding?" said Dean. "No way." An image of the new gun drifted into his mind. It was close by. Maybe I should use it now, he thought. I wouldn't have to put up with any more of this.

She could see how angry he was and knew she had to proceed carefully.

Letting the door close, she moved to him and pulled his head to hers, kissing him the way she'd kissed him in the window. After a moment, he broke away.

"You kiss me like that and then you tell me you're still not sure?" he asked, wild-eyed.

"I never claimed to be logical. I *am* sure," she said, as though it were out of her hands. "I have to go home." She took him in her arms like a mother caressing a child.

"Call me," he whispered.

"I might not be able to, so I don't want to promise," she said gently, stroking his head.

He couldn't let her go just yet and decided to surprise her.

"I got what you wanted," Dean murmured.

She hugged him tighter, grinning. "You did?"

He looked up at her and nodded.

"Why didn't you tell me?" she asked.

"The way you've been acting, I don't know, I was thinking about keeping it myself."

It scared her, but she decided to bluff.

"If that's what you want," she said, starting away.

"No. No," he answered, caving. "I got it for you, and I'm good to my word. You want it?"

"Not quite yet," she said simply, coming back and hugging him again. "Could you maybe . . . deliver it? If I promise to give the delivery boy an extra-special tip?"

Dean smiled in spite of himself.

"Show a little faith," she urged gently, slowly taking down his zipper and getting to her knees. "I have such a good feeling about all this. I just need a few more days, maybe a week. Can you put up with me that long? We'll have the rest of our lives afterward."

"*Mi* karma, *su* karma," said Dean, who couldn't take his eyes off her lips. "I'm in this for the long haul."

She rolled his pants down around his knees. "What did I do to deserve you?" she asked as if the sun rose and set in him. He blushed.

"Don't give up five minutes before the miracle, you wonderful man," she said, exploring him with her tongue, answering, quite literally, Dean's most recent prayer. "We're almost home."

It didn't take long. When she left, he drifted over to his dresser, opened a drawer, reached under a pile of socks, pulled out the

.38, and snapped the silencer off and on, off and on, without looking. He was getting good at it.

Ferdy Levin had been Joe's editor at the *Dispatch* for seven years, and he and his wife Caroline were famous for their inner sanctum dinners, always with a dozen eclectically chosen guests. Knowing how the cognoscenti coveted a seat at Caroline's table, Joe had managed to phone to tell her that he'd be coming without Mary Beth.

Ferdy's Spring Street loft had four huge, wide-open, postmodern rooms. The place seemed utterly at odds with Ferdy and Caroline, whom one would have expected to live on the Upper West Side in something decayed and professorial. Instead, broken columns, partial walls, and angular lighting gave their place the feel of a high-tech set for a Michael Crichton movie.

Caroline, who favored place cards, sat Joe between Liz Smith and Elaine Kaufman, owner-manager of the East Side celebrity hangout that bears her first name. Joe was almost punchy with fatigue and grateful for their nonstop, raucous conversation. Liz had heard about Joe's P.S.'s and asked for a comment. He told her that they were composed on a Ouija board. She laughed and didn't seem to notice, or graciously ignored, the riot taking place between his ears. A few people were smoking, aggravating Joe's cravings, which had kicked in mercilessly.

On his way to the guest bathroom, he grabbed a Winston from a crystal bowl Ferdy always kept filled. Resigned to rekindling his habit, he locked the door of the powder room and struck a match. As he was about to inhale he remembered that his smoking could cost the Mets the pennant, and tossed the cigarette into the toilet.

He was incapable of enjoying himself. All he could think of was getting home and possibly seeing Amy. He made too many excuses for Mary Beth, bragged modestly to Liz about the C Channel job, and left early, reminding Ferdy he still had a review to knock out when he got home.

"Sorry to be the messenger," said Ferdy at the door, "but you're under orders to cool it with the P.S.'s. Edgar said — and I quote — 'Remind that prick that his job is to review television. If he wants to be a columnist, he can do it on his own time for some other rag.' The mayor's been on Edgar's ass, Joe. The city can't have tourists worrying about drinking the water. And Edgar has an old friend on the board of the grocery workers union who took offense at your P.S. about bag packers."

"Edgar should get a life," said Joe. "I'm a union member myself. I have nothing against bag packers in general. Just bad ones."

"I don't have the strength to fight with Edgar," said Ferdy apologetically. "Caroline's not well, and I'm . . . distracted."

"She looks fine," said Joe, surprised. "What is it?"

"Her ticker," said Ferdy, who seemed suddenly on the verge of tears. "Go. We'll talk. She's okay. Just had a bad checkup, she says."

"Call me if there's anything I can do," said Joe. "Really."

Ferdy shrugged helplessly. Joe took his leave and hailed a cab on Spring Street.

As they rode uptown, Joe's scrawny, surly driver slurped something through a straw in a plastic-topped cup, then tossed the whole thing out his window as they sped across Fourteenth Street. Joe looked back and the cup bounced, joining the already accumulated debris on the street, the plastic top and straw rolling away like sagebrush.

Keenly aware that he needed a night for emotional regrouping, Joe promised himself he'd avoid the kitchen when he got home, and that under no condition would he accept "Amy's" invitation to come over. He was desperate to confront her with her lie, but he knew his limits. He couldn't get by on another sleepless night. He'd find her tomorrow.

He watched an advance tape of a tense new episode of *ER* and by 11:30 he'd managed to write — and even proofread — a review. He faxed it and sent slightly revised versions to the Philadelphia and Milwaukee papers so that each could claim an original piece by Joe McBride. With perverse glee, he attached the following:

P.S.

I don't approve of murder. But at least deluded people think they have a reason to kill, and occasionally juries agree. But is there ever *an excuse for littering? Have I missed something?*

I'd like to lock an angry postal clerk in a room with litterers, and, you know, do something nice for the environment.

He put on pajamas, brushed his teeth, and got into bed. His housekeeper, Zabida, would be coming tomorrow, and the sheets, which smelled of Mary Beth, would mercifully be changed.

He lay in bed for an hour trying to avoid glances at the faded glow-in-the-dark dial of his watch, thinking only of cigarettes and women. Unable to stand it, he got up, threw on a pair of jeans and a sweatshirt, rebrushed his teeth, and, going forthrightly back on his word to himself, walked out his kitchen door and proceeded down to the apartment of the woman whose name he didn't know.

CHAPTER 20

As promised, the back door was open. Barefoot, he moved in, making his way silently through the kitchen. He walked into the living room. It was empty.

"It's Joe," he called tentatively. There was a soft light coming from under the door to the bedroom. He walked to it and pushed the door gently. The hinge squeaked, and a platinum blonde sitting on the bed snapped her head toward Joe and grabbed her heart.

"Oh, my *God*," she shouted, her hand over her mouth. "You better be Joe McBride or I swear I'm gonna scream bloody murder!"

"I am, I am," said Joe, who felt like screaming himself.

"Jesus!" she sighed, recovering a little. "This apartment's about as secure as a 7-Eleven. How the fuck did you get in here?"

"Sorry," answered Joe. "I came in through the back door — "

"She left the back door open?"

"That's the arrangement we had," explained Joe sheepishly.

"In *this* city? She's nuts. Loree Battochi," she said, rising and moving to him. "The little sister." She shook his hand and then, remembering something, picked up an envelope with Joe's name on it that had been on the bed. "I don't usually show up during the week, so Nannie didn't know I'd be here, and, anyway, I guess this is for you."

"You call your sister Nannie?" Joe asked hesitantly, clearing his throat.

"Well, you know, most people call her Annette, but she's always been Nannie to me," said Loree.

He took the envelope and started back the way he'd come. Noticing that the letter had been torn open, he stopped.

"I read it," she said unapologetically, blowing on the shiny white nails she'd been filing. He remembered her husky Long Island accent from the night she'd barged in drunk.

Joe nodded. She was dressed in plaid silk slacks featuring hips that apparently ran in the family and a classic white short-sleeved blouse tied at the waist showing a few inches of nicely tanned belly. Just what I need, thought Joe — an absolute, out-and-out stunner. Pretty women seemed to be growing on trees. She had a thin string of cultured pearls around her neck and stud earrings that might have been diamonds.

Joe pulled the letter out of the envelope.

"I shouldn't have opened it," she said, "but, hey, I see a letter with no street address and just some guy's name on it . . . so sue me, I'm curious. I gotta get going, which means you gotta get going, too," she added, all business, walking into the living room. It was impossible not to watch her leave.

He yanked out the letter, almost ripping it as he unfolded it.

Dear Joe,
I followed you out to Queens. I hope in time you'll see that while I'm not Amy Goode, I'm not all bad, either. (Ha, ha.)
You turned me inside out. I didn't expect that. I thought I could steal an evening and just enjoy you and . . . I don't

*know what I thought. However (deep breath), things with
Dean are proving more complicated than I thought. I can't
quite see straight and I need to get away for a few days.
When I come back you can yell at me and I'll do my best
to explain.*

*It was cowardly to invite you over and not be there. I
guess that's another thing I'll ask you to forgive me for.*

Nannie (that's me)

Joe exhaled, folded the note, pocketed it, and walked back into
the living room. Loree had lit a cigarette and was sitting on the
arm of the couch, toying with the jigsaw puzzle, which was starting to take form.

"Was that you with her when I came in the other night?" she
asked. "I was a little, shall we say, tipsy. You were kinda hiding
out in the kitchen?"

Joe nodded.

"Nannie strikes again," muttered Loree, looking up at him.
"Sorry."

Trying to absorb the note, Joe shrugged and looked down at
the puzzle.

"I think it's *The New York Times*," Loree said, her hand hovering over the puzzle with a piece she couldn't fit. "I have a feeling
it's from the day we were born or something."

Joe's headache started to come back.

"She told me it was a gift from *you*," he said.

"Oh, my God," said Loree, her jaw dropping. "Of course. Then
it is *The New York Times*. I can't believe she still has this. I gave
it to her, like, five years ago. We're both puzzle mavens. Jigsaws
are usually our default birthday present to each other."

"May I have a drag of that?" Joe asked, nodding at her cigarette, a nonfilter that smelled astonishingly good to him. She held
it out. He reached for it, but paused remembering the Mets had
an eight-game winning streak going. He left it dangling in her
long fingers. "Never mind," he said smiling tightly.

She raised her eyebrows and took a long drag.

"Is Battochi your married name?" Joe asked, breathing in a mini-hit from what she unthinkingly blew in his direction.

"Yeah," she answered. "Maiden name's Pritchard."

"She told me her last name was Goode."

Loree grunted ironically. "Nobody ever said my sister doesn't have a sense of humor."

Joe looked out the window, lost. Amy Goode had become Nannie Pritchard.

"You seem nice," Loree said picking up another puzzle piece, "and I humbly suggest that you turn tail and forget about her." She stubbed out her cigarette with a punctuating exhale of smoke. "Of course now that I've said that, she probably sounds all the more interesting. I don't know. Never mind. Do what you have to do." She dropped the puzzle piece to the side.

Joe stood, a million miles away.

"So, uh, I guess you know the way out," she said, getting up and trying to be polite.

Joe noticed her spiked alligator shoes, the straps adorning her feet like ankle bracelets, and a tattoo of a spider above her right anklebone. There was also a tiny silver ring pierced into her navel that Joe, who'd been trying to avoid staring at her bare midriff, hadn't noticed before.

He took a step or two toward the back door.

"Don't feel bad," said Loree, stopping him. "She started pulling this stuff when we were teenagers. Messing with people. Guy-people, mostly. She used to play tricks on my boyfriends — the usual twin stuff. I did it, too. But she's branched out from just pretending to be me. Amy Goode, huh?" She blew out some more smoke. "I wonder if there's a real Amy Goode."

"A cop at the Ninety-ninth Precinct in Queens," said Joe.

Loree, who was lighting another cigarette, laughed and choked a little. "That's a stretch," she said, waving away some smoke. "Nannie's an actress. I kick in half the rent or I don't think she could keep this place. She doesn't work a whole lot — she'd kill me for sayin' that — and I keep telling her to give it up and come out to Garden City, but, you know . . . she has a *dream*." She shook her head and gathered a purse and white cashmere sweater as though she were leaving. "Hold it, wait a second. McBride? Are you the TV guy?"

Joe nodded.

"So my sister bagged a critic," she said. "Ain't life grand?" She examined him more closely. "You don't look like your picture in the paper."

"Neither do you," he said with a nod toward the silver-framed photos in which Loree was a redhead.

"I'd been everything but a blonde," she laughed with a shrug. "And I got news — they *don't* have any more fun than I did as a redhead — or a brunette for that matter. But, hey, maybe my luck'll change tonight. I read your stuff from time to time. Whatta you got against sitcoms?"

"Nothing," Joe said, defensively. "It just gets harder to find good ones."

"Oh, come on," Loree snapped back. *"Frasier, Seinfeld?"*

"Sure," said Joe, unconsciously relieved to be talking about something he understood, "but for every decent show there are these endless lousy ones."

"You're nice to the actors, though," she said, nodding. "I gotta say that. You don't go all ballistic on them, like some of your, whatta-you-callits . . . ?"

"Peers," he said.

"Peers, right."

"I got over that when I reviewed plays for a while," Joe said, trying to talk through his discomfort. "It's tempting to be clever about actors, but I finally learned that if a play doesn't work, it's usually the writing or the direction."

"Well, bully for you," she said, heading toward the door. He wondered if she was aware that the outline of her tiny, thong underwear showed beneath her slacks. She stopped and turned to him. "If you're not gonna leave, I will."

"Sorry," Joe said, taking a step away. "Is there . . . anything else I should know about your sister?" he asked with a haggard smile.

"Maybe I'll cancel my next girl's night out," Loree answered. "You can buy me a drink and I'll tell you some bedtime stories about the Pritchard girls." She checked herself in the mirror by the door. "Listen, me and my girlfriend are meetin' downtown to play. Kind of a mini girl's night out. I don't think she'd mind if you joined us. You can be an honorary girl. You look like you need to get your mind off you-know-who."

"Isn't that 'you-know-*whom*'?" inquired Joe halfheartedly.

"Like I give a rat's ass," said Loree impatiently. "You comin'?"

Joe glanced at his watch. It was a little after one. "Past my bedtime," he said.

"This is when the clubs are just gettin' started." Loree shrugged.

"I think I've had enough entertainment for this particular lifetime," he answered, numb.

She closed the door and walked back toward him, stopping a little closer than Joe felt comfortable with and looking him in the eye.

"At least she has good taste," said Loree, flashing a grin. Joe felt as if his feet were nailed to the floor. "You sure you wouldn't like to come downtown?" she repeated, as if it were no big deal.

"I'm sure of absolutely nothing in this world," answered Joe, whose headache had made a vivid re-entry. "But I have some work to do, and with a little help from Saint Paul over there" — he looked to the portrait on the wall — "I'm gonna do it. So, yes. Thanks for . . ." He stopped, realizing he had nothing to thank her for but adding to the wreckage of his emotional state.

He turned to move away, and she stopped him with a hand on his shoulder, pulling him around, leaning into him, hugging him. Her breasts, soft but firm against him, felt entirely too good. He pulled away.

"You ever wonder what it'd be like to be with twins?" she asked as though she were inquiring about the weather.

"Not till tonight," Joe replied, stepping away from her and heading toward the back door. "Nice meeting you," he called.

"See ya 'round," she called back.

Joe went to bed, pulled the covers over his head, and managed an hour or so of sleep. He awoke a little after three, and in what had become his Pavlovian routine, walked to the kitchen. It was dark and he didn't see anything at first, but then, in the window below, he was able to make out parts of two bodies silhouetted in the faint TV glow. Joe's chest tightened at what he assumed was Nannie with Dean. He retreated into the shadows and looked closely. It *was* Dean, and, as he turned his partner to embrace her from behind, Loree's platinum hair caught a trace of light as she threw her head back and cried out so loudly that Joe could hear, even though the windows between them were closed.

"Oh . . . you . . . *mother*," she wailed. "*Please* not so hard. Please be gentle."

Sensing she was frightened, he did as she asked.

"There. Yes," she purred. "That's . . . so . . . much . . . better. Come on, let's move away from the window."

"No," he said, holding her there. "I like it here."

"Oh, Mother of God, that's good," she said.

"Blaspheme in your other life, but never with me," he warned, slapping her face hard enough for her to know he was serious.

She twisted, reached behind her and grabbed his torso with both hands, pulling him closer again. "Tell me something," she said. "Is this better than with her?"

"I won't answer that," Dean said, his breath short.

They worked their way to the floor and out of sight of the window. In the midst of her climax, he moved his hand to her belly, grabbed the ring in her navel, and twisted it hard, saying, "Don't give me orders."

She shrieked, kicking him with the heel of the alligator shoe she hadn't removed. "Get out!" she screamed in pain. "*Out! Now!*"

Picking up the .38 where he'd left it, a thin trail of blood seeping from where her heel had met his abdomen, he backed out of the kitchen. She looked down at her navel, then followed him out, only to find the .38 pointed at her eyes. He moved it up and down her body as though he couldn't decide where the bullet should enter.

"Get out," she ordered again.

"I oughta shoot," he said, tears streaming, but moving to the door nonetheless. "This is killing me. You hear?" She stared him down and his voice trailed off as he dropped suddenly to the floor at her feet. "I'm sorry," he sobbed.

"Tell me," she whispered urgently. "Who do you like most?"

When he didn't answer, she pulled away, walked quickly to the living room, grabbed the silver frame with the three pictures, brought it back, and shoved it in his face. "Choose."

"No . . ."

"*Choose!*" she screamed.

"Why?" he demanded, backing away.

"Because I have to know!"

He grabbed her neck and pulled her to him, pressing her lips too hard. "Loree," he whispered sadly as he broke the kiss, "I choose you."

She pulled him closer. They quieted and held each other.

"I'm sorry I hurt you," he whispered, his fingers gently touching her belly.

"I'm sorry, too," she said.

Exhausted, she released him, gathered his clothes from a heap where they'd been tossed, walked to the front door, opened it, and threw his stuff into the hallway.

"Go home," she said, turning to him almost good-naturedly. "I'll call you very soon. I promise."

Gun in hand, he shook his head, moved into the hallway, and began dressing.

"Your wish is my fucking command," he muttered, down on himself.

"I know," she whispered, watching him. "And I love you for it."

Joe stood in the kitchen, ashamed that he'd watched. It was quiet across the way and the shadow players had disappeared. He turned from the window.

So, he thought, Dean was having it off with both of them.

An idea came and he jerked his head back to the window. It was dark. Maybe Dean had left. It was a tremendously long shot, but he ran to his bedroom, stepped into his running shoes, and without lacing them, grabbed his keys, ran out, and rode the elevator down.

Looking first in all directions, he took off east on Ninetieth Street and ran full speed for a block and a half before realizing the futility of trying to find someone who, for all he knew, was still up in the building with Loree.

He made his way back turning things over in his mind. Did Nannie know about Dean and Loree? Was that the unexpected complication she'd referred to in her note?

Back in his kitchen, he decided to make milk and honey. Pathetic as it was, he admitted to himself that he yearned for Nannie. As he poured milk into a saucepan, Loree appeared again in the window, naked, her back to him.

He stood still, taking her in, unable to move, recalling her drunken taunt through the bedroom door.

"Pardon my sister, Mr. Whoever-You-Are. She's so rude she wouldn't even . . . introduce us. Are you cute?"

His phone rang and the answering machine clicked on. Joe's heart jumped.

"I want to bury the hatchet, Joey," implored his mother's voice, calling again from Wisconsin, apparently as sleepless at this hour as her son. "Let me have a look at your palms, sweetie. I'd like . . . to talk to *you,* damn it, not a machine. . . ." She coughed noisily. "I know, I know — I should stop smoking. But it's all I have left. Smoking and you."

Joe, an only child, listened, eyes on Loree, her body catching a glint of light and glowing with perspiration as she made her way about the kitchen, apparently oblivious to Joe. He heard his mother's phone clank on something as it slipped from her arthritic hands and she clumsily hung up.

He forced himself to turn from the window, grabbed the phone, dialed his mother's number, got a busy signal, slammed down the receiver, and turned back toward Loree.

She was gone and the curtains were closed.

CHAPTER 21

JOE struggled out of bed on Tuesday morning, went to the kitchen, reflexively checked for signs of either neighbor, and noticed the zero on the display of his answering machine. Nothing from Mary Beth or Nannie. Zombie-like, he scarfed down pancakes at Jackson Hole, constantly looking out its tall glass windows in hopes of spotting Nannie or Dean. He taxied to Silvercup Studios in Queens and the guard simply waved him upstairs.

"Mr. C Channel," the guard chuckled, shaking his head as Joe went by. Sumitra, in the same clothes as yesterday, led him again to Brutus Clay's office, though by now he could have made it on his own. Punch-drunk with fatigue and the disorientation wrought by his twin demons, he hoped that Clay's energy would be more revivifying than the pancakes, which had formed a knot of indigestion somewhere in his small intestine.

Sumitra opened Clay's door and Joe did his best to walk in freshly. The first thing he saw was a portion of tanned long legs leading to the short skirt of an expensive, dress-for-success suit. If this had been a quiz show, Joe would have guessed whose thighs they were before the buzzer, but his upward glance voided any suspense. It was Sandy Moss.

"The Joe-ster!" exclaimed Clay, clapping his hands. "Most excellent! Come in. Sit. Or better yet, stand, since there aren't any more chairs. David, make a note: more chairs!"

"Yes, sir," said David Teng, who stood a few steps from Clay's desk, clipboard in hand, ready for anything.

"Do you know the *fabulous* Sandy Moss?" Clay asked as Sandy swiveled around to greet Joe.

"Hi, stranger," she said, rising and greeting him with a businesslike hug. "Move go okay?"

"Yeah, sure, fine," Joe answered, lying through his teeth.

"Sit, sit," urged Clay, rubbing his hands. Then, remembering the dearth of chairs, he offered his own, pulling it around from behind his desk and placing Joe next to Sandy. Clay sat cross-legged in front of them as though he were about to tell a bedtime story.

Joe was so busy trying to seem alert that he hadn't done justice to his curiosity about Sandy's presence. Or perhaps he was in some early stage of denial. Clay stared at them for a moment with a happy-dopey expression, too excited to speak. Joe waited.

"Anchor," said Brutus Clay finally, with a momentous nod in Joe's direction, as though the blade of Excalibur had touched Joe's shoulder. Joe blinked and waited. Clay looked to Sandy and his eyes closed a bit as though the sun had brightened. "Co-anchor," he dubbed her.

Joe's eyes widened the way they might have if he'd been pleasantly surprised, which he wasn't. Was he now sharing his half hour with Sandy Moss, journalist lite?

"John Tesh," reaffirmed Clay, with that same nod at Joe, "and Mary Hart," he added, completing the equation with an equal-time glance at Sandy.

They both looked to Joe, their presentation complete.

Joe cleared his throat. "Well," he began, biting his upper lip and sucking on it dementedly. "How can I say this, Brutus — may I call you Brutus . . . ?"

"If you must," said Clay, disappointed.

"I mean, where do I start?" Joe continued, eyes fixed on Clay. "I thought it was *my* show."

"Oh, it is," chirped Sandy, oozing deference. "You're the only reason *anyone* will tune in. I'm just the, I don't know, the comic relief."

"Demographics," said Brutus Clay firmly, as though it explained everything. "Between the two of you, our sponsors are overjoyed. Joe does the serious, edgy, pushing-the-envelope-of-criticism stuff — and Sandy . . ."

"I sit around and look pretty," she said, with an easy shrug.

"Now if *I* said that," Clay exclaimed, "wham! Sexual harassment. I love it!"

"If anybody's going to do any sexual harassing around here," said Sandy, "it'll be me." They laughed like old comrades.

"Seriously, Joe," Sandy went on, turning to him, "the only reason I'll even be on the show is to feed you, set you up, support you. I mean, if there were ever an Emmy in this for me — and, okay, I know I'm getting ahead of myself here — it would be in the 'supporting' category. I'll be out on location, on the set of shows you're reviewing, doing what *I* do, which is interviewing celebrities. The body of the show, the *substance,* will all be you." The jacket of her suit was V-cut, and she wasn't, judging by infinitesimal flashes to which Clay and Joe were being treated, wearing anything underneath. Joe was astonished to find that he had utterly overdosed on cleavage.

"When . . . did all this happen?" Joe asked, trying to sound merely curious.

"Sandy charged in here yesterday," said Clay, effusively. "My God, she's a determined woman. . . ."

"He tried to throw me out," laughed Sandy.

"I told her in no uncertain terms that this is *your* show, Joe.

She said she admired you and wanted to be a part of what we're doing. I have to tell you, I resisted. I actually buzzed for security to come and . . ." He searched for a word.

"Remove me?" suggested Sandy.

"But she walked over, calm as you please, took the phone out of my hand, and hung it up. Can you believe that?" He laughed a smitten laugh at the memory. "What can I tell you, Yosef, she *fought* for this. Which I certainly hope you take as a compliment. I admit it doesn't bother me that she's an attractive woman. You're a fairly attractive man. I started to put a different two and two together. Look at Laurin Sydney on CNN, or Leeza Gibbons. Or the women of *Friends*. Smart, yes. Hip, sure — *but* — it doesn't hurt that they look fabulous in tank tops."

He seemed to rest his case.

Joe glanced at the ceiling and tried to imagine what it would be like working side by side with Sandy Moss. He never wanted to see an attractive woman again.

He reminded himself that an offer of sorts was on the table. There was a possible future in TV to consider. And the money. It was a pretty sure thing that Mary Beth wouldn't be kicking in half of the beefy new mortgage; his child-support payments were due for a court-scheduled inflationary increase, and Mollie's tuition seemed to inflate exponentially each year.

Brutus and Sandy were staring at him.

Feeling as though any semblance of control over his destiny was vaporizing, he willed himself into a state of acceptance. It was money for Mollie. Like Dialing for Dollars: Money for Mollie. Simple. His income-producing abilities weren't otherwise encouraging. A book he'd written about the networks had been well reviewed but had sold roughly as well as books about cement.

"Sandy has some ideas, Joe," said Clay, shaking his head as though he couldn't believe his good fortune. "Really on target."

Was he implying that Joe's ideas had missed?

"Sandy's going to do the show topless," announced Clay.

Joe looked over at Sandy, who raised her eyebrows.

"I beg your pardon?" Joe stammered.

"He's *kidding*!" said Sandy sharply, with a tsk-tsk glance at Clay.

"*I* wasn't kidding," said Clay, disappointed. "But I guess you were." Sandy looked at him like a schoolteacher who's caught an eighth-grader with busy hands beneath his desk. "Well, not precisely topless," Clay went on. Sandy listened as though this were about someone else. "Although I confess that if I could talk her into it, I would."

"Not at *all* topless, Brutus, you dirty young man. But sure, I might — like if I'm interviewing on a beach — wear a G-string and a little top. I mean, you see that on *Baywatch*." She was very businesslike, setting the record straight. "But that's *it*. Understood?"

"Can't blame a fellow for trying," Brutus Clay said sheepishly. "There's bleeding nudity on Showtime, HBO, Cinemax, and public access, so this is quite modest, really. But okay — anything else you'd like to add, Sandy?"

Sandy gave a little shake of her head, all the while keeping her eyes on Joe.

"So," said Clay with an eager smile in Joe's direction, "what do you think?"

Joe searched what was left of his heart and soul. Stalling, he said, "I think it may outdraw the networks."

"That's what we think," said Sandy decisively.

Clay took Joe's comment as a yes.

"Why don't you two go with David and have a look at the sets?" suggested Clay, ending the meeting and ushering them toward the door. Sandy uncrossed her silky legs and took Joe's arm as David Teng held the door open. Joe still didn't feel he'd said yes. He and Sandy followed David down a series of long corridors.

"Isn't it crazy?" said Sandy. "I just thought of the most outlandish thing I could. He asked me, 'What can you bring to this job that no one else can?' I told him, 'Nerve, experience, and a heart-stopping wardrobe.' I couldn't believe I was saying it, but, well . . . what can I tell you? I've always been shamelessly ambitious. I already have a designer friend working on a line of clothing for the show."

"All translucent?"

"I can never remember what that means," said Sandy, refusing to take the bait. "See-through or opaque?"

"Whatever," Joe said, invoking a term he loathed.

David Teng kept a respectable distance as he led them down another labyrinthian hallway.

"It isn't even nudity," Sandy went on, squeezing Joe's arm a little tighter. "It's just, well, pushing the envelope. If we play this right, nobody'll watch *ET* anymore."

"Where does that phrase come from, 'pushing the envelope'?" Joe asked irritably. "I mean — what's the envelope?"

"Don't go there, Joe."

"Where?"

"What's wrong with tarting up the interview process — I mean, as long as we do it in an upscale, high-fashion, well-lit kind of way? Why wait for Deborah Norville to think of it?"

"What's your mother going to say when she sees this show?" Joe asked, not knowing a thing about her mother, but actually sort of curious.

"Oh, it'll kill my parents," said Sandy, as David led them down some steps and into a studio. "But that's their problem."

"This is the main room, Joe," said David, pushing open two swinging metal doors with SILENCE in big letters on both sides. The studio was small, dusty, and hot. "Here's our action central desk. It'll be your home base." It was a straightforward, newsroomy, fake mahogany desk with a huge TV screen behind it and a mural-photo pastiche of Gleason and Carney, Mary Tyler Moore, Edward R. Murrow, Milton Berle, the Fonz, Johnny

145

Carson, Walter Cronkite, Farrah Fawcett, Archie Bunker, Ed Sullivan, and more.

Joe took David aside. "Can we talk for a few minutes alone?"

"Sure," said David.

Sandy noticed their whispering. "You guys have a lot to discuss," she said. "Joe, should we maybe have lunch? I mean, we could use a little quality time. We've got a lot to think about."

"You can eat in your dressing rooms," suggested David. "They're freshly painted."

"My room in fifteen minutes?" suggested Sandy. Joe nodded distractedly as she walked away, her long mane swinging behind.

"Listen, David," Joe said. "I want the show to open with my reviews. Schedule her segment at the end. I'm not following a half-dressed Sandy Moss."

"Actually, we thought we'd schedule her at the top. Sort of rope in the audience."

"No way. Her segment goes last."

"I'm not sure how Mr. Clay will respond to that. He envisions this incredible kind of byplay between you two." He walked behind the anchor desk. "Here's where you'll sit."

As David turned away to show Joe his chair, Joe swung around and pushed through the doors and up the stairs. After a few wrong turns, he barged into Clay's office. Brutus, on a call, waved at Joe to sit.

"Dad, I think your little dare is going to cost you ten million big ones, because if Sandy Moss doesn't become the biggest name in TV — oh — " He glanced at Joe. "*And* Joe McBride! If Sandy *and* Joe don't become the biggest names in TV, my name ain't Suzy Glutz."

He hung up and turned to Joe. "I see the look on your face. You think it might be demeaning. You're a respected writer. She's a . . . I don't know what she is, but whatever she is, she certainly *is*. I ask you, Joseph: What would you, as a TV writer, say about

Everybody's a Critic if you weren't a part of it? Would you tell people *not* to watch, say, Jane Pauley conducting interviews in a string bikini?"

"You think Sandy Moss is up there with Jane Pauley?"

"They're both *babes*," returned Clay, as if stating the obvious. "Smart ones. Haven't you ever mentally undressed Jane Pauley? I sure used to. But listen, Yosef, assume — which I am — that TCC succeeds. What do I do for an encore? I'm glad you asked, because my *next* project is to rescue one of New York's fading newspapers from oblivion."

Joe leaned forward. Clay looked out his non-window far into the non-distance.

"How'd you like to be managing editor of the *Dispatch*?"

Joe stared. Clay was serious. "Something to think about," he added with a wink. "If our audience share gets into double digits, I win ten million smackers. Enough for a down payment on a cash-poor tabloid."

David Teng stuck his head in.

"Miss Moss is waiting, Mr. McBride."

"Go. Plan," said Brutus Clay. "I need outlines for the first three shows. Oh — Sandy's segment leads off. Any problem with that?"

"That's what I came back to talk about."

Clay folded his hands in front of his chest. It made him look incredibly compact. Joe was sure he had an expensively acquired black belt in something.

"Nothing to discuss," Clay said, resolute. "She's the opener. Then she does a cozy sort of Hugh Downs–Barbara Walters wrap-up with you."

"What'll Sandy wear for that — a negligee?" Joe asked.

"Go. We'll talk tomorrow," Clay said, shooing Joe with his eyes. "Don't keep that woman waiting," he added, turning away and answering one of the desk phones that had multiplied over-night.

"I'm afraid you're on your own," Joe said without moving.

Clay cupped his hand over the receiver. "What on earth do you mean?"

"I'm sure," said Joe, "that Sandy Moss is about to become an icon of desire to millions of men, and a role model to young cable-equipped women everywhere. But" — he paused to be sure of himself — "I'm afraid she'll be doing it with another co-anchor."

Clay stared in disbelief. "Don't be ridiculous," he said with a lopsided smile. "Don't be a . . . critic, for God's sake."

"I'm afraid that's what I am," Joe said.

Clay shook his head with a pitying look in his eye.

"I'll probably kick myself," Joe went on. "But what can I tell you? I have a pop-culture gene missing. I just don't want to end up as some kind of patsy for Sandy Moss and have to go to the gym six days a week so I can interview, say, Gillian Anderson with *my* shirt off. Not that that wouldn't be fun."

"What's the problem?" Clay whispered, annoyed, still holding his hand over the phone.

"Last-minute attack of scruples, I guess," Joe replied.

"Scruples?" said Brutus Clay, with a dismissive huff. "I've been vaccinated. Be careful, Joe. No one reads newspapers anymore."

"Tell me about it," said Joe. "But print news is where my bread's been buttered all my life, Mad Dog."

"You mastodon," said Clay sadly. "You wooly mammoth. You're extinct. Get out."

Joe moved toward the door.

"I was kidding!" Clay said, hanging up and doing a one-eighty. "Come back, Yosef. Let's talk."

Joe stopped but didn't turn.

"You're wavering, Joe," said Clay, enjoying it. "And why not? You'd be a fool to walk away from overnight celebrity, not to mention a shot at editing your own paper." Clay sounded as though they were the oldest of buddies.

The first miracle Joe had ever consciously been aware of came next: an image of Mollie, Ferdy Levin, and God sitting on a couch watching *Everybody's a Critic* formed in Joe's mind, lending him just enough momentum to walk out the door without looking back.

CHAPTER 22

Brutus Clay's limo was conspicuously absent at the front door of Silvercup Studios. Joe managed to find a cab and when he got to his building, Zabida, his housekeeper, was standing outside by the main entrance.

"Oh, no," he said, remembering. "How long have you been waiting?"

"Only a couple of hours," said Zabida good-naturedly.

"I forgot to get a key to you," said Joe, shaking his head. "Oh, brother. I'm so sorry, Zabida. You should've gone home."

"It's all right, Mr. McBride. You just moved. Everything is jumbled up, yes?"

"You have no idea," he said, unlocking the door and holding it open for her.

"I figure you need me today maybe more than usual, Mr. McBride. It's a nice day. It's all right." They got onto the elevator.

"You're true blue," said Joe. "Thank you." She blushed.

Zabida had been coming twice a week to the various places Joe had lived the past few years. She worked the other three days for

Gayle in Hastings, cleaning in an unfashionable way — thoroughly, deeply, even lovingly.

"It's wonderful," said Zabida, looking around the apartment. "But big, Mr. McBride!" No matter how many times he'd asked, she wouldn't call him Joe. "Miss Mary Beth must love it. Yes?"

He tried to nod merrily.

He checked the machine. Buddy Monk, a director and the closest thing Joe had to a best friend, had left a message.

"Listen, Joseph, I know we talked about dinner, but a script arrived with an offer for an eight-hour miniseries that you'd probably hate to watch as much as I'd hate to shoot, but I'm kinda short on shekels these days, so I gotta read it. I'll call you tomorrow or the next day. Don't light up. Later."

For the next hour he tried to catch up on deadlines as Zabida worked silently. Ferdy called to remind Joe about a review he needed of a new USA cable movie, the cassette of which had been delivered yesterday. Rhonda Spivak and Andy Zeserson, Joe's *Philadelphia Inquirer* editor, made their daily calls to press Joe for output. Andy asked curtly if he was supposed to be amused by Joe's last P.S.

He was filling the pot with water for coffee when his machine beeped and the exhaustion in his mother's voice stopped him cold.

"Joe-boy, why don't you come and take a look at your lake? And why don't you make it soon while you're at it? I'm getting some vibrations and I need to read your right hand. By the way, I remembered that Wayne Newton was a guest once on Sonny and Cher's show. Remember? No, you don't. Well it was *Sonny*, of course, who was headed for Congress all along. TV signals do strange things to me." She shook her head. "I miss you. Oh, never mind. I just couldn't . . . let go without . . . I'm sorry, forget it." She hacked a gruesome cough and hung up.

Joe wanted to call back, but hungry, stubborn, and sensing that a conversation with his mother might create enough guilt to tilt him into a breakdown, he ordered out for a small pepperoni pizza. While on hold, he looked down at 9B. In the dusky late afternoon, there was no sign of life there. He didn't know if he was grateful or not.

He watched the animated *Hey, Arnold* on Nickelodeon for a children's-TV review he'd been working on, and simultaneously viewed the USA movie, an unexpectedly funny one with Stockard Channing. The pizza came, delivered by a Pakistani whose mastery of English didn't include the distinction between pepperoni and the peppers that adorned the delivered pie. Joe tipped him anyway only to discover that the pieces, as usual, weren't cut all the way through. He managed to rip a half-cut, uneven slice away, spattering tomato sauce onto his shirt in the process. He wrote a favorable review of the USA movie, adding a P.S.:

> *Does someone teach pizza people not to slice the pieces all the way through? Is this willful?*
>
> *Or is it an existential statement on the futility of life? 'Cause otherwise, I don't see how someone whose whole fucking job is to slice pizzas, wouldn't slice the fuckers all the way through.*

There was still no light across the way. He walked out his kitchen door, down the stairs, and knocked on her back door.

No reply.

He went back and called Buddy Monk, whose machine answered. "Buddy," he said. "It's Joe. I'm gonna smoke any minute now, but I know if I do, the Mets'll stop winning and I can't live with the guilt. Talk me down."

Impulsively, he decided to call Mary Beth. He had her mother's number on the computer.

"She doesn't want to speak to you, Joe."

"This is ridiculous, Mrs. Wise. Her stuff is still here. . . ."

"What can I tell you?"

"Nothing, obviously. Would you please ask her to call me?"

"I'll give her the message," her mother said, hanging up firmly.

He tried Mollie.

"Daddy!" she answered merrily. "Daddy, Daddy!"

"That's me."

"Only three more days till a you-and-me day — right?"

"Right!"

"Yayyy! I'm coming Friday, right?"

"Friday night," Joe repeated, a thought taking shape.

"Here's all my kisses, Daddy. I'm tired." She smacked the phone loudly and hung up.

He made another call, at least as impulsive as the one to Mary Beth, then recorded a new answering machine message, explaining he'd be out of town for two days, "unreachable." Inside of an hour, laptop and overnight bag in tow, he boarded the last flight to Minneapolis with a connection to Duluth.

H E reached the Twin Cities on time and was one of three passengers on the last flight from Minneapolis to Duluth, a twenty-four seater so rocked by turbulence that Joe began conjugating the verb "to smoke" as a way of keeping his nausea at bay. When the turbulence worsened, he promised himself that if the plane landed safely, he wouldn't lose his temper with his mother and would even let her read his palm if she insisted. They touched down a little before ten and Joe dashed through the virtually empty Duluth airport to the unattended Avis counter. He rang a service bell and a slight man in his fifties limped out, seemingly in pain, but covering it with north-midwestern good cheer.

"Well! You musta come in from the Twin Cities," he said, as though glad to see Joe.

"How'd you know?" asked Joe, wondering if the Avis man was psychic too.

"Only flight that lands here after nine o'clock," the man answered. "I was fixing to close up. Credit card and license, please. Full-size?"

"Make it a compact," Joe said.

The man punched buttons. "Need a map?"

"I think I could do it in my sleep," Joe answered.

In ten minutes, he was outside the Duluth-Superior city limits, speeding north and east on Route 2, pushing the blue Escort in hope of making the ninety miles before the last ferry left for Madeline Island at 11:30.

He was en route to a place synonymous with summer pleasure, the place his father, too, had summered as a boy, the place his family had always been happiest, where his parents had settled in retirement, where his father had died and was buried, and where his mother was hinting she might soon do the same. Joe hadn't been there for seven years, five due to summer scheduling conflicts, the last two because of the feud with his mother.

As though in the company of the Ghost of Summer Past, he felt years peel away as he sped the Escort around the lower perimeter of Lake Superior.

He made Bayfield by 11:27, too late to stop for a snack, and drove right onto the *Nichevo II*, the old ferry that ran during the off-peak season. April in northernmost Wisconsin was like February in New York. Joe buttoned the top of his suede coat, got out of the car and let the icy breeze blow straight into his face. He watched the lights of the Madeline Island town dock get closer as the *Nichevo* glided by the porches and yards of lost friends and old summer loves.

He hadn't called his mother, afraid that contact by phone might thwart his intention to see her. As the *Nichevo* bumped gently into the Madeline town dock, a young crew member lassoed two huge, rusty cleats with thick stern lines and undid the boat's safety chains, dropping them with a loud clank as Joe started the Escort. He was the first off, moving down the dock as the wide oak planks rumbled familiarly beneath his tires and his nostalgia gave way to sadness and fear.

Where the paved road changed to dirt, he rounded a corner,

passing empty summer houses, finally spotting the familiar sign, MCBRIDAL SWEET, the letters of the old pun fashioned from tiny pine cones, the "a" dangling from its place and hanging askew. The Escort turtled over the ruts of the driveway.

There were no lights on. The front door and porch were on the opposite side, facing the lake. A pine-walled, single-level, barely winterized summer cottage built by his father's grandparents in the 1890s, the house had three small bedrooms around a living room, and another tiny one off the kitchen. Joe walked up to the back door. It wasn't a door he had ever knocked on, but he rapped gently.

It seemed to get chillier as he waited. He knocked again, a little louder. He thought about leaving, spending the night at the old motel, and then slipping away on the first boat. But on an island of a hundred and fifty people, news of his visit would reach his mother and hurt her more than whatever outcome was in store. He knocked again.

A light went on in her bedroom, then in the kitchen.

"Who is it?" her voice whispered loudly.

"Hi, Mom."

"Oh my Lord in heaven!" There was a pause. She turned the old brass knob on the inner door and pushed the screen door open, her hand shading her eyes in disbelief. "Joe-boy?" she said. She half closed the door in his face, then opened it again. "I'm so mad at you I can't breathe. I don't care, I don't care. Come in out of that chill! I hope you didn't ride outside on the ferry. Oh, Joey — you rat! Let me get a look at you!"

They stood apart. She had, if such could be said, a convenient coughing attack, since neither of them was quite ready for hugging. Recovering, she touched Joe's cheek, peering at him sideways with a grim smile. She looked pale. At seventy-three, her over-tanned face had become parched and wrinkled, but the green Irish eyes still had light in them. There was a slight stoop to her shoulders. That was new. She was in an old pair of her dead husband's plaid flannel pajamas and a clashing tattered pink robe Joe had given her years ago.

She couldn't take her eyes from his and he couldn't look at her.

"You're here." She pinched both his cheeks as though he were a baby. "You little brat!"

"Well, I got your messages."

She took a step away. "Did I . . . guilt-trip you?"

"It sounded . . . important."

"Well, it is important," she said cheerfully. "Let me see that palm." She grabbed at his right hand and he laughed and let her take it, rolling his sleeve up a little.

"Move," she declared simply, tracing her finger along the lines of his palm.

"What?" he asked.

"Time to live in a new place," she said, looking down and scowling.

Joe laughed. "Ma," he said. "I just moved. Like, a few days ago."

She dropped his hand and shrugged. "Move again," she said.

"Yeah, right," answered Joe, taking his hand back. "Maybe it's Sonny Bono who should have moved, Mom." She looked at him, shrugged again, and, coughing hard, began to rinse a coffee cup that had been left by the sink. Joe took a few steps into the kitchen.

"How . . . serious is it?" he asked.

"Don't make me talk about it. Take off your coat and stay a while," she said as she'd said to anyone who'd ever set foot in her house as far back as Joe could remember. "Are you hungry?"

"Yeah. I didn't have time to stop at the A&W or I would've missed the boat."

"I have some cheese and a little braunschweiger. You always used to like that."

"Any Wheat Thins?"

"Of *course*."

"Sold," Joe said. She got the cheese and liverwurst while Joe gathered the plate, knife, and crackers, their age-old division of labor. He sat and she stood, serving him at the Formica-topped table they'd bought the year Joe was born.

"Ma. I came a long way. What's wrong?"

"My lungs. In a word. In two words: my lungs. I can't talk about it, I get crazy angry." She moved to the kitchen window. "And if you tell me to check myself into that hospital in Duluth or, god forbid, Ashland, I'll slap you sideways."

She had done that more than once when Joe was a kid. It had stopped when he outgrew her at the age of eleven. She was five-one.

"What does the doctor say?" Joe asked.

"He wants me in the hospital. But I said no. Not after what I went through with your father." She touched the top of Joe's head. "Am I dreaming this? Are you here?"

"I'm here."

"I've been having such dreams."

Joe was afraid she'd share one. She was prone to recounting her encyclopedically detailed dreams, and they never made a stitch of sense to him.

"You want to watch TV?" she asked. "There's an old Nelson MacDonald movie."

He blinked. "You mean Nelson Eddy?"

"And Jeanette whatchamadoodle," she said. "Come on."

She took the crackers and cheese and led him through the living room to the master bedroom. One of his father's hooded fishing sweatshirts was hanging on a peg where it had roosted as far back as Joe could remember. It seemed eerily like a shrine.

"Still no cable here, so we only get two channels. But the Minneapolis station has good movies."

"Shouldn't you be sleeping?" Joe asked, looking around the

familiar room that wasn't much bigger than the double bed that dominated it and where his great-grandparents had slept. There was a bureau, a little TV table, and a window that looked through the porch to the lake.

"I'm taking this stuff that clears my lungs out and makes me feel, I swear, like I guzzled ten cups of coffee. Oh — you want coffee? I just made some."

He decided to spare her a spiel on caffeine. She fiddled with the TV dial. The set didn't have a remote control, which Joe found almost comforting. A commercial for a cruise line was in progress.

"Life was better before remote control," he said, almost to himself.

"I wouldn't know," she pointed out. They watched Kathie Lee frolic in a Norwegian ship's pool. "With this awful global warming," his mother said, as though the commercial had reminded her, "it's going to be in the seventies up here all year 'round — maybe as soon as next winter."

"Really?" he asked without sarcasm.

His mother believed virtually everything she heard on TV or radio. Joe had always felt it was part of what drove him to become a critic.

"I read your reviews, you know, even when I'm not talking to you. You don't like *American Edition.* I don't know why."

"It's *60 Minutes* without the fact-checking," Joe replied.

"I wouldn't have known about the plague if I didn't watch that show," she said, settling back on the bed. Joe fluffed a pillow up against the headboard and lay next to her, the box of Wheat Thins between them.

"What plague?" he asked, determined not to correct or criticize.

"You don't know? There was a plague in the Midwest. From bad corn. Or was it pork? I can't remember. Where have you been? I didn't eat corn or pork all last winter. If it hadn't been for *American Edition* — who knows? Now, isn't that what television is supposed to do?" she asked Joe as though he were a panelist on her debate show. "Isn't it supposed to *inform*?"

"I guess it is," he replied, munching and watching Nelson Eddy croon to Jeanette MacDonald with the sound off.

"Well, there, you see?" she said conclusively. "There was no plague on *this* island. They didn't sell a whole lot of Fritos down at the market, I can tell you, but not one person in town died."

This, he thought, is how my mother processes information.

"Too bad they didn't do a show about lung disease," Joe said.

She ignored that and they watched as she sipped from a mug of cold coffee. Tomorrow she'd complain, as always, of not having slept well.

At around one, she dozed off, and Joe managed to maneuver himself off the bed without waking her. The mattress was as old as the house and even more creaky, and it required a silent sideways roll his father had taught Joe, perfected in the days when Dad came in late from philandering and got up to fish before dawn.

Joe went to the tiny back bedroom off the kitchen and changed into flannel pajamas he'd brought, then went back to turn out his mother's light and make sure she was well covered.

She opened her eyes with a start and coughed hideously, grabbing wads of Kleenex from a box on the bed as though her life depended on it, then spitting up some rancid-smelling stuff. She threw the tissues into a waste basket in the corner that was filled to the brim with balled-up Kleenex.

"You're here. Oh dear me, Joe-boy. Thank you." Her lip trembled and she pulled on his arm, moving him into a hug, holding on surprisingly tight for someone who'd never been big on hugs. "Go on down to the dock and look at the stars. You always used to like that. Take a Hamm's draft. I keep your brand around."

"Hamm's isn't my brand."

"Used to be."

"You never asked. You just bought whatever was on sale."

"I was on a budget. Something rich people don't understand." His father had been a fireman and she had driven a school bus. Joe had never been able to convince her that he wasn't rich.

"Why don't you say 'rich people who divorce their wives'?" he suggested.

"You said it, not me." Without looking at him, she went on. "How 'bout we bundle up, hit the dock, and look at stars. Whatta you say?"

It was something the small family had done when Joe was little. He re-dressed, adding a scarf over one of his father's winter coats. She threw a parka over her robe, pulled on long john bottoms and boots, grabbed a flashlight, tagged him, and said, "You're it! Last one to the dock is a monkey's uncle." She lumbered off through the back porch and down the steps to the lake like the ten-year-old she was most comfortable being. Joe followed, accepting his monkey's-uncle-ness, which she proclaimed joyfully as they plopped onto their backs, looking up at the stars. A coughing fit seized her, but she had her pockets stuffed with tissues and it passed. They lay, their heads a foot apart, the waves from a slight northeast breeze lapping the pilings of the dock.

"I'm never leaving," Joe said, inhaling deeply. "Look at that, you can see both Dippers."

"Why're you here, you big galoot?" she asked, giving him a schoolyard swipe with her nearest hand. The sky was a deep blue-black with more stars than Joe thought it could hold. The wind had died. The moon was waning, but still dancing on the water. He heard "Brown-Eyed Girl" playing from a house on the mainland.

"Van Morrison," he said quietly.

"You always loved the Beatles," she murmured.

He didn't correct her.

"You're not here because of me. You're here because of you," she said after a few minutes. He started to protest. She turned her head and grabbed him fiercely, "I'm your mother! Don't try to pull a fast one! I don't know much, but I know *you*. You're in some kind of pickle, you're — oh, dear God, no. Are you in love again? I don't think I can take it. Are you?"

He told her about the move, then, reluctantly, about Mary Beth leaving. He didn't mention the only thing he'd done recently that he felt good about, figuring she'd berate him for turning down a TV job. With a combination of disgust and good sense, she listened without interruption, her silence drawing him out. He was in need of confession, and he finally offered an abridged version of Nannie.

"You slept with her?" his mother demanded.

"Never mind."

"Where does this leave you with Mary Beth?"

"I wish I knew."

"What do you *want*?"

"I'm not sure."

"You listen to me!" she barked, standing up. "I'm about sick of this! Your generation thinks it's honorable not to know what you want. Stop behaving like you're on one of those soap operas you won't admit you watch. Your father was always running around falling in love with this and that. At least he *thought* it was love. He'd get all starry-eyed and cry and I'd cry and threaten to leave — but I knew you needed a dad, and he always got over it. Why is it so hard for you jerks? Look at you! I wish I was big enough to give you a thrashing. Do you know how long it's been since I've seen Mollie? I hate you for that. I hate you! Just go on back to that stupid city where nothing grows, and sit in front of a TV set and call it work, if that doesn't take the cake. I look at you and I see a little boy with his . . . dootie leading him around like a leash that's yanked by whatever pretty thing comes your way. Did *I* teach you that?"

Joe stood up to leave.

"You talk about about how busy you are, but you have time to stand in your kitchen at all hours of the night waiting for some woman to show up and ruin your life. You get paid to criticize — well, take a good look at yourself, whimpering and pretending not to know what you want. Reminds me of your father, I swear to God it does." She crossed herself quickly. "He stood there like that one night — just like you're standing — and you know what I did?"

"What?" he asked.

She got up suddenly and took a mighty run directly at him, leaning over into a crouch like a halfback and barreling into him with everything her weakening frame had. It was enough, together with the element of surprise, to send him reeling backward. He reached out to catch his balance, but he was falling, and there was nothing but cool night air between himself and the lake.

It was frigid beyond belief, the water having thawed less than a month before. The lake was always too cold, even in August, but this was something else. He was only about waist-deep, but perversely, recklessly, he plunged in and swam away from the dock. Knowing he couldn't take the cold for more than a minute or two, he swam out beneath the surface till he was over his head. He paused for a second and considered inhaling a big, long, final breath of ice water. Frightened, he kicked himself to the surface.

"Now you happy?" he gasped. "You want to kill me? Or is it Dad you're trying to punish?"

"Get back in here, Joseph!" she yelled, covering her face. "Right now!"

"Not till you forgive me," he called, treading water and starting to turn blue.

"Forgive yourself!" she spat at him. "That's your whole problem." She turned around and ran up the stairs. His bluff called, Joe swam in and peeled off his freezing clothes. She returned to the bottom of the steps with a huge orange beach towel that had been around for decades and threw it at him, still holding a robe and a pair of his father's thick wool slippers. He dried off furiously, trying in vain to keep himself covered.

"I haven't seen you naked since you were, I don't know, ten," she said. She walked up to him, studying his body without embarrassment. He was almost dry. The windless air felt warm compared to the water.

"Nice body," she said with a certain pride, handing him the robe. "Good dick," she added, like a stuffy academic. It cracked her up.

"Good *dick*?" Joe repeated amazed, but now laughing too. "Is that any way for a mother to talk?" He pulled on the robe.

"I should have told you that when you were about ten," she said, dismissively. "You'd probably still be with Gayle."

"No, I'd probably be with someone who looks and acts just like you."

She had a coughing spasm, hacking as if it came from a whale. "You know," she managed, finally, "sometimes I wish you could just crawl back inside me and we could start over."

He tied his robe's belt.

"I was raised strict Catholic," she went on. "As bad as things got with your father and me, we always put our holy vows first. You seem to think you can renegotiate everything."

He put on the slippers, feeling almost warm. The moon had taken a dip to the eastern horizon, and as he put his arm around his mother to head back up to the house, he looked across at Bayfield to the north and something stopped him cold.

It appeared as if the horizon were the top of a hill, and a huge unseen car was climbing that hill, soon to move into sight and shine its headlights at them. Within seconds, the entire northern shore was dotted with phosphorescent green floodlights that seemed to be slowly readying themselves to focus on Joe and his mother, who held on to each other and watched. Dozens of giant rays of light reached the top of the horizon.

"Aliens," whispered his mother, terrified. "I knew it — I *predicted* it!"

It occurred to Joe she might be right.

"Oh dear God," she said, hushed. "No. It's the northern lights."

It took Joe a second to hear her. "Are you sure?"

"Ssh!" she said. "There are people who've lived on this island all their lives and never seen them. The last time I saw them was with your father right after you were born. Oh, no. No!" She doubled over suddenly and began to cry, heaving sobs that brought on another coughing fit.

"What is it?" Joe asked, frightened. The lights turned greener, more intense.

"Oh, Joe, let me see your palm in this light." Joe hesitated. "Give it here, you brat!" she ordered. Unable to take his eyes from the lights, he let her have his hand.

"Yup," she said conclusively, trembling. "Sure." She took his face in her hands and looked at him hard. "Now you listen to me, you bugger. Move!" She hugged him fiercely and they watched the light fade as suddenly as it had appeared.

CHAPTER 24

THE next day, Wednesday, Joe and his mother played gin rummy, took a long walk, and finally talked about her illness. She was adamant about not going to the hospital. While she napped, he drove to the market for more Kleenex and her favorite TV dinners. Wrapped in blankets, they had tea on the screened porch at dusk and watched *The Price Is Right* and *Jeopardy!*. She knew Joe had to leave in the morning on the first boat. Aside from work, he needed to be home to get ready for Mollie's Friday visit. After their TV Salisbury steaks, they called Mol, and she and her grandmother had a long talk about the northern lights. Joe's mother and Gayle spoke for a while, too. Joe told Gayle he'd pick up Mollie at 5:30 Friday afternoon.

"She was a friend to you, Gayle was," said his mother when they hung up. "This Nannie person isn't your friend. She wants to hurt you."

"How do you know?"

"Because she did." She coughed loudly. "You'll always be able to find a lover, you're good at seduction. But you'll never find a friend that way."

At dawn on Thursday, Joe awoke, started to run a bath, then thought better of it and made his way down the back steps. Knowing he'd never go in if he toe-tested the water, he jumped directly into the lake clutching a yellowed bar of Ivory, as his father and he had done every morning in summer. He could barely stay in long enough to rinse off the soap, but he breathed in the mineral-fresh scent of the lake as it chilled him terrifically. Running up the stairs two at a time, he noticed his mother, watching at the living-room window. She seemed to be looking through or past him, as though she expected her husband to follow Joe up from the lake.

He had a reservation on the seven A.M. ferry. His mother followed him to the town dock in the '61 Fairlane he'd learned to drive in. Madeline Island tradition holds that loved ones come to the ferry and "kick off" those who are leaving, forming a ragtag chorus line and ceremonially high-kicking departing friends or relatives as the ferry disengages from the town dock.

It was drizzling and a fog had lumbered in. A big fuel truck and Joe's car were the only vehicles on the boat. Joe set the emergency brake and walked back to his mother. They each did their best to behave as though they'd see each other again.

The *Nichevo*'s engines rumbled. The guy from Tuesday night, already back on duty, began untying the heavy lines.

"Hiya, Miz McBride," he called, trying to tip his woolen cap. "How ya feelin'?"

"Not too shabby," said Joe's mom.

"You give us a call if you need anything, you hear?" said the guy, walking away and leaving them alone.

"Thanks, Jeff," she called. Joe stepped onto the boat, inches from where she stood on the dock, and faced her. "And thank *you,* brat head," she added.

"Don't mention it," he said forcing a smile. A seagull lighted near their feet, grabbed a speck of something, and flew off.

"You wondering why you bothered to come?" she asked without looking at him.

"No."

"Oh, sure you are!"

"You want to argue about *this*?" he said, hunching his shoulders to fight off the chill. "Why does everybody think they can read my mind?"

"Because you're such an open book, Joe-boy." She wiped a few strands of hair from his eyes and he pulled his head away as he always had. "Even with all our nonsense, your father and I always knew we'd stay together. But you, Joey." She sighed and shook her head. "You need to get on your knees to . . . something."

He stared past her eyes, not noticing the slight movement of the boat.

"I didn't tell you enough stories when you were little," she said out of nowhere. "You always wanted more, and you critiqued the ones I did tell you. I'm sorry I didn't tell you more. I used to get so . . . tired."

The *Nichevo*'s fog whistle blew.

"It's okay, Ma," he said.

She swallowed. "Don't forget," she said hoarsely. "On your knees!"

He had waited too long for a final hug. The ferry was pulling away. His mother backed up a few steps on the dock as the *Nichevo* pulled out, its slowly churning propellers creating a fast-widening, glassy floor of water between them.

His mother put her arms around two imaginary co-kickers on either side of her, ran forward to the edge of the dock, and sent Joe off with a big kick. The effort made her cough. She recovered, waved stiffly, and stood there.

Joe looked back several times during the half hour trip to Bayfield. His mother never moved.

At the Duluth airport he returned the car and sat out a flight delay, checking Matt Roush's TV coverage in *USA Today*. He called his machine. There was a message from Buddy Monk.

"Sorry we keep playing phone tag, Joseph. Is there some connection between you smoking and the Mets winning that I don't fully comprehend? Call me."

There was a "Hi, Daddy!" from Mollie and an impatient message from Ferdy Levin about Joe's P.S.'s, but nothing from Nannie or Mary Beth.

He dialed New York City information, then had them autodial the number they found. A digitized voice requested $1.25 and he plopped in five quarters.

"Ninety-ninth Precinct," a woman answered after a few rings.

"Is Amy Goode there?"

"Amy's out," said the woman curtly.

"Do you know where I can reach her?"

"We don't give out numbers. She'll be in this afternoon. Is this an emergency?"

"No. I'll be in the city by late afternoon," Joe said. "I'll call back."

The commuter plane finally took off and they lurched through some distinctly unfriendly skies toward Minneapolis, where Joe barely made his connection. On the flight to La Guardia, he opened his laptop and managed to eke out a feature on game shows, guiltily putting to use some of the time he'd spent with his mother.

On Joe's doorstep, he found a small manila envelope with 10D scrawled on it. He put down his bag and laptop and picked it up. A piece of a jigsaw puzzle dropped out onto the floor. It was solid white. On the back was written, "Put me together."

Joe spoke out loud, trying to calm himself. "Whistle a happy tune," he muttered. "Focus." He picked up his bag and computer as well as the usual pile of videocassettes in various overnight envelopes and walked inside, his arms overflowing.

Every bit of Mary Beth's furniture, every box of her clothing, every pot, pan — indeed, every vestige of her — had been picked clean, leaving the place more empty than Joe could have imagined.

chapter 25

T HERE was a note on the bed with Mary Beth's engagement ring scotch-taped to it.

Dear Joe — I'm not cut out to be an East Side stepmom. I thought I was, but the retreat did a Humpty Dumpty on me, and I'm afraid the king's horses and men are having the usual problems. I know you're disappointed, maybe you even hate me. I also know you and Mollie deserve better than I can give you right now. I wasn't going to do it like this, but I called and the machine said you were out of town, so I took the easy way out. There's much more to say, but not here. . . . Mary Beth

Joe's disorientation was complete.

If frequent-flyer miles were awarded for Dear John letters, he thought, I could make it around the world for free.

He called the Ninety-ninth Precinct.

"Amy Goode, please," he said. There were a few clicks.

"This is Amy," said the firm voice he remembered from the other day.

"I'm sorry to bother you," Joe began, trying to keep himself composed. "We met briefly on Monday morning. I'm the guy who came in to say hello. Remember?"

"Oh, yes. Mr. . . . . ah . . . Dean?"

"Yes," said Joe. "Wow. You have quite a memory."

"It helps in my line of work."

"The thing is," Joe said, chuckling awkwardly as if it were no big deal, "my name is really Joe McBride."

There was a silence.

"Why would you give me a different name?" she asked pleasantly. Joe felt immediately that he was being tricked into a confession of some sort.

"Because," said Joe, berating himself for not having thought of an answer in advance, "I'm a big fat jerk."

She laughed, once, very cleanly. Joe felt it was, ultimately, a noncommittal laugh, and he was no more comfortable than before.

"What can I do for you, Mr. McBride?"

"I wonder if you know a woman named Nannie Pritchard. Does that name ring a bell?"

"No," she said, considering it. "I don't think so. Why?"

"It's kind of a long story," Joe said. "But when I met her, she told me her name was Amy Goode, and that she was a cop at your precinct. Undercover."

"Really?"

"Yeah. I had no reason to doubt her, so I . . . dropped by the other day to say hello, and instead of her, I found you."

There was more silence at the other end.

"Could be a joke of some kind," she considered. "Technically, I guess it's impersonating a police officer. Did she try to do anything in an official police capacity with you — or to you?"

None of the things that Nannie had done to Joe — images that flitted through his mind like a sped-up movie — qualified as official police business.

"No," answered Joe. "I did see a badge at her place, though."

"You did?"

"Yeah, but I didn't really look closely at it. It could've been fake, for all I know."

"So you can't be sure it was a specifically faked NYPD badge?" she asked.

"No."

"Or a stolen one," she continued, thinking out loud.

"Sorry," said Joe. "I just glanced at it."

"I can't very well get a search warrant on the strength of what you're telling me, Mr. McBride," she said wearily. "But maybe you should come in. Are you free tomorrow? I'd like to hear more, but I have to be in court in a few minutes. Do you feel like you're in any danger?"

Joe had only his mother's palm reading to go on, and since her predictions were wrong half the time, he just said, "No," though he was feeling increasingly queasy.

"What time tomorrow?" asked Joe.

"Nine-thirty? Is that too early?"

"I can be there," he said.

"It's the side entrance, off Corona Avenue," Amy Goode explained. "They'll buzz you in. My office is up two flights."

"Okay. See you tomorrow."

"Thank you, Mr. McBride," she said cautiously. "I think."

She got off the elevator and walked around to the back of the lobby. Next to Dr. Bass, the dentist in 1A, she found apartment 1B, whose front door was smudged with children's fingerprints. A toddler's tricycle was overturned on a doormat that read VAYA CON DIOS. She rang the bell. In a few seconds Ramón, looking harried in an apron, answered.

"Yes, Miss Loree?" he said, wiping his hands on the apron.

"My sister asked me to give you this."

She handed Ramón a half-gallon Tupperware container of vegetable soup.

"For your wife," she explained.

"*Sí?* Yes?" said Ramón brightening. *"Sopa?"*

"Sopa?" repeated Loree.

"Soup, I mean," he explained, examining the container, beaming and shaking his head with gratitude. "Yes. My wife love her soup. I am not so good for the cooking."

He stood, grinning, and she did her best to grin back.

"Tell your sister — tell her *please* that Mila and I are thanking her. Very kindly." He nodded several times quickly.

"I hope she feels better," said Loree uncomfortably as she backed away.

"Gracias," said Ramón. "She is an angel, your sister."

Yeah, right, she thought to herself as she nodded and smiled meekly back at Ramón.

JOE woke up three times before morning and each time was unable to resist the kitchen window, but there was no sign of activity down there. A little after dawn, he had a nightmare about his mother. Unable to get back to sleep in his curtainless bedroom, he sleepwalked to his desk and tore a cassette from a UPS blue envelope. It was the latest "Best of Uncensored Bloopers," in which a brunette Loni Anderson beamed a wifely smile while her screen husband enthused over shiny linoleum in an ancient Mop & Glo commercial. This was followed by out-takes of Sally Struthers hawking late-night adult-education correspondence courses and Jamie Lee Curtis wrestling an apparently drugged alligator on an old "David Frost Presents *The Guinness Book of World Records.*" Joe managed to plonk out a review, adding:

P.S.
Maybe we aren't what we eat; maybe we're who we have sex with.

He inhaled a bowl of Cheerios and a cup of Ovaltine without so much as a glance out the window, and told himself that if he could resist looking down there, the Mets would pull off a triple play that night.

He worked till nine, showered, shaved, and dug out a clean shirt and corduroys he'd packed in their cleaners bag and hangers. He wrestled with the twist that the cleaners used to hold hangers together, twisting it more and more tightly closed before discovering he was turning it in the wrong direction. He yelled in frustration like a Sumo wrestler and tried yanking it off, but all he did was thread the paper coating from the twist, cutting himself on the wire beneath. Cursing the cleaners, he grabbed a windbreaker and headed to Queens. The sky was overcast, the air damp and chilly. Spring seemed to be on hold.

He was buzzed into the side entrance of the precinct building and, as directed, worked his way up two flights of rounded, castle-like winding stairs. The second floor hallway had beige tile walls and oak doors with windowpaned upper halves. He peered into a few offices before finding Amy Goode. To his surprise, her nose was buried in a copy of the *Dispatch*.

He was about to rap on the door when he noticed the picture hanging over her desk. It was St. Sebastian — almost identical to the one in Nannie's apartment. He scanned the walls quickly. There were Mary Magdalen, St. Kevin, and Thomas à Becket.

Amy Goode looked up, smiled, and waved him in.

"Hello," she said, standing and shaking his hand firmly. Joe was so relieved not to find her attractive that he almost hugged her. She held up the paper. "I was doing a little research. I agree about pizza slicing, by the way."

"Thanks," Joe said. "My publisher doesn't."

"You didn't tell me you were *that* Joe McBride."

"You didn't ask," said Joe. "Not everybody in the city reads me. If they did, the *Dispatch* wouldn't be fighting for its life."

"I can't say I know much about your world. I don't watch a lot of TV."

"Well, I'm not sure I would, either, if I wasn't paid for it," Joe said.

"Really?" she answered, sitting and motioning him into the leather chair.

"I didn't mean that," Joe said, recanting. "I love TV, but I get defensive around people who don't approve of it, as though I might have to . . . uphold it."

"Sounds exhausting," she said. Her bleach-blond hair was down today, and dressed in a knee-length skirt and striped oxford-cloth blouse, she looked less severe. She noticed Joe staring at St. Sebastian. "I'm kind of a sucker for the saints," she said.

His head snapped back to her and some blood drained from his face.

"Are you all right, Mr. McBride?"

"I'm a bit of a mess, actually," Joe admitted.

"You want a glass of water or something?"

"Do you think maybe we aren't what we eat?" Joe asked as if it were the next item on their agenda. "That maybe we're who we have sex with?"

"You've lost me," she said politely.

"I'm kind of on overload," Joe replied, almost to himself. "I guess I'll print a retraction."

She recrossed her legs and cleared her throat. "Did you sleep with this Pritchard woman?" she asked carefully.

Joe looked at her uneasily. "We . . . traded karma, yes," he said.

Not sure what to make of that, she put down the paper. Joe stood and moved to the portrait of Becket.

"Let me take a wild guess," he said. "You studied divinity at Union, took an exchange semester at a seminary in England . . ."

"How . . . did you know?" she asked, astonished.

"... and your thesis was called *The Search for the Divine in Everyday Secular Life*."

"I never got as far as writing a thesis," she said. "I decided to become a cop. But you sure have my attention," she added, attempting a smile that faded quickly.

Joe stood as far from her desk as he could in the small room. "This woman has the same pictures in her place that you have here. She described herself as a sucker for the saints."

The real Amy Goode looked out the window, squinting as though scanning her memory. "What does she look like?"

"Five-six, light brown hair," said Joe. "Classic features, blue-green eyes ... "

"Body?"

Joe paused, embarrassed. "Really ... well proportioned," he answered. "But subtly so." Detective Goode listened intently. "When I saw you on Monday," he went on, "I was so startled I just left. I had an appointment and I was totally disoriented and I ... I couldn't deal with it. I would've called sooner, but, well — my life has been sort of disintegrating for the last week."

"I'm sorry."

"The night I ... was with her — Saturday — she actually went so far as to tell me she was working here. I mean, she was daring me to find her out."

"Nannie Pritchard," repeated Amy. "Probably not her real name. Have you seen her with anybody else?"

"Just her twin sister — "

"She has a *twin*?"

"Yeah. Loree. L-o-r-e-e. They're quite a pair. Loree says Nannie's pulled things like this before, with boyfriends and guys, but she didn't imply anything serious, or dangerous. I probably shouldn't have bothered you, but I just wanted to talk, 'cause, well, I thought you should know."

"Thanks," said Amy, poker-faced. "I'm not sure what we can do. She's not ... stalking you?"

178

"Only in my dreams," answered Joe.

"Let's see. She hasn't defrauded anybody but you — at least not that we know of. Maybe she's telling other people she's me, but this is the first I've heard of it. It's . . . weird, but I'm not sure it's a police matter. Yet." She straightened her skirt. "Tell me about you," she said. "If you don't mind."

"Twenty-five words or less?" he asked. She smiled wanly. "I'm divorced," Joe began. "I have a daughter who's five. Her mother has custody. They live in Hastings. Let's see, what else?" He looked at the ceiling. "My mother is dying and my fiancée just broke off our engagement." He moved around and looked out the window where a throng of kids was filing out of a school enjoying a fire drill. Remembering the puzzle, Joe took the piece out of his pocket and explained its history. Amy shook her head.

"Okay. This kind of gives me the creeps," she said. "Open that bottom drawer." She pointed to a battered oak chest near the window. Joe yanked the drawer open. It was crammed with jig-saw puzzles of various sizes, shapes, and complexities.

"It's my hobby," she said. "I love puzzles." She exhaled. "Sometimes I leave the office unlocked. She must have gotten in here."

"Maybe I should call a private detective."

"I don't know, that's up to you," said Amy. "What we seem to have is a *possible* criminal without a crime. I haven't noticed anything missing here."

Her phone rang and she answered it impatiently.

"What?" She listened for a few seconds and muttered, "Come on, Roxie, it can't wait ten minutes?" She looked at Joe, shook her head disapprovingly, and made the universal gesture for mas-turbation. "Right, right. *Okay*," she added and slammed down the receiver.

"I've been, shall we say, *summoned* by this bitch of an assistant DA who has a history of busting my chops. I should've stayed home today. This is gonna take a while. Let me give you my home

179

number. Call me if you find out anything more, okay?" She wrote it down and handed it to him. "I'll do a little checking, too." She stuck out her hand to shake his. "It's good that you came."

"Really?" he said. "I feel like an idiot."

"No, no," she said, not too convincingly. "You did the right thing. Let's, well, keep our eyes open."

Joe left the precinct office and, low on cash, took the subway home, changing at Fifty-third Street. Distracted, he peered out the window of the un-air-conditioned No. 6 IRT train through a blur of lights and subway girders as the local whizzed uptown. Lost in thought, he didn't realize he'd missed his stop until the train pulled in at Ninety-sixth Street. He got out glumly, trudged up some urine-drenched stairs, and walked to Ninetieth Street, reaching the front door of his building just as a perspiring young man in a gray sweat suit, dark glasses, drooping mustache, and backwards Jets hat approached. The guy fiddled with a huge set of keys, flipping through them in a frustrated search for the right one. Impatient with everything, Joe waited for a second before pulling out his own key.

"I'll get it," he said brusquely, turning the lock and pushing the outer door open.

"Thanks," the young man said, pocketing his clanking wad of metal as Joe unlocked the inner door. "I gotta get some of those colored plastic markers for my keys. Get organized, you know what I'm sayin'?" He seemed to look at Joe for the first time. "You're new in the building, aren't you?"

Joe nodded vacantly.

"Cat got your tongue?" said the guy as he walked in ahead of Joe and headed for the A/B elevators, the ones leading to Nannie Pritchard's. Joe decided to go up and ring Nannie's doorbell, so he followed the man into the elevator. The guy punched 7, Joe hit 9. The elevator cab shuddered and began a hellishly slow climb.

"Do you by any chance know somebody named Nannie Pritchard?" asked Joe, desperate for information.

The elevator stopped at the third floor, but no one was there.

"Ghosts," whispered the young man.

Joe blinked as the doors closed. "I guess you didn't hear me," he said. "I was asking — "

"Good-looking brunette?" the guy interrupted. "Lives upstairs with her sister?"

"Yes," said Joe, trying to appear at ease. "Right."

"Know her," said the guy, nodding hard. "Her sister, too."

The elevator wasn't moving. Joe pushed the 9 button three times with terrific force, but nothing happened.

"It has a mind of its own," said the guy, first pushing the DOOR OPEN button, then the one marked DOOR CLOSE. He offered his hand, and Joe, not knowing what else to do, shook it. "I'm Hank," the guy said as the elevator lurched upward at its snail's pace. "Hank Potter. Of the seventh floor Potters." He smiled. "You *are* the new tenant, aren't you?"

Joe returned a half smile. "Joe McBride."

"We're just, you know, simple Christian folk," said the guy. "Have you accepted Jesus Christ as your personal savior?"

Joe's eyes widened. "Excuse me . . . ?"

"Never mind, never mind," said the guy affably. "That's between you and the Lord. By the way, don't you live on the other side of the building?"

"Oh — yeah," laughed Joe, trying to mask his discomfort. "I'm just calling on . . . Nannie."

The elevator stopped again at six. The doors opened and a harried young woman with a baby stroller started in.

"Going up," said Joe to the woman, who exhaled impatiently and pulled the stroller back. The doors closed and the elevator chugged up to 7.

"Anyway — yeah. I know Nannie a little," said the guy, whose name was not Hank, whose hand touched the silencer of the .38 tucked into his belt at the small of his back. "What about her?" The elevator arrived at the seventh floor and he stepped out, holding the door open.

"Well," said Joe, fumbling and feeling like a bit player on a *Twilight Zone* rerun. "I just wondered if she's . . . around, you know . . ."

"Couldn't tell you. But Loree's spoken for," said Dean with certainty. "The other one . . . I couldn't tell you. See you," he added pleasantly, letting go of the door.

Joe smiled weakly as the doors closed. He rode up to nine, walked the three paces to 9B's door, and rapped on it. After a few seconds he knocked harder. There wasn't a sound inside. He rang the bell, but apparently it was broken. He walked back to the elevator. The floor indicator showed that it was moving slowly toward the lobby, so Joe headed for the stairs, opening the exit door and starting down, just as Dean, out of breath from sprinting up two flights, wiped his brow with the Jets cap and froze around a corner, ten steps above where Joe stood. Dean tried to control the sound of his breathing, his hand touching the .38, and waited until he heard Joe move down the stairs before peeling off the scratchy mustache, pocketing it, and quietly continuing his trek to the roof.

27

WHEN he got back to his place, Joe checked the machine. There was a message from Gayle asking him to call as soon as possible.

"It's me," Joe said when Gayle answered. He wondered if there were other men in her life who said that when they called her. "What's up?"

"I need to talk to you about this weekend," Gayle said.

"Okay . . ."

"Two things. First, Mollie's been asking for a play date with Jessica, so I wonder if you wouldn't mind setting one up for Saturday."

"Tomorrow?"

"Is Saturday tomorrow? Oh, right. I should've mentioned it before, but I know how much you like your time with her, and I thought she'd forget about it. But she asked twice this morning before she went to school. Would you mind?"

Jessica had been Mollie's best friend before they'd moved out of the city. Fortunately, she lived close by and was a well-behaved, likable kid. Her parents, heavily socializing investment bankers, were never around, but Carly, her sitter, was terrific.

"Okay, I'll set it up," Joe said. "Actually it'll give me an hour or two to finish some writing. What's the other thing?"

"Well, I don't want to concern you, but . . . Mollie's been going through something that just started the past few days. I thought it might pass or I would've told you sooner."

"What?"

"She has these new fears. She's terrified she'll have nightmares, even though she almost never does. It's typical, it turns out, for five-year-olds. She's starting to wake up to the real world and get a glimpse of how vulnerable she is. She saw a quicksand scene in *The Jungle Book* and now she thinks there's quicksand every-where, and she watched a cartoon where some ooga-booga fifties natives threw Goofy into a volcano, and she's afraid people are going to break into her room and do it to her. It comes and goes, but I need you to be prepared for it. It's worst when it starts getting dark."

"What do I do?"

"She needs what may seem like a ridiculous amount of assur-ance that she's safe. Can you give her that? Without making her feel silly? It's really important, Joe. Otherwise, you're in for a long weekend. When she starts with this stuff, it just snowballs."

"Wow," Joe said grimly. "Okay. Thanks."

"Remind her that she has guardian angels working round the clock. Remember? It makes her feel better."

"Right," Joe said, "What's her main guardian angel's name?"

"Angela," replied Gayle disapprovingly. "How could you for-get that?"

He was feeling more and more as though the sky were falling. But he steadied himself by calling and arranging the play date for the next day at noon. Carly said she'd take them to Hog Heaven, a kid-friendly restaurant on Third Avenue that Mollie loved, then to the park at Ninety-sixth and Fifth, an old haunt.

Joe ran out to the Food Emporium and bought boxed juice, peanut butter, jam, pancake mix, maple syrup, milk, eggs, ketchup, and some fortune cookies, Mollie's latest favorite dessert.

When he got back there was a message from Andy Zeserson, his *Philadelphia Inquirer* editor.

"Joe, what's this shit about pizza cutting and you are who you sleep with? Our copy editor wanted to lose it, but I reminded him about your goddamn no-cut deal. So — I hope you're pleased. I need that piece on the networks' space shuttle coverage."

Joe found linens and made Mollie's bed, placing a new Pooh bear he'd been saving for her on top of the pillow. He hurriedly tacked up an *Anastasia* poster and put down the colorful rag rug Mary Beth had, in her mercy or neglect, left behind after her purge. The room, woefully underdecorated, came alive a little.

He jury-rigged some curtains that had been earmarked for the bedroom and hung them on the kitchen window in case either or both twins showed up undressed, then reminded himself to leave the answering machine turned down in case Nannie called while Mollie was there.

He forced himself to spend the next few hours at the computer. At the end of his review of the coverage of the recent space shuttle flight, he added:

P.S.

Warning to dry cleaners who use garbage bag twists to fasten hangers together: From now on, twist them clockwise only. Violators will be neutered.

He faxed it off to all three papers, straightened the place up, put the groceries away, and took off for Grand Central where he caught the 4:20 to Hastings.

As the train pulled in, he had the preposterous and, of course, unrealized fantasy that Gayle and Mollie would be there to meet him. He got into a run-down station wagon taxi and rode up to the Tudor house on Scenic Drive that Gayle had gotten a deal on when the previous occupants had moved suddenly. He rang the bell and Mollie opened the door almost instantly.

"Daddy!"

"Look how big you are!" exclaimed Joe, picking her up and squeezing her. Gayle appeared. She'd never been heavy, but she'd lost weight and it agreed with her. Her black hair had been cut short and Joe was surprised to see that it was a good look for her, complimenting, as it did, her brown, oval eyes, olive skin, firm chin, and long, Modigliani nose. Her nose was beautiful, Joe had always thought, but it had a slight crookedness toward the top that a woman with less self-esteem might have had whittled away for a price. Barefoot, drawn but attractive in a cut-off sweatshirt and well worn jeans, she seemed in less of a hurry to get rid of Joe than usual.

"Hi," she said with an almost cheerful smile.

"Hi . . . good haircut," Joe observed, pointing vaguely in the direction of her face.

"Oh. Thanks," she answered shyly as they gave each other, for Mollie's sake, kisses on the cheek.

"How are you?" she inquired, concerned. "You look tired." Her hand went up to his face instinctively and straightened his hair.

"No, I'm great," Joe answered, trying to talk himself into it. "I made the play date with Jessica. Lunch at Hog Heaven tomorrow."

"Yay!" whooped Mollie.

"Thanks," said Gayle warmly. "Here's her bing," she added, referring to the small, ragged, pink blanket that had been part of Mollie's life since she was weaned and without which she had never gone to sleep. *Bing* was the sound Mollie had made as a baby when she wanted Gayle's breast. When Gayle weaned her, she cleverly introduced the blanket, naming it *bing*. It gave Mollie instant comfort, and Gayle and Joe kept track of its whereabouts the way a diabetic keeps track of insulin. Gayle folded the frayed pink cloth carefully into a small suitcase and inventoried its other contents with Joe. "Bear, stuffed whale — a new favorite — snacks for the train ride . . ."

"Thanks," Joe said. "I forgot snacks. . . ."

"I knew you would," she said, going on. "Crayons and coloring books. Some other books that might come in handy in case of f-e-a-r." Joe nodded.

"Fear?" said Mollie, looking up at Gayle.

"She's spelling," Gayle said to Joe. "I keep forgetting."

"What about fear?" asked Mollie.

"You and Daddy can talk about it on the train," said Gayle with a smile, ushering them out. "Please, please keep track of her bing. . . ."

"Of course," he whispered, amazed she felt the need to re-mind him.

"There's a sweatshirt in there, and a jacket. I don't know what the weather's doing. They said it would be sunny today."

It wasn't.

"I told you to stop watching weather reports," Joe said. "You can't trust people who refer to snow as 'snow activity.' "

"We don't have weather anymore," chimed in Gayle with a grin. "We have 'weather systems.' "

"It's word inflation," Joe said, shrugging.

Mollie glanced from one parent to the other, contentedly taking in their almost-banter. Gayle smiled at Joe as though she'd for-gotten how easily they were capable of enjoying each other.

"Have her back by five on Sunday?" she said.

"Absolutely," Joe agreed. They gave each other a little hug and Joe noticed a trace of warmth from Gayle, which calmed and in turn surprised him.

On the train he and Mollie colored. They talked about her fears, and she drew them, putting herself into the pictures —

Mighty Mollie, beating back the objects of her alarm with the help of her trusty guardian angel, Angela. Joe told Mollie that Mary Beth was away for the weekend. He couldn't bring himself to relate the whole thing, fearing it would upset her and spoil her first trip to his new place.

As they colored their way toward Manhattan, the sun went down over the Hudson without an onset of Mollie's fears. With Mollie happily absorbed in her coloring book, Joe dozed for a few minutes and in a quickie dream saw pieces of a black-and-white jigsaw arguing with each other, refusing to fit.

To save on cab fare, and because Mollie begged, they took the subway uptown. Joe held her hand tightly, but she loved the noise, the crowds, everything about it. She was a city kid by nature. They got off at Eighty-sixth Street and walked to the new building hand-in-hand, playing I Spy. Mollie laughed and babbled about her friends. Forcing Nannie, Loree, Mary Beth, and his mother from his mind as best he could, he tried to let go and give his daughter what she needed most — his undivided attention.

They rounded the corner onto Ninetieth Street and Joe pointed to his place.

"There it is!" he said.

As Mollie looked up, everything Joe didn't like about the building came to the fore. It seemed dingy and gray by night, its once-white brick sullied by decades of filthy New York breezes.

"Daddy?" she said. Joe looked down at her. She motioned for him to stop and bend over so she could whisper in his ear. "Would anybody sneak into that building and cut off my head?"

Thrown, but trying not to show it, Joe took a deep breath. "No, sweetie," he answered, remembering Gayle's advice. "That'll never happen."

"Would anybody cut off my arm, or my hand?"

"No. Never."

"Would they hit me so hard that I died?" She was fighting off tears.

He looked her straight in the eye, masking his alarm, and said, "Absolutely not. You're completely safe here."

"Okay," she said bravely. The tears receded. She blinked and exhaled loudly.

Joe put his arm on her shoulder, led her to the door, and they ducked in out of the chilly early evening air.

In an eerie replay of the moment when he'd first laid eyes on her, Nannie scooted through the door behind them in her Lycra bicycle pants and Yankee hat.

"Well!" she said merrily. "Whom have we here?"

Half excited, half frightened, Joe ushered Mollie toward the elevator and put on a cheerful face.

"Well," he said clearing his throat. "Uh — this is my daughter, Mollie." He turned to his neighbor, hesitating to use the name Nannie, which he'd never called her.

"I'm one of your dad's new neighbors," she said, bending over and talking to Mollie at face level.

Mollie reached out a hand as she'd been taught and said, "How do you do," shyly but clearly.

"I'm . . . Nannie," she said, looking at Joe apologetically, then back to Mollie. "It's very nice to meet you, indeed." It seemed to Joe that Nannie was close to tears, which disarmed him. "You and your dad are invited over to my place for milk and honey or hot chocolate any time. I'd love to talk a little with your dad and it just so happens that I make the best hot chocolate on earth, and that's a fact!" She had regained her composure.

The words "hot chocolate" widened Mollie's eyes and she looked up at Joe, pleasantly surprised.

"Can we, Daddy?"

"We'll see," Joe said, both glad to see her and sorry they'd met. Mollie, who was usually shy with strangers, grinned at Nannie, reached up, and playfully whisked off her Yankee cap. Nannie's hair fell around her face in that way Joe now found maddeningly attractive and he looked at the lips into which he'd contentedly disappeared so recently. She beamed at Mollie, and Mollie swung around and plopped the cap onto her father's head.

"Looks better on you," said Nannie.

"Yeah!" said Mollie with a happy chortle.

Joe took it off, doing his best to smile, and handed it back to Nannie. He pressed the button for his elevator and Nannie did the same for hers. Mollie, several feet away, played with something on the bottom of her shoe.

"This is impossible," said Joe. He wanted to say how hurt and bewildered he was, but Mollie was too close. "I met Loree," he added quietly as they waited for their respective elevators.

The color seemed to drain from Nannie's cheeks. "And . . . ?" she asked.

"She's . . . certainly a handful."

"Tell me about it," said Nannie. "I asked her if she'd met you, and she said no. She drives me up the wall." Then, under her breath, she added, *"When can we talk?"*

"It'll have to be after the weekend," Joe whispered with a nod at Mollie.

"I miss you," she whispered back, fighting tears again. "I'm *so* sorry."

The elevators arrived. His mind swirled with questions as she got on.

"See you . . . later," said Joe.

"Not if I see you first," she said almost cheerfully.

"Not if I see you first," repeated Mollie, laughing. "That's funny."

"Bye, Mollie," Nannie called as her elevator door closed. She gave Joe a sad little wave and looked at him through the elevator window as she rose out of sight. He smiled vaguely, in utter conflict with himself.

"I like her," said Mollie as they rode up. "Can we go for hot chocolate?"

"We'll see," Joe said evasively.

"When I'm queen," she frowned, "grown-ups won't be allowed to say, 'We'll see.' "

The next hours were a much-needed antidote to the previous days. Joe drew the new curtains across his kitchen window, and he and Mollie munched chicken fingers and broccoli with dollops of ketchup on the side. She ate heartily, which always made Joe feel better. They watched *Hey, Arnold,* her favorite animated show, and he read to her. She even liked her room. She got into striped pajamas that reminded Joe of the ones Nannie wore when he first saw her through the window. No matter how he battled it — maybe *because* he battled it — Nannie leaked into almost every thought.

When it was time for lights out, Mollie's fears returned.

"Daddy, would anybody sneak in here and hurt me?"

"No, sweetie," he assured her as Gayle had directed. "That'll never happen. We're ten stories up, the windows are locked, our front door is locked, and there are two more locked doors downstairs. You're completely safe." He tried to put from his mind thoughts of break-ins, murders, and the multitude of horrors parents want to assure their kids will never happen. Feeling something of a liar, he soothed and calmed her until her terror subsided and the what-ifs and questions stopped. He flipped on a night light and she pulled the covers over her head.

"You know why I do this, Daddy?" she asked from beneath the sheet.

"Why?"

"Because I'm afraid. It really helps."

He patted her back soothingly until she fell asleep.

He went to the kitchen and did the dishes, leaving the curtains drawn. The phone rang. Knowing the machine didn't pick up till the fourth ring and not wanting Mollie disturbed, Joe grabbed it.

"Hello?" he said, keeping his voice down.

"Hey, cowboy," said a voice he didn't immediately recognize. "Have you come to your senses?"

It was Sandy Moss.

"Hi, Sandy," he said, trying to keep it light. "Yeah, I *did* come to my senses. That's why I'm not doing the show. How's it going?"

"We have an offer out to David Bianculli to replace you. He's here in the metropolitan area, and Brutus likes him a lot. You wouldn't happen to have his number, would you? I want to sort of twist his arm."

Bianculli was the highly regarded *Daily News* critic, a stand-up guy with a wife and two kids.

"Why do you have to twist his arm? When I first met Brutus," said Joe, "he told me Bianculli wanted the job."

"He was bluffing," admitted Sandy.

"Are you actually calling me to get David Bianculli's home number?"

"Well, I thought you might want to reconsider, since David hasn't given us an answer yet."

"Did you describe the show to him?"

"Brutus did. David came in for a meeting, and I was in Brutus's office to greet him."

"Topless?"

"Very funny. *No.* I said hello and left. Brutus gave him the pitch and made the offer. You think he'll do it?"

"Depends on how high his mortgage is," Joe ventured.

"Come on, Joe. We'd have a ball together. I apologize for getting this show behind your back." She laughed. "Can you hear how contrite I am? I'm just absolutely the picture of contrition. How 'bout meeting me for a drink?"

"You mean you're all alone on a Friday night?" he asked.

"Just like you," she said.

"Actually, I'm not. My daughter's with me for the weekend — and she's just gone to sleep. I should too."

"Joe, I think if you got in touch with Brutus first thing Monday, he'd take you back. But I'm going to call Bianculli and twist his arm in case you don't come around."

"I don't have his number," Joe said, lying. "But I'm sure you'll dig it up. And when you do, go easy on him."

They hung up. Joe dialed Buddy Monk in search of support. Buddy was out, so Joe readied himself for bed, wondering if he could get to sleep without so much as a peek at Nannie's window. He went in to check on Mollie. With her twists and turns, the sheet had fallen down enough so that her face was visible. He threw a light quilt over the sheet and gazed down at her. Gayle always said that Mollie and Joe looked exactly the same when they slept.

He pulled up a chair by her bed and studied their mutual face, doubting he'd ever looked as angelic or carefree. He was grateful for her very presence, which helped him keep his attention focused on the small but significant world inside his apartment.

At the same moment, his neighbor in 9B sat next to her coffee table, staring at the jigsaw puzzle — complete but for the single missing piece — in a serene euphoria.

"Perfect," she said.

CHAPTER 28

MOLLIE and Joe made their Saturday morning ritual pancakes, followed by a fortune cookie, individually wrapped in plastic. Mollie asked Joe to read it for her, and he substituted, as he and Gayle always had, "You will have a small wedding in your own backyard."

"*Again?*" she said with amazement. "I always get that."

"Must be true, then," he said, poker-faced.

They played Chutes and Ladders and toyed with the *101 Dalmatians* CD-ROM. A little before noon, he got her dressed and took her to Jessica's apartment on Eighty-eighth between Madison and Park, a stone's throw away. Mollie was ecstatic to see her old friend, and she let Joe drop her off without so much as a whimper. Jessica's parents were out, but Joe told her longtime sitter Carly, a kind, stalwart Nova Scotian in her early twenties, that he'd pick up Mollie at about three.

He walked home quickly to view tapes and hammer out more material for the ever hungry mouth of the *Dispatch*. With the distractions of the past few days, he'd been fighting and stretching deadline after deadline. He showered, set the timer on one of the VCRs, and struggled, as always, to unwrap a new blank cassette, muttering and gnashing his teeth at the near impossibility of ripping the cellophane that clung to it, eventually succeeding in clawing it off.

Being with Mollie had improved his mood, which helped him through a review of a TV film with Susan Lucci.

> *I'm a closet Susan Lucci fan, okay? While no one in this cast can rise above the material, Ms. Lucci, who's not likely to bring home her a prime-time Emmy for this particular effort, is, at least, easy on the eyes.*
>
> *P.S.*
>
> *Let's talk about this plastic shrink-wrap that strangles everything from ketchup bottles to spices to video cassettes. The plastic is there, as I'm sure you know, to protect you from being poisoned.*
>
> *Not long ago some psycho slipped a dash of cyanide into some yogurt and invaded a batch of Tylenol. The result? Everything in our markets and drugstores is now fortified against murderers by an impenetrable layer of plastic.*
>
> *This is the food-packaging equivalent of every person on the planet carrying a gun in order to keep us safe from each other. So the psychos, unable now to slip syringes into our yogurt, turn to sniping from highway overpasses, or gassing subways.*
>
> *Shrink-wrap doesn't go away, folks. It's plastic, it lives forever, it's immortal. If you burn it, its smoke erodes the ozone layer, creating skin cancer. In the name of safety, we're making ourselves less safe. I predict we'll ultimately kill more people with shrink-wrap than would ever have died from poisoned Tylenol.*
>
> *Stop watching programs that advertise shrink-wrapped*

products. This leaves you with PBS, public access, C-SPAN, and the movie channels. Happy viewing!

He pulled off his shoes and fell into bed for a nap. He was awakened when his answering machine clicked into action an hour later.

"Mr. McBride? This is the Central Park Precinct. Your daughter's friend and her baby-sitter are down here. I'm sorry to tell you this, but your daughter is missing."

CHAPTER

29

Joe ran out into traffic on Madison Avenue. Every cab he could see was taken, so he jumped into one that was idling at the corner. The driver was just getting seated after buying a cup of coffee at a Korean market.

"You don't see my light?" the cabbie snarled, slamming his door. "I'm off duty."

"Listen," Joe said, barely able to breathe, "my daughter's in trouble. Please, *please* take me to the Precinct on Eighty-fifth Street in the Central Park transverse. It runs east-west, straight through the park."

"I'm off duty, pal."

"I'm not getting out of this cab. This is an emergency."

The driver yanked the meter down. "My good deed for the day," he sighed.

"Thank you," Joe said. "Go down Fifth, make a right on Eighty-fifth . . ."

"I know where it is," the driver interrupted, as though Joe had just thrown up on him. They rode up Madison, across Ninety-first Street, and took a left onto Fifth. Joe looked out the window and fought off thoughts of what was possible. A few days before, he'd seen stories in the tabloids about a little girl who'd been abducted, raped, forced to dig her own grave, had her fingers cut off, and was stabbed to death.

"So — what happened?" asked the cabbie. He was in his late forties with a square face, a Marine butch haircut and two days' growth of prematurely gray beard. "Your daughter into drugs or something?"

"My daughter is five," Joe said angrily.

"What kind of trouble can a five-year-old get into?" the cabbie demanded.

"She's lost!" Joe wailed. "She's missing! Just drive the car."

The guy sped up and wove through the clogged traffic around the Guggenheim Museum with a surprising newfound concentration. They arrived at the precinct office in minutes. Joe handed the driver a ten.

"On the house," the cabbie said, waving Joe away. "New York takes care of its own."

Too upset to respond graciously, Joe jumped out, slammed the door with a distracted "thanks," and jaywalked across the busy street as a van swerved to miss him.

He made his way into the small station house, the oldest precinct in the city and even dingier than the one in Queens. There were uniformed cops everywhere. Joe identified himself to the officer at the desk and was ushered through a door marked Community Affairs into a small, windowless room with four steel desks cramped in where there should have been two. The room looked as though it hadn't been painted since La Guardia was mayor. A uniformed officer was huddled with a half dozen underlings, briefing them, and Joe realized they were setting off into an already-organized search. The noise of a hovering helicopter mixed with the barking of dogs. Behind one of the desks, a plain-clothes cop sat with Carly and Jessica, who were holding each other, sobbing.

The plainclothesman was a small, fair, tightly built man in his forties with trim Brylcreemed hair and the face of an ex-choirboy. He got up, apparently recognizing Joe, and introduced himself quickly.

"Mr. McBride? I'm Detective Kerrigan. I seen your picture in the *Dispatch* a million times. Sorry to meet like this . . ."

"Oh, Mr. McBride!" Carly called when she saw Joe. She ran over and threw her arms around his waist, clinging and keening and choking. Whatever had happened, she clearly felt it was her fault.

"Carly?" said Kerrigan awkwardly. "Why don't you try to relax and let me explain what happened. Okay?"

"I'm so . . . sorry," sobbed Carly, who couldn't catch her breath.

"Just tell me what's going on," Joe said, trying not to shout and only partially succeeding. Carly cried louder and Jessica held on to Carly's coat and did the same. Kerrigan put his hand on Carly's back.

"They were in the park," Kerrigan began.

"We went after lunch," blurted Carly between sobs.

"Up at Ninety-sixth and Fifth," continued Kerrigan. "They walked into the park to go to the playground there . . ."

Carly charged in again. "Jessica and Mollie kept talking about playing hide-and-seek. There were a lot of people around and Mollie was anxious to hide and I was yelling after her, reminding her not to run out of my sight. But then — suddenly everybody was screaming and making a commotion . . ."

"Apparently a dog had bit a kid a few feet away," said Kerrigan, trying to take over. "This kid was howling in pain, and the dog, a big rabid rottweiler, ran toward the girls."

Carly chimed in again. "I grabbed Jessica's hand to steer her away from the dog, and I, like, spun around to get my eye back on Mollie. But I didn't see her. People were running and yelling and hitting the ground. It was like someone was shooting a gun or something, Mr. McBride. It was just a total panic." She wept. "I held on to Jessica to make sure she was safe. I was pretty sure I knew where Mollie had gone, but when I turned around, I couldn't see her.

"I was *sure* she'd go to the tire swings, so I ran in there. I couldn't see her anywhere! We ran out, but I was afraid to let go of Jessica, so I wasn't moving very fast. We yelled and called, but it was, I don't know, Mr. McBride . . ." She coughed and gasped for air. "I ran farther into the park, but I should've gone back to the street. There was a kid's birthday party on the lawn with a loud radio playing, so maybe she couldn't hear us calling . . . oh God, oh God. I'm so . . . sorry!"

Beset by grisly images of Mollie's possible whereabouts, Joe was dreading the call to Gayle.

"We don't know if she ran off by herself," said Kerrigan.

"She wouldn't do something like that," Joe said, flicking away a tear as though it were a speck of dirt.

"With all due respect, Mr. McBride, you can't be sure of that," said Kerrigan.

"I know my daughter," insisted Joe, who realized he no longer knew her as well as he once had and was entertaining hazy thoughts of Nannie's possible involvement. "What happens now?"

"Our boys are combing the park and adjacent streets. The helicopter's about to go. We got dogs standing by. Let me just ask you a couple questions, Mr. McBride. Sit down — please."

He sat next to Jessica and Carly. A tanned, tight-lipped cop with a weight lifter's body stepped forward.

"This is Detective Riolo," said Kerrigan. Riolo tipped his cap. "He'll be in charge of the command post we've set up. The NYPD takes missing persons very seriously, Mr. McBride. Kids your daughter's age — under-sevens, we call 'em — they're our highest priority. We got blue suits from all over Manhattan North, we got guys from homicide . . ."

"Homicide?" Joe repeated.

"No, no," Kerrigan said, brushing aside Joe's fear. "It's just that our homicide guys are some of the best we got, that's all." He took Joe by the shoulders. "We'll find your daughter. Have you got a picture of her?" Kerrigan asked, sitting again.

Joe slipped one out of his wallet. It was Mollie in pink ballet tights doing a close approximation of fifth position. Kerrigan handed the photo to Riolo, who hustled away.

"We'll get it copied so everybody has it," Kerrigan explained, sitting again.

Joe felt as if he were being prepped for major surgery.

"Does she have a favorite place in the city?" Kerrigan went on. "When my daughter got to be five, she wanted to go everywhere by herself. It made me and my wife nuts. Is there a special place Mollie might gravitate to?"

"She hasn't lived in the city for almost a year," Joe said, "and she wasn't even four when she left — my wife and I are divorced — so I don't know how much she remembers. But we used to love that playground at Ninety-sixth Street."

"Who has custody?"

"My ex-wife," Joe answered.

"We'll need her number," Kerrigan said.

Joe scribbled Gayle's number as he spoke. "I only see Mollie two weekends a month. I just moved into a new place and this was her first time in it."

"Your address?"

"Twenty-three East Ninetieth."

"I know that building. How long you lived there?"

"Just since last week."

"We'll have the place canvassed," Kerrigan said, ripping off a piece of paper and handing it to another officer. "Ronnie, you and Al knock on every door at Twenty-three East Ninetieth. If anybody doesn't answer, find out from the doorman — is it still a doorman building?" he asked Joe.

"No," said Joe.

"If somebody doesn't answer, get hold of the super and find out who's away — probably a few of 'em in the Hamptons — or buzz 'em on the building's intercom." Joe was somehow relieved at the thought of Nannie or Loree being questioned. The cops took off. "Is Mollie on any medication, Mr. McBride?"

"No."

"She strong? In good health?"

"Yes," Joe answered.

"Good," Kerrigan muttered barely audibly. "Does she know your address and phone number?"

"Oh dear God," Joe said. "It's a new address and number for her. If she calls my old one, she'll get a recording, but it may just confuse her . . ."

"Does she know her mother's number?" Kerrigan asked, writing all the while.

"I'm sure she does," Joe answered, his mind flooded. "Yes. Yes — but she may not know her area code. She's never in her life been without either her mother, me, or a sitter."

"Is your new number listed?"

"No," Joe said. "If Mollie could get to a phone, she'd try to call home in Hastings. But I doubt she'd be able to figure out a phone booth on her own, and she might be too afraid to ask for help." Joe shook off more tears, fearful he'd start in like Carly and Jessica, and knowing he had to keep his head straight.

"May I use your phone, detective? I better call my wife," he said, unconsciously removing the *ex* from *ex-wife*.

"Over there," Kerrigan said, pointing to an old pay phone. "No, what am I sayin'? Use this." He grabbed a desk phone and held it out for Joe. "This isn't my office. I normally work Homicide, but everybody was out at a parade when Carly came in. Dial nine."

Gayle, remarkably calm, went straight into emergency mode, saying she'd drive in right away and meet Joe at the apartment. Kerrigan questioned her over the phone for ten minutes. When he hung up, he led Joe outside.

"You see the manpower we got here, Mr. McBride? Let us do what we do. You can stay, or you can wait at your place. Here's the precinct number, here's my beeper number, here's the Command Control Center number — that's the room we were just in."

Joe nodded and heard an amplified voice from outside.

"Central Park Precinct is endeavoring to find a lost child, Mollie McBride, Caucasian, age five, weight forty-one pounds, height forty-four inches. Light brown dirty-blond shoulder-length straight hair. Last seen wearing denim overalls, a pink *Pocahontas* T-shirt . . ."

"Mr. McBride?" Kerrigan's voice shook Joe from ricocheting thoughts of death by drowning, rape, and torture. "Let me just ask you — could you excuse us for a second here, Carly? Why don't you take Jessica out to look at the buildings. Jessica, did you know that this *whole* place used to be a stable? For horses?"

The thought had clearly never occurred to Jessica, and it distracted her enough that Carly was able to steer her toward the door.

"Johnnie," said Kerrigan, calling to a slim young officer. "Go with Carly and Jessica here and see if you can find some of the Twinkies I saw in the fridge. Then get 'em drinks if the goddamn soda guy filled the goddamn machine, pardon my French. G'head, girls. Officer Kennedy here'll show you where the horsies used to be."

Kennedy led them away. Kerrigan spoke as soon as they were out the door.

"Is there anything else you might want to tell me, Mr. McBride? I hate to say this, but any idea about somebody who would have reason to, you know, take her?"

Joe stood with his back to Kerrigan.

"Mr. McBride? You okay?"

Joe turned and faced him again. "There's something I . . . forgot to mention."

"Have a seat," Kerrigan said. The little room was so busy and noisy that there was an odd sense of privacy. Kerrigan rapped his hands on the desk, trying to appear more patient than he was.

"I met a woman last week . . ." Joe began.

"Uh-huh," Kerrigan said unobtrusively.

"She lives one floor below me in the new building. Uh . . . this may be *very* far-fetched, but, I don't know, I just thought I should . . ."

"Sure," said Kerrigan, friendly.

It occurred to Joe that his need for sex had led him inevitably, maybe fatally, to this moment.

"This woman and I had an affair . . ."

"Had?" said Kerrigan. "It's over?"

"Yes, it's over. But I thought you should know . . . that she told me she was someone else."

Kerrigan's face registered nothing. "I see. She gave you a phony name, and you found her out?"

"Yes."

Kerrigan blinked. "Why do you think she did that?"

"She apparently has a history of it. She has a twin sister who I met a couple of days later who told me . . ."

"A twin," said Kerrigan. "Wow. Lookers?"

"Actually, yes," said Joe.

"Who did she tell you she was?"

"She said she was Amy Goode, which is, in fact, the name of an undercover cop in Queens."

"I've heard of her," said Kerrigan. "Does she know about this?"

Joe took Kerrigan through the last week of his life. For Mollie's sake, he left nothing out.

Still writing, Kerrigan picked up a phone with his left hand and dialed 411.

"The number for the Ninety-ninth Precinct in Queens, okay sweetheart?" He waited, then dialed. "Detective Goode, please," he said. "Uh-huh. Okay, now listen up. Get a message to her to call Detective Tom Kerrigan at the Central Park Precinct ASAP. It's urgent. About a missing under-seven. Right. Sure, I under-stand." He left the number, put down the phone, and stretched to both sides as if working out a kink in his back.

"She's on a stakeout and they may not be able to go in and get her without blowing her cover. Up in the fuckin' woods some-where in Jersey."

"I have a home number for her," Joe said. "At my place."

"Phone it in as soon as you can, all right?"

"Sure," Joe answered.

"And the twin's last name you said is . . . Battochi? In Garden City?"

"It's unlisted," said Joe. "I tried."

"You got this Nannie's number?"

"Unlisted," Joe answered. "But she's in 9B."

Kerrigan picked up a phone again and dialed. "Too many fuckin' unlisted numbers in the world. I got a friend at the phone company, though," he said. " 'Scuse me just a second, will you? This has to be between him and me." Joe stood and backed a few feet away. Cops working the other three desks in the room moved around him as though he were a statue.

Kerrigan hung up and waved Joe over, scribbling more notes. "My friend has a way to check the activity on Miss Pritchard's phone for us. Might not turn up anything, might turn up a lot.

He needs a couple hours, though. This Pritchard woman sounds . . . interesting, let me say."

"I didn't mean that I think she actually . . ."

Kerrigan cut Joe off politely. "If your daughter's been abducted, it may not be the most obvious person. I'm not sayin' this Pritchard woman is, like, you know, the *least* likely suspect. Hey, maybe she's just a harmless prankster, maybe she's out of her lively little gourd. Maybe, you should pardon what I'm sayin', she's just a whore. . . ."

"No, no," Joe said simply, the thought never having occurred to him.

"It's my job," Kerrigan said, "to make sure someone talks to her, that's all."

"Of course."

"Don't get your shorts overadjusted about this woman. Life isn't usually that logical. It probably has nothing to do with her. Unless it does. Shall I take you and the girls back?"

"Please."

They walked outside and Joe gathered up Carly and Jessica, who were playing with an old hula hoop and nursing frosty cans of cream soda. Kerrigan dropped Carly and Jessica at their place. Joe went in and tried to reach Jessica's parents, but they were on a golf course and wouldn't be back, he was told, "till after cocktails." Joe offered to take them to his place, but Jessica seemed to be comforted by being home and Carly had finally calmed down. Joe left his number, gave them hugs and assured them both, separately, that it wasn't their fault. Kerrigan left instructions for Jessica's parents to call as soon as possible.

They drove by the park at Fifth and Ninety-sixth Street where Mollie had disappeared.

"Would you mind pulling over?" Joe asked suddenly.

Kerrigan waited while Joe ran up to the playground. The last families were gathering strollers and leaving. The sun was going down and Joe thought of how afraid Mollie must be, wherever she was.

Police with dogs and flashlights roamed in teams beyond the fenced-in jungle gyms, swings, and slides. Joe walked over to the familiar row of five empty baby swings. He pushed one. It wobbled away, then back, then away again.

"Higher!" he heard Mollie say, as if she were there, being pushed by him — often for as long as an hour — on any number of afternoons they'd spent there. "Higher!"

As his hands met her back with each push, she could feel he was there, quite literally, and he would lose himself, concentrating on pushing her perfectly.

"Your only kid?" Kerrigan's voice asked. Joe turned to see the cop standing behind him.

"Yeah," Joe said, watching a purple sunset gather over a little hill that rose up to meet the reservoir.

"My daughter just got married," Kerrigan said, lighting a cigarette. He offered one to Joe, who took it but didn't light up. "When the priest said, 'Who gives this woman in marriage,' I thought about just not answering. Like I could keep her from, you know . . ." He exhaled a long stream of smoke. Joe caught a tempting whiff.

"You have any idea how the Mets did last night?" Joe asked.

"They beat the Giants. Two-zip. Why?"

Joe gave the unlit cigarette back to Kerrigan.

As the empty swing slowed to a stop, they walked out through tall, black, wrought iron gates.

"We had somebody ring nine B's bell," said Kerrigan. "It was out of order. He knocked a few times. No answer. Does Miss Pritchard maybe go away for the weekend?"

"I have no idea," Joe said. "I know so little about her, it's pathetic."

"I met my wife twenty-three years ago, and I don't know much about her, either. Don't be hard on yourself." He flicked away his cigarette.

"That's littering," Joe said distractedly, stopping and watching where the butt landed.

"What?" Kerrigan asked as Joe focused on the smoldering cigarette, marking its location with his eye.

"Somebody has to pick that up," Joe said as though sleepwalking. He bent toward it.

"Oh," said Kerrigan. "Okay. Yeah."

Joe picked it up and held it until they reached a wastebasket, then dropped it in.

"Thanks," Kerrigan said.

"Don't mention it."

It was dark now and they wandered out of the playground and over to the adjoining area where the dog had run rabid.

"I feel like walking," Joe said at the corner of Ninety-sixth and Fifth. "It's just a couple blocks."

"Go right home, okay? We'll be talking to you," Kerrigan said.

Joe closed the car door for Kerrigan and headed down the cobblestone path on the west side of Fifth Avenue. The squad car zoomed away with lights blazing.

About to pass the Church of the Heavenly Rest, he noticed its doors were open. Knowing Gayle would be a while before reaching the city, he made his way to a rear pew, and, as his mother had directed him two days before, got to his knees.

UNABLE to imagine his life having value without Mollie, he of-
fered himself in exchange for her, left the church feeling a failure
at everything, including prayer, and ran to his building.

As he entered the lobby, a uniformed policeman snapped almost to attention.

"Excuse me," said the officer. "Do you live in the building?"

"I'm Joe McBride, the father of the . . . lost child."

"Sorry, Mr. McBride. I'm Officer Morosini," said the cop, a
barrel-chested man in his thirties with a mustache and long side-
burns. "Anything you need, sir, you just let me know."

"Thanks, Officer," Joe said, moving to the elevator. "Any
news?"

"Afraid not," said Morosini quietly. "Hang in there."

When Joe got to his apartment, he made for the answering
machine. There were two messages.

"It's Andy Zeserson, Joe. What is this shit? Who the fuck cares
about *shrink-wrap*? You think I don't have better things to do on
Saturday night than read your neurotic ramblings about *plastic*?

I need a column on your Emmy picks first thing Monday. And no more of your fucking little P.S.'s, okay?" There was a beep.

"Joey? It's Mom. I just had one of those silly motherly feelings that . . . I don't know. Are you all right?"

Everybody in my life, Joe thought, is psychic — except me. He started to call her, but decided it was too soon to upset his mother in her condition. Maybe there'd prove to be no reason to alarm her.

There was nothing from the police. He dialed Kerrigan, gave him Officer Goode's home number, hung up, and ran out the back door and down a flight of stairs.

Putting his ear to her door and hearing nothing, he dashed back up to his kitchen, got a glass, trotted down again, cupped it gently where it said 9B, and listened. All he picked up was the buzzing of a fluorescent hall light.

When he got back to his place, the intercom was ringing. He answered and Gayle's voice announced flatly, "It's me."

He paced a tight circle in his foyer, then moved out to the hallway by the elevator. The doors opened and Gayle emerged, drawn and red around the eyes, in jeans and a tan leather jacket over a green V-neck sweater. She moved close to Joe but made no contact.

"We'll get through this," she said. She followed Joe into the apartment and daubed at her cheeks with a wadded tissue. "I couldn't believe the traffic. Where's Mary Beth?"

"Away for the weekend," he said.

"Thank God."

"Come in."

"No word?" she asked.

"Nothing."

She walked in and sat on the living room couch as though she'd been there many times before. "A neighbor's waiting by the phone at my house," Gayle said. "She'll spend the night if she has to in case Mollie calls."

Joe nodded. There was a moment of screaming silence.

"Do you have anything to drink?" she asked finally. "I need something."

"There's stuff in one of these boxes," Joe answered, pulling the tape off one. "Scotch?" he asked, finding some Johnnie Walker.

"Fine, anything," Gayle said, as though annoyed that he'd kept her waiting so long. He went to the kitchen for a glass. The phone rang and he answered.

"Before you say a word," said Sandy Moss, "let me just tell you what I'm wearing on the first show . . ."

He hung up.

"Who was that?" called Gayle.

"Wrong number."

He poured a hefty drink, added water, and handed it to her. She downed it, took a breath, shook off the heat of the Scotch, and jerked her head at him.

"I'll never forgive you for this, Joe. If anything has happened to my daughter, I swear to God I hope you . . . die."

"What kind of talk is that?" he said. "I wasn't even there!"

"She's your responsibility. When she's staying in the city — which she will never do again if I have anything to say about it — she's your respon — "

"Wait a minute!" Joe broke in.

"Don't interrupt!" she shouted.

"She goes on play dates in Hastings, doesn't she?" he shouted louder. "You're not with her every single second of every day."

"I'm very careful about who she's with. . . ."

"This was Carly and Jessica, for God's sake!" Joe said, rising and moving away from her. "We used to have play dates with them all the time. If you're going to start blaming, get out."

No one spoke for a moment.

"I should've moved to — I don't know — California," Gayle said, shaking her head. "I should've gotten as far away as possible."

"Be quiet."

"Fuck you," she said. "Give me another drink."

"I need you sober."

She looked around, taking in the room for the first time. "Where's the rest of your furniture?"

"Still in boxes," he lied.

"Nobody packs furniture in boxes. What are you talking about?"

He took a deep breath and exhaled, realizing he didn't have the energy to lie. "Mary Beth's gone. She cleaned everything out. It's over."

"Oh," said Gayle. She raised her empty glass to her lips and coaxed a final drop from it. "Sorry."

"Yeah," he said.

"Serves you fucking well right."

"Why don't you get out?"

"It's not my fault that Mollie is missing, Joe — okay?" Her voice was rising again. "I'm her mother, okay? I gave birth to her, *okay*?"

"I wish to God *I* could have given birth to her," Joe yelled. "As if just contributing my lousy sperm and doing most of the parenting while you checked out on a daily basis with one psychosomatic illness after another — "

Gayle went for the Scotch bottle. "Okay, Joe. Life is fair, you're fair, you've never done anything wrong, and I should get down on my knees and thank you for everything you've done for me, like taking up with one of my oldest friends, you son of a bitch . . ."

She charged him, like his mother on the dock at Madeline Island, swatting at him with her glass as though she might erase him. He grabbed her wrist.

"Stop it!" she demanded, wincing. "That hurts. Really." She looked frightened. He stopped squeezing but held her wrist, pulling her face to his.

"You never thought I was safety-conscious enough with Mollie," he whispered. "But this wasn't my fault. . . ."

She found the strength to break away and slapped him hard with her free hand. He stood, absorbing it, pondering how easy it would be to kill her. He was out of his mind.

"You always talk about fault," she raged. "You're so afraid someone will say something — *anything* — is your fault! God forbid Mr. Perfect does something wrong."

"I defend myself because you're a blamer. You stop and I'll stop."

"Deal," she said. Her shoulders started to heave and she dropped to the couch. "Oh, God," she said in a near-silent squeal. "Where is she?"

Joe sat and put his arm around her. It was the first contact they'd had, outside of their quick-peck kisses, in a long time. She held on tight.

"I didn't mean I wanted you to die," she sobbed. "I think *I'd* want to die if . . . I don't know if I can live through it if . . ." She lost it and Joe held on.

"I thought she might die the moment she was born," he said quietly, cradling her.

It had been a nightmare birth, three weeks premature, complicated by Gayle's fever during labor and an incompetent midwife, resulting in an emergency caesarean. Mollie's first days had been in intensive care.

"I remember looking at her when they took her into the ICU," Joe went on, "all bloody and crying and ugly and beautiful and I thought it might be the only time I'd see my daughter alive." He was shaking, suddenly unable to get enough air. "You were still under anaesthesia, and I was afraid she'd die before you ever saw her."

"Oh, God," said Gayle, holding Joe closer.

"I couldn't believe how alive and . . . part of everything I felt," he continued. "I've always been terrified something would happen to her."

"Really?" said Gayle, surprised. Her eyes opened wide and she looked into Joe's. "I thought it was just me."

"I can't stand the thought of . . ." He trailed off, lips fluttering.

"How did we get here?" Gayle asked, looking around. "Sitting in your — what is it now — your bachelor pad? And me in the suburbs. Where's the Scotch?"

"Right where you put it down," he answered. She began pouring again. "Don't get drunk on me," Joe warned.

"I'm not the one with the drinking problem," she said, taking a swig. "Oh, God. Do you have any coffee?" she asked suddenly. "I feel woozy."

"There's half a cappuccino in the fridge," he said. "But you have that weird thing with caffeine . . ."

"What are you talking about?"

"When you drink coffee on top of booze, it always makes you sleepy."

"Not always," called Gayle, already in the kitchen, removing the cold cappuccino and taking a slug, wincing.

The fax machine tweeted in the office area, followed by the hissing of a connection.

"Incoming, incoming!" Joe said, covering his ears and bending over.

"What's that," said Gayle, downing the rest of the coffee and moving back to Joe in the living room.

"A fax," Joe explained. "Someone wants to know what I thought of the latest episode of *Buffy, the Vampire Slayer* or wants me to send them an interview with Jerry Springer or Pamela Anderson Lee or Jenny McCarthy. Our increasingly illiterate public wants to know how Jenny prepares for a role, who's the latest hunk in her life, what's it like to make love in front of a film crew . . ."

"You're ranting," said Gayle.

"God forbid I should rant," he said. "You could never take it if I was afraid or anxious."

"I couldn't take whining," she sniffed.

"Okay, I'll pretend I'm fine," he said angrily.

"*That* we were good at," she said in a faraway tone.

The fax machine signaled the end of the transmission. Joe ignored it.

"Could it be something about Mol?" she asked.

"The police don't have my fax number," he said, rising and going to his office nook.

"*Where's that Seinfeld interview?*" he read aloud from Andy Zeserson's fax. "*And give the motherfucking wiseass stuff a rest.*"

"How's Andy Zeserson?" Gayle asked.

"Still doesn't have a sense of humor," Joe answered, balling up the fax and tossing it into the fireplace.

"It's chilly in here," said Gayle. "What motherfucking wiseass stuff?"

Joe didn't answer. A car alarm went off in the distance.

"Where do you suppose she is right now?" asked Gayle, looking into the empty fireplace.

"Maybe she's all right. Maybe she just . . ."

"She's *not* all right," snapped Gayle. "You can never stand for anyone to suffer. You have a pathetic threshold of pain."

"I'm not going to take your bait. . . ."

"Oh, of course not. Because that wouldn't be *nice* and we can't have you ever, *ever* be the bad guy about *anything,* can we?"

"Is this what happens when you have a couple of drinks? I'd forgotten."

"You don't get it, do you?" she said, her voice rising again but with less control. "I'm not going to be a mother again. And I can't live without her. You don't know. You don't take care of her every day."

"You can have my bed," Joe said, changing the subject. "I'll sleep on the couch or in — "

"May I see Mollie's room?" Gayle asked, wiping her eyes.

"Sure," he answered, leading her in and suddenly wishing he hadn't. Gayle's decorating skills were extraordinary, down to the tiniest details. "It's nowhere near finished," he said. "But she slept like a log last night. No waking. No fears."

"I don't remember what it's like to have four straight hours of sleep without having to go in and tell her she's safe, or sing endless lullabies," said Gayle with an edge to her voice. "Wouldn't you know she'd come *here* and sleep through the night." She sighed and looked around. "I can't believe she felt safe in here."

"That's just it. She *wasn't* safe," he pointed out, standing by Mollie's bed and reaching in to straighten the sheet. "She must be thinking, 'Mommy and Daddy told me I was safe, but I wasn't.' I wonder if she'll ever trust us again if she . . ."

Gayle patted him on the back and he shut himself up. She sat on the bed.

"Oh my God," Gayle said, panicking. "Does she have her bing?" She broke down again.

"It's okay, it's okay — she took it with her," Joe reassured her. "She hid it in her pocket, though. She said it makes her feel like a little kid and she didn't want Jessica to see it."

"Really?" said Gayle quietly, fingering the sheets with a puzzled expression. She bunched up her mouth, lay down, held the pillow to her face, and they sat in silence.

"Are you happy?" she asked.

He looked away. The only times he'd been happy recently were walking down the street playing I Spy with Mollie and, he had to admit, making love to Nannie.

"I used to ask you if you were happy and you'd say yes — quite often," said Gayle. Joe moved around the room picking up the loose pieces and game board of Chutes and Ladders. "Were you lying?" she asked.

He slid the game into a cupboard. "I was happy when Mollie was born," he answered. "I thought we'd make it."

"You never had time for me," said Gayle. "I got sick of begging. You thought you could come out of your office for five minutes, feel me up or have a quickie, and everything would be okay."

The car alarm finally stopped and they heard the wind rustle through the vent of an air conditioner.

"I saw my mother," Joe offered.

"I know," Gayle said, brightening a little. "I spoke to her, remember?"

"Oh, right," Joe answered. "When . . . Mollie . . . comes back, you know what I think we should do?"

"What?"

"You'll think I'm crazy, but we should — the three of us — visit her on the Island." Gayle's eyes narrowed. "Or you and Mollie should. Mom likes you more than anybody."

"We're not a family anymore, Joe," Gayle said quietly. "Don't get carried away because I'm here."

"I'm not carried away . . ."

"If Mollie hadn't disappeared, you wouldn't be talking about going to see your mother — which I'd love to do, by the way —"

"Mom's dying."

"What?" she said, stricken.

"She won't go to the hospital."

Gayle smiled tightly and shook her head, familiar as she was with his mother. "I just think if whoever's running this show grants us the chance," Joe went on, "you and I might muster whatever it takes and bring our daughter to see her grandmother while we still can."

Gayle curled up on Mollie's bed.

"I can't get comfortable," she said, squirming, then sitting up suddenly. "Oh, man! I drank too much. Don't leave, Joe. I won't attack again." She swung off the bed, knelt, and folded her hands in prayer, her mouth involuntarily pulling down at the corners. She grabbed Joe's hand and tugged him to his knees to join her. After a moment, she opened her eyes.

"I want to go to the park," she said abruptly.

"Now?"

"I have to see the place . . . where it happened. Maybe I'll figure something out if I see it."

"The police have been combing the area for hours," Joe protested. "You're drunk. Why don't you lie down and relax — "

"*You* lie down and relax, you asshole!" she shouted. "I'm not drunk. I'm her mother. Her mother! Come on. Get your coat."

"I'm not going," said Joe, ignoring her provocation. "The cops could call any time."

"Fine," she snarled. "It's the little hill at the entrance at Ninety-sixth Street, right?"

"You're not gonna find anything, Gayle."

"I can't just sit around anymore," she said, heading into the foyer. Tears streamed down her cheeks. "I have to see that place, that's all."

"Okay," said Joe quietly, her feelings triggering his. "Just don't catch a chill." He opened the small hall closet, grabbed a gray, weathered, *New York Dispatch* sweatshirt and thrust it into her hand.

"Thanks," she whispered, turning the brass doorknob of Joe's front door. "I won't be long."

"Be careful crossing Fifth," said Joe as she stumbled slightly in her path to the elevator. "The bus drivers are like maniacs coming down there." She nodded with a grateful, thin smile, her face wan and pale yet beautiful. He marveled with a writer's momentary detachment that despair could be so perversely becoming. The elevator arrived and Gayle got on, waving back at Joe without looking at him. He stood in the hall for a moment, the stillness broken only by the scraping of the elevator's cables as they brushed and bounced against the walls of the shaft.

Terrifically thirsty, Joe closed the door and went to the kitchen for some cold water. Through the mostly drawn curtain, he saw a light in Nannie's window. Blood rushed to his face. Had the light been on all day? Was someone there? He poured a glass of water from a bottle in the fridge and downed it.

Something bright fluttered into his field of vision and he pivoted toward it. The light in Nannie's kitchen was going off and on, off and on. He stepped to the window and drew the makeshift curtain a little. Loree was standing there, in a green jacket over a sparkly yellow blouse, flicking the light switch. When she saw Joe, she left the lights on. With an urgent and distinctly unflirtatious expression, she beckoned him to come down. He didn't move. She beckoned again and walked out of sight.

Thinking he might get some information out of Loree, he took the phone off the hook so that Kerrigan would get a busy signal and keep trying if he called. He dashed a note on a Post-it for Gayle, saying, "Went to the ATM for cash." Figuring he'd be back before her, he stuck the note onto the front door just in case.

Letting himself out the service exit and careful to leave it unlocked from the outside, he made his way down to 9B.

H ER door was open. Joe walked through the kitchen and down the hallway.

"In here," he heard her say from the living room.

As he rounded the corner, Loree had her back to him and was headed into the bedroom.

"Sorry, just give me *one* second," she whispered. "Be right back." As she went in, Joe noticed the puzzle on the coffee table. It appeared to be finished, so he moved around to get a look at it.

It was a reproduction of a page from the arts section of *The New York Times,* reduced in size to about two thirds. One corner piece, the one in Joe's pocket, was still missing. He absently took it out and popped it in, his eye scanning the text on the puzzle.

It was dated June 15, 1994. He read the most prominent headline on the page.

Misguided Performance Mars Promising New Play
by Joe McBride

His brain turned over for a few seconds before it clicked. It was a review he'd written during his brief tenure as third-string drama critic at the *Times*.

He felt his limbs go cold as he read his words.

J. A. Alper's new play See Through *opened last night at the Minetta Lane. This wasn't just a bad hair day in the theater — although the interminable evening included a parade of atrocious wigs — it was, sad to say, a bad directing day, a bad casting day, and a horrendous acting day. Why did Mr. Alper, who made a brilliant debut last fall with his comedy on the lives of aging Gen-Xers, allow the woefully miscast Annette Fontana to take on the play's central role?*

"Annette Fontana," said Loree, coming out of the bedroom, "is my sister's real name. I think she's mad at you, Joe." She'd removed the jacket and was wearing jeans and a yellow blouse so transparent that her body seemed spray-painted. Her eyes were fixed on Joe, and her free hand was draped around the waist of Dean.

Joe began to back out of the room.

"I don't think so," she said in a sharp whisper, raising a revolver with a silencer and pointing it at Joe, who froze. "Go on back. Read the rest."

"That's okay," he said.

"Simon *says* read the rest," she ordered, waving the barrel of the gun. Joe moved carefully back toward the puzzle.

"Out loud," she ordered.

Joe looked down and began.

"In a pivotal role requiring edgy sexuality and an aura of danger, Miss Fontana comes up with neither. It's difficult to imagine this clumsy, leaden-toned actress as a sexual siren. She may have a future in character roles, but she's simply not a leading lady. This is an actress who lacks the inner fire

*or, frankly, the physique to lure a man into the kind of ca-
lamitous relationship Mr. Alper has written. Duty compels
me to report that Ms. Fontana is unconvincing during almost
every moment of the play and is simply in over her head.
Frankly, I was relieved when she left the stage. In a role that
should be all intrigue and secrets, Ms. Fontana is an open
book — and one, I'm afraid, that's much too easy to put
down."*

Joe looked up at Loree.

"My sister and I are a lot closer than you think," she said. "We
look out for each other."

She reached up and yanked off what Joe now realized was a
stupendous wig. Dean helped her as she patiently undid a batch
of pins and let her real brown hair tussle free, shaking out the
tightly wound curls and dropping the pins onto the glass-topped
coffee table.

"How about that?" she said in Amy's voice. "You can actually
hear a pin drop." Holding the gun on Joe, she put her arm around
Dean's neck, pulled him to her and kissed him long and deeply,
her eyes wide open and gazing through Joe.

"Leave us alone for a few minutes, okay?" she asked Dean,
straightening her blouse.

Dean looked at Joe. "Hi," he offered as he opened the bedroom
door quietly. "We already met. The name's Dean, not Hank."

"Go!" said Nannie Pritchard in a sharp whisper.

"You be nice," warned Dean, lashing back and pointing a
threatening finger at her. She stared him down and with a flick
of his long hair he regained his composure. He looked at Joe.
"God be with you, guy," he said as he disappeared into the bedroom.

"Hi, Joe," she said after a few seconds. Joe thought she looked
as scared as he felt. "We have a lot to talk about. Do you like
my blouse? I wanted to be pretty for you. What do you think?"

"Are you going to . . . put that down?" Joe asked, eyes on the gun.

"I really doubt it," she said, taking a cigarette, lighting it, and inhaling a long drag. "You believed in Loree, didn't you?" He didn't answer. *"Didn't you?"* she repeated, raising the gun a little.

"Well," he said carefully, "I saw you both."

"No. What you saw was a glimpse of Dean, in this wig. If you'd been less polite and gotten close enough to sneak a better look, you might've been on to me. Dean's so thin — his butt looks as good in capri pants as mine, and he had Loree's trench coat on. Plus I was blocking your view of him as best I could."

"But . . . I heard her," said Joe.

"I did both voices in the hallway," she answered, jerking her head to one side, and placing a hand on one hip, her body language taking on Loree's cocky lilt.

"You have a guest?" she said as Loree. *"I guess you got luckier than me. Can I meet him?"*

In a split second, every trace of Loree drained from her face, replaced by the calm straightforwardness of Amy.

"No. Absolutely not," she said, repeating what she'd said in the hallway that night. *"How many times has the shoe been on the other foot, Loree? Just go to bed."*

"It's too noisy in the bedroom," said Loree, re-appearing on Nannie's face with a smirk. *"I want to sleep on the couch."*

"Not tonight," she replied as Amy, switching roles with dazzling speed.

"Well, I'll be," taunted Loree. *"Miss Goody-Goody steps out!"*

Finished, she made a little curtsy as if an audience were applauding.

"But — wait a second," said Joe, trying to get a grip. "I heard her in the bedroom."

"I prerecorded Loree's voice and Dean hit the play button on cues I worked out with him. That was Dean on the bed with the pillow over his head when you went to the bathroom." She shook her head. "Couldn't you just kick yourself? He watched us through a peekhole that night. Knowing I had an audience was great. I love an audience."

Joe looked down at the photo of Nannie and Loree on the coffee table.

"Pictures are so easy," she said, following his glance. "Everybody's doing it these days. I could've put Elvis in there with me if I wanted to. Remember when *TV Guide* put Oprah's face on Ann-Margret's body? You call yourself a journalist — you should know." She shook her head at Joe. "I'm a really good actress, don't you think?"

Joe stared back.

"I hate to have to beg for a fucking compliment," she said, nervously taking a drag of her cigarette, "but then I've had to learn not to be proud. *Don't you think I'm a good actress?*"

Joe nodded slowly.

"Thank you," she said. "Now — "

"My daughter's in trouble," he sputtered. "I have to get home. . . ."

"No, you don't, Joe. Relax. Mollie's in the bedroom. With Dean."

J OE'S stomach began to heave.

"Mollie's asleep," Nannie said. "I got downstairs this afternoon just as you and Mol were leaving the building." She sighed. "I called to you, but you didn't hear me. That's dangerous, you know, that kind of overabsorption in your kid. I will *never* allow myself to be distracted when I'm with Mollie. I followed you to where you dropped her off, and then I had a cup of coffee at Jackson Hole. A few minutes later Mollie and her friend and the sitter walked by. I followed them."

Joe bent over, his intestines raging.

"Stand up straight!" she ordered and he somehow managed it. "And don't yell or anything. She might wake up."

He tried to stop his legs from shaking.

"Mollie has no idea anything's wrong and she likes me — remember? You're so lucky I followed her. When that dog spooked everybody and Mollie couldn't find Carly, *I* was there. Talk about fate. I picked her up and got her away and calmed her down. She was very worried about Carly and Jessica so I told her we were going to play a really fun game. I said that Carly and Jessica knew you were meeting us here for hot chocolate and that you might be a little late. When we got here, I pretended to phone Jessica's apartment so Mollie wouldn't worry. Then I told her you'd been called to the newspaper for a meeting and you'd be joining us as soon as you could. We played cards — she beat me at War, she watched TV. She watches too much TV, Joe. I'm going to have to clamp down on that. She cried for you a little, but I assured her everything was okay and that you'd snuggle with her and put her in her own bed when you got back. I'm good with kids. She cried some more, but I think she was just overtired, so I dressed her in one of my shirts and that seemed to comfort her, so I put on a matching one. She really liked the whole mother-daughter thing. I told her we'd wear lots of matching outfits from now on and she fell asleep in my arms after I put a little valerian root into her third hot chocolate. Dean carried her in there and put her on my bed. I'll wake her in a few minutes, but not yet, okay?"

Joe swallowed. "I don't believe you."

"*Never* say those words to me again!" she hissed, motioning him toward the bedroom with the gun. She walked a few steps behind and they stopped at the door. "Go on, open it."

Mollie was sprawled on the bed, sleeping soundly, the sheet partially over her head. Joe knew that for the first four or five hours she was asleep, almost nothing ever woke her. Dean sat in a corner chair, wide awake and looking at Nannie. After a few seconds, Nannie closed the door.

"Can I take her home now?" Joe asked as gently as he could.

"Yeah, right," she said, motioning him back to the living room.

Joe's mind, far from racing, was in sharp focus. He had to make sure Mollie slept through as much of this as possible. He clung to the possibility that if Nannie was telling the truth, Mollie might not have suffered any lasting trauma yet.

"Get away from the couch," she said. He backed off a few steps. She aimed the gun at the chintz couch and squeezed the trigger. A pinched popping sound came from the gun and feathers exploded from the seat cushion. "The silencer sure works," she said matter-of-factly. She twirled the chamber, shot again, and more feathers flew.

"There are four more rounds in here," she continued, fanning the chamber. "Would you like to play a little Russian roulette, Joe?"

"What . . . do you want?"

"I hate to admit it, but I'd miss never kissing you again," she said softly.

Joe was standing almost at attention. Never breaking eye contact, she slowly advanced a few steps toward him. Then, seeming to catch herself, she stopped and backed up again.

"There are twenty-five or thirty critics who review Broadway," Nannie said, "but you know as well as I do that *The New York Times* is the only one that counts, the one that *everybody* reads, the one that can close a show, or make a big, overnight hit. You can get raves from everybody else, but if the *Times* doesn't like you, you usually close. It stinks, but everybody in the New York theater lives with it. When my play opened, we thought Frank Rich would review us, but he was off in England. And Ben Brantley was sick that night — so we got *you*. *The New York Times* is the Bible, Joe. In three little paragraphs, you nuked my career.

"The play closed the day after it opened," she continued, almost in a daze. "I didn't get sent on anything for months. No one would return my agent's calls. A few months later, the agency let me go. The only person who'd represent me was an old guy with a cheap office over Times Square whose last client had just died. So I went to some classes and did a few plays in places where they don't pay enough for cab fare. I saved every dime so I could have a little work done on my body. When this building went co-op, I couldn't begin to scrape together the down payment, so I had to stay on as a renter. They harass me, they won't fix anything, they turn off my heat 'cause they know if they can get me to move they'll sell this place in a second. The only reason I ever have hot water or heat is because the super likes me.

"I always thought I'd get you back by being so good in a play or a TV show that you'd have to eat your words. And then, wonder of wonders, you moved into my building. Of all the gin joints in all the world, I thought. At first I was furious. I felt invaded. The fact that you, of all people, could afford to buy a place here —it made me kinda nuts. But then I thought, hold everything, this is an opportunity. I'm not a quitter. Whatever doesn't kill you makes you stronger, you know? Hell, Joe, your review inspired me. I mean, this woman you see before you, this woman who has the power of life and death over you right now, Joe — this woman whose body, let's face it, has been on your mind since the moment I pulled my pajama top off in the window — this sweet bitch has worked at her craft. And here was a chance to show you, the man who so cavalierly ruined me, to show you just how far I've come as an actress. As Dean would put it, Joe, 'Ya hear what I'm sayin?' "

Joe stared blankly, then, realizing that her question was not rhetorical, nodded slightly.

"I decided to *make* you eat your words, but in a positive way. One thing I'm not, Joe, is a negative person. I decided to serve up a real virtuoso turn — better parts than anyone, any *man,* could ever write. Not one, but *two* roles. Two women I'd make you believe in, lust after, and — yes, folks — obsess about."

She paused to light a cigarette, never taking her eyes from his and managing the job one-handed, the gun still squarely addressing Joe's skull. "Now here's where I have to confess to being a little naive. I mean, silly me, I actually thought that when you saw how far I've come, how convincing my work is, you might even do something for my career. Like write a piece on this smashing, tantalizing babe with the talent to make Joe McBride, or anybody else for that matter, believe *anything.*"

She smiled and shook her head. "But you don't write about

actors that you know." She laughed derisively. "No. Uh-uh. Mr. Integrity only ruins the careers of people he *doesn't* know. Well, all I can say is that even though you believed I was Amy Goode, the charming but kinky girl next door who turned out to be a cop . . . and even though you believed I was Loree, the slutty twin — Dean did, too, by the way, and Ramon, the super, so don't feel bad . . . and even though this afternoon your little girl believed I was her motherfucking savior . . . even with all that, you know what, Joe?"

"What?" he said on cue.

"The fact is you'll never know who I am!"

"What do you want?" Joe said hoarsely. "An apology? Because I — "

"How do you like this puzzle? Cool, huh? There's a company in Ohio that makes jigsaw puzzles out of anything you send them. Pricey, but don't they do a nice job?"

Joe looked into her eyes, trying to find a way to connect.

"I'm sorry," he said plainly.

"Me, too," said Nannie as if she meant it.

"Can I please just take Mollie and put her in her bed? I'll come back — I swear — and we'll talk."

"Take off your clothes, Joe."

"Listen . . ."

She waved the gun. "You don't want this going off, killing you *and* waking Mollie, do you? Dean said these old silencers aren't always a hundred percent reliable. Take off your clothes, my sweet, critical man."

He unbuttoned his shirt slowly.

"I'd love one more of those endless kisses we're so good at," she mused, "but I have a feeling you'd try something." She pointed the gun at different parts of his face, studying possibilities. Joe removed his shirt.

"Look at me, Joe," she said almost earnestly. "You've been thinking about these breasts, these lips, this face, and these legs since the day we met. And you want to know what's *really* sick? I crave you too. Off with your pants."

He stripped down and stood before her.

"Too many choices," she said, pointing the gun at her own ear. "What do you think, Joe? Have I blown it? 'Cause I could just shoot myself and be a hero, get everybody off the hook."

The thought of Mollie waking seared his brain and made him feel as if he was screaming even though he wasn't making a sound. One thought at a time, he urged himself.

"Why don't you just put it down?" Joe said as simply as he could.

She seemed to consider it, although the gun was still pointed at him.

"Okay," he said, resigned. "I guess that was a stupid thing to suggest."

"I'd have to agree," she said, a glint of charm making its way through her steely smile. Joe stared back at her, his eyes softening in hopes that hers might too. No one spoke for a few seconds.

"How about one last hot milk?" he suggested. "For old time's sake?"

She smiled. "You sweet, romantic idiot," she said. "Sure, okay. But quietly. I don't want to wake Mollie."

She ushered Joe to the kitchen, walking on the balls of her feet and motioning him to lean against the counter while she got out a pot, poured some milk, and turned on the stove, all the while training the gun on him.

Joe thought of rushing her, but realized she might get off a shot first. Even with two of six bullets gone, he didn't like the odds.

He looked up at the darkness of his own window. While Nannie lowered her eyes and spooned honey into the familiar mug, Joe saw the dim form of Gayle walk into his kitchen. Gayle reached for the light switch, but looked down before turning on the lights.

She saw this: her ex-husband, naked and in the company of a

woman in a see-through blouse. Because Nannie had her back to the window, Joe wasn't sure if Gayle could see the gun.

He knew that if Gayle turned on the light, Nannie might see it, and there was no telling what could break loose. But Gayle froze. Joe looked at her as best he could, unable to see her face clearly.

The second miracle of his week followed. Gayle did not turn on the light.

GAYLE stood across the way, her body silhouetted in the near darkness. Joe knew he couldn't make any sort of contact with her without Nannie noticing. Wishing he hadn't left the Post-it about going to the ATM, he tried to put from his mind the loathing Gayle must be feeling.

He stared at where he thought his ex-wife's eyes were. He hoped she knew that if she'd "caught" him in some sort of illicit act, he'd never be able to look her in the eye.

"We don't have much time together, Joe," said Nannie, her hands shaking as she poured milk into the mugs. "One way or the other, this night will end. What'll we do?"

Gayle slipped away from the window. A light went out in his office nook, making it completely dark in his kitchen. He couldn't tell if Gayle was watching or not.

Nannie kept Joe in her peripheral vision while bending to take two spoons from a drawer. Joe thought again of rushing her, but she was still far enough away to recover before he reached her.

"Careful, it's hot," said Nannie, pushing a mug toward Joe.

"Now, me — I don't mind hot," she added, placing her left palm over the stove's flame and holding it there for several seconds. "It isn't that it doesn't hurt. It's that I choose not to mind it." She turned off the burner and offered him the milk. Stunned, he took it, and, though he didn't have the slightest appetite, raised the cup to his lips. He thought about tossing the near-boiling liquid at her, but she seemed to be oblivious to pain at this moment.

"Let's go into the living room," she said. "And on second thought, put that mug down. I don't want you getting any ideas." She moved a few steps out into the hall, carefully motioning him to follow. They were now out of Gayle's sight.

"The last supper," she said, taking a few steps further away from him. "The prisoner ate a hearty meal of milk and honey. Did you think of this place as the land of milk and honey, Joe? That night we were together?"

"Can't I take my daughter home?" he asked again. "We can pretend this never happened." She didn't answer.

He tried to figure his options. The only choice was to stall. Everything else included the possibility of shooting.

"We have a terrific passport for Mollie, with a new name and everything. And Dean knows how to get rid of a body. I'll have a new name, too, and I'll be a busy, creative, working mom. Don't worry, Mollie'll love it. This city is no place for a kid. And Joe, I know who I am. I mean, I'm not a split personality or anything. That was just acting. When I want to just be me, I can."

"Listen," Joe said, doing an imitation of a person who was comfortable with what he'd just heard, "I'll never repeat any of this if you let . . ."

"I can't have children, Joe," she interrupted. "I had a hyster-ectomy a few months after your review came out. The doctor said my condition had been affected by stress. I thought about suing you, but critics, it turns out, are really well protected from libel laws. So I let go — which of course is the key to everything. Little by little I gave up my resentment, my hatred, my need for revenge.

233

And then you showed up and all my hard work went down the drain. The anger came right back. So I thought, What's the worst thing I could do to you? Hurt you? Ruin *your* reputation? I decided to get close to you, do a little research — like I did when I played a cop in a play and followed Amy Goode around for two weeks. I was so good at it, she never even knew. So I decided I'd find out what would hurt you most. But I'm kind of a method actress and I couldn't get into the role unless I let myself explore what there was about you I could really like. And there *are* things about you to like. I mean, you're charming, goddamn you, and you love your daughter, and you certainly understand the lost art of foreplay. Wow. Yes. You know what the scariest part was? When I told you I could love you, God help me, at that moment it felt like it was true."

She spoke as though they were old friends having a late-night chat. "Did you ever break a promise you made to yourself? What am I *talking* about? You're divorced. Well, I had an epiphany today: There isn't going to be any more divorce in Mollie's life."

Joe nodded as though what she was saying was perfectly reasonable.

"Listen to me yak. Who cares?" she said sadly, shaking her head.

"I do."

"Why don't you put your clothes on? I don't want them to find you in an undignified way. I hate this. Go ahead, get dressed."

As he reached for his shirt and began buttoning it, he heard Mollie cough. He froze, knowing that coughing almost always woke her if it began in the middle of the night.

"That's Mollie," Joe said.

"Oh, shit," whispered Nannie.

"May I go to her?" Joe asked. "I think I can get her back to sleep. But if she wakes up and I'm not there, she'll start hollering."

Mollie coughed again, this time more deeply.

"I don't like this," said Nannie, agitated. "She has to be weaned away from you, but . . ." She sighed. "In good time. Go ahead. I'll follow you." They started toward the door. Joe had his hand on the knob when she stopped him with a whisper.

"I have a headache so I'll make this simple," she said. "If Mollie doesn't go *right* back to sleep, I'm going to point this in your direction and pull the trigger. My nerves are gone. Okay?"

Looking down the barrel, Joe nodded and turned the knob.

Dean looked up as Joe opened the door. He was standing over Mollie rearranging her covers.

"Don't do that!" Joe whispered. "You'll wake her."

"Come here, Dean," Nannie said.

Dean walked out and stood next to Nannie as Joe stepped toward Mollie.

CHAPTER 34

WHILE Nannie and Dean watched through a crack in the door, Joe knelt by his daughter. She coughed again, but didn't open her eyes. From past experience, Joe knew she needed to blow her nose to stop the postnasal drip that was making her cough. Joe remembered there were tissues in the bathroom. He got up, found the box amid the array of Nannie's makeup, and quickly returned to Mollie's side.

He slid his arm around Mollie's neck, carefully pulled her up a little, and tried to reproduce the soothing tone he always used in the middle of the night when he gave her medicine. "Hi, sweetie. Daddy wants you to blow your nose." Without opening her eyes, she took the tissue from his hand and blew. So far so good.

She blew hard a second time and the sound and action of it made her eyes open halfway.

"Daddy," she mumbled, glad to see him.

"Hi," he said, doing his best to seem normal.

"We waited for you, but I fell asleep."

"I'm sorry," Joe said. "My . . . meeting went late."

"Nannie's nice. I had three cups of hot chocolate. Is that okay?"

"Sure. Now go back to sleep."

"Are we having a sleepover?"

"Yes, but we have to be very quiet. . . ."

"Will you lie next to me, Daddy? Till I fall asleep?"

"Of course." He curled up at her side. He couldn't shake a chill and hoped that Mollie didn't feel his trembling. He could make out a piece of Nannie's shoulder through the open crack of the door. Nannie's eyes moved into his line of sight and she raised her eyebrows at him impatiently.

"I wasn't afraid with Nannie, Daddy. She's nice," Mollie said through a yawn.

"That's . . . great," Joe whispered softly. Terrified he'd lose control, he took deep breaths to stop his shaking. After a few minutes, Mollie's breathing became heavy. She was asleep again.

Joe waited a moment to be sure, then stood carefully and went to the door, re-joining Nannie. Dean was now sitting on the living-room couch.

"Nicely done," she whispered, closing the door again. She backed Joe a few feet toward her service door, away from where Mollie lay.

He kept his mouth shut and looked at the gun, now pointed at his mouth. If there were four bullets in it, the odds were two-to-one that her first shot would stop him. If he beat those odds, though, he might wrest the gun from her before she got off a second shot. She lifted the gun slowly, holding her arm out straight and looking at him through the gun's little sight as though he were a great distance away and she wanted to be sure she wouldn't miss.

"Dean," she said. "I think it's time."

Joe straightened up as best he could and faced her.

"You sure?" asked Dean.

"Yes," she said, irritated. "Go to the roof and see if every-thing's okay."

Dean moved toward the front door. "Don't be in a hurry is all I'm sayin'," he urged, stopping with his hand on the knob. "Can I tell him something?"

"What?" answered Nannie impatiently.

"I wasn't sure this was such a good idea," Dean explained to Joe. "But then she showed me that review you wrote on that cable movie." He shook his head with disdain.

Joe blinked. "What movie?" he asked carefully.

"What movie?" repeated Dean disgustedly as though Joe must be faking. "That one called *Three Women* that made heroines out of mothers who killed their unborn."

Joe thought for a second. "I didn't say they were heroines," he protested as reasonably as he could. "All I did was praise the movie for dramatizing both sides of the issue."

"Whatta you mean?" Dean asked, confused, looking toward Nannie.

"Just get going," Nannie said sharply to Dean.

"It's a tough issue," said Joe, ignoring Nannie, trying to keep the discussion alive. "Nobody *likes* abortion — "

"Maybe I should see the movie," Dean suggested to Nannie.

"Out!" she spat, her voice rising.

"She said you sent yourself straight to hell for that one," Dean continued, although Joe thought he detected a trace of doubt in his voice. "So . . . nothing that happens tonight matters — ya hear what I'm sayin'?"

"Well," said Joe. "What I hear is that you're a man of con-science."

"Oh, please," said Nannie, under her breath.

Dean looked hesitantly to Nannie and then back to Joe, before walking out the front door and closing it quietly.

Nannie looked at Joe as though expecting him to speak, but he didn't.

"He's a little zealous," she said, "but he's good with kids. Now, Joe — I want you to count down from ten. When you get to one, I'm going to pull the trigger. It's better Dean isn't here. He's the remorseful type. Now . . . count."

He hesitated. She steadied the gun and whispered, "Simon *says* count."

He made himself breathe. "Ten," he said, finally. "Nine . . ."

"It's almost like *you're* pulling the trigger," Nannie said rationally. "You get to be your own executioner, in a way. When you say 'one,' it's over. Keep going."

Instead of his life flashing before his eyes, all Joe saw were shadows of what lay in store for his daughter.

"Eight . . ."

"Good . . ."

"Seven . . ."

"Your last deadline, Joe . . ."

"Six . . ."

"You sound sexy. You know that . . . ?"

"Five . . ."

There was a knock on the back door, a foot from where Nannie stood, and then the door swung open.

W ITH the door diverting Nannie's attention for a split second, Joe surprised himself. Having figured the odds, having begun a literal countdown to his own execution, two chances in six that the first chamber would be empty suddenly seemed good enough.

He experienced it in a kind of slow motion. At first Nannie's head turned toward the sound of the door, but she quickly collected herself and forced her full attention back on Joe. As the back door opened slowly, Dean swept through the front entrance yelling, "No!" He flew right by Joe, lunging at the gun in Nannie's hand. Gayle peeked in the back door, holding a knife from Joe's kitchen.

"Don't!" Dean cried to Nannie. Nannie did her best to keep the gun trained on Joe. Dean, seeing her intention, sprinted toward her like a Secret Service agent and got between Joe and the gun just as Nannie squeezed the trigger and the .38 popped silently. It took a second for Joe to realize that he hadn't been shot as Dean slammed against the wall and looked up at Nannie, holding his thigh in agony.

"Somebody took the planks away," he moaned.

Gayle moved into the room as a now purple-faced Nannie pulled the trigger a second time at Joe, who lunged to grab the end of the silencer.

This time the click was hollow and metallic. No other sound cut the air until Joe grabbed Nannie's arm and cracked her wrist against the wall, dislodging the .38, which fell to the floor. Gayle stood frozen. Joe grabbed Nannie and swung her into the wall. Her forehead smacked against the edge of the door frame and she went down, holding her good hand against the gash on her head.

Gayle, bewildered and terrified, held the knife raised.

"No!" Joe said, holding Nannie as Dean writhed. "Pick up the gun."

Stunned into silence, Gayle grabbed the .38 from the floor and held it on Nannie and Dean. Joe had Nannie in a hammerlock, her wrist apparently broken.

"Oh, God," she cried in pain.

"Quiet!" Joe whispered.

Her body went limp. Blood trickled from her head to the floor.

From the bedroom, Mollie called, "Daddy! Can you come here, please?"

"Gayle," Joe said. Dazed, she looked at him and blinked. "Listen." Gayle started to speak. "Don't ask questions," Joe ordered. "Give me the gun. I'm going to take these two into the living room. Mollie's in that room — there."

"Daddy!"

"Mollie's okay," Joe continued feverishly. "She just woke up." Gayle was in shock and seemed faint. "Look at me," Joe repeated. "Gayle!" She found his eyes. "Mollie has no idea what's going on. I can't explain. Just do what I ask. Okay?"

Gayle nodded. She seemed more alert. Joe reached out a hand and she placed the gun in it.

"Take Mol back to my place. Then call downstairs and tell the police to come up to nine B."

"Daddy!" called Mollie, more insistently.

"Go," Joe said to Gayle.

Gayle was frozen, staring at Joe as though they'd never met.

"Don't make me explain, dammit!" Joe said. "Go on!"

She started for the bedroom door.

Nannie looked at Dean. "Don't you say a goddamn word!" she barked. Dean stared back at her.

Joe shoved them, shuffling and barely able to stand, into the living room so Mollie wouldn't see them on her way out. He pushed Dean into a chair. Nannie bent over the sofa and started to cry. Joe pushed her mouth into a pillow to quiet her, making sure she could breathe. Blood stained the pillow in pea-sized spots. She tried to scream and Joe pushed the pillow harder.

He heard Gayle and Mollie move to the back door.

"Mommy, are we *all* having a sleepover?"

"Uh-huh," said Gayle blankly, ushering Mollie down the hallway.

"I want to say bye-bye to Nannie," protested Mollie sleepily.

"I don't think so," answered Gayle.

"Mommy!" Mollie shrieked suddenly. "That's blood! Oh, Mommy! Is Nannie all right? Where's Daddy?" She began to wail as Gayle pushed her through the door and it closed behind them.

Joe's family, such at it was, was safe.

He released Nannie, letting her stand.

"Shoot me, Joe."

He wasn't back on firm ground yet. He just stared at her.

"Please," she urged in a strangled whimper.

Dean sat shaking his head, tears in his eyes. Joe wondered how long it could take for the police to arrive.

"I meant it when I said I was sorry," Joe said.

"I know," she answered.

They heard footsteps in the hallway and Officer Morosini rushed in.

"Are you okay?" he asked Joe, simultaneously seeing Nannie and Dean.

"I think so," Joe said. Morosini moved to Nannie, made her lie down on the floor, and improvised a bandage for her forehead, which was still bleeding almost as much as Dean's thigh.

Dean sat eerily quiet, his mind churning.

"Call nine-one-one," Morosini ordered Joe, who moved to the phone. By the time he'd finished the call, Kerrigan and Detective Riolo had arrived with two uniformed cops in tow.

"What the fuck is going on?" Kerrigan demanded when he saw the room.

Nannie raised her head slightly, defiantly pointed at Joe, and announced, "This man shot my boyfriend."

Everybody's head whipped around to Joe. "He shot him," continued Nannie in righteous indignation, "with the gun he's holding on me."

Joe was too stunned to speak.

"He would've killed him," said Nannie a little groggily, beginning to cry harder. "And he would've killed me, too, if his ex-wife hadn't come in here and saved my life. He's a monster!" she screamed, holding her injured wrist up to the gash in her forehead. "Look what he did to me!"

Joe realized in a flash that Gayle had virtually no idea about any of what had happened. Beads of sweat popped from his temples as he imagined what Gayle's version of tonight might sound like.

"Officer," Joe said, trying to keep calm.

"Just a second," interrupted Kerrigan politely, pulling his own revolver. "Drop it," he said to Joe, who released the .38. Riolo bent to pick it up.

Kerrigan walked into the bedroom with the two uniformed

cops and came right out. The cops all seemed to be making an effort not to stare at Nannie's blouse.

"Nine-one-one's on the way," said Officer Morosini.

"Okay," said Kerrigan, who was still breathing hard. "You want to tell me what happened, Mr. McBride? I know your daughter's all right."

"*She* fired the shot," Joe explained trying to think clearly, indicating Nannie. "I'm not sure who she was trying to hit, but she hit him."

"Oh brother," said Nannie, as though Joe had just whipped up the most preposterous story imaginable.

Kerrigan looked at Nannie, then back at Joe and Dean, then gloomily over to Riolo and the other two. "Fellas, take a few pictures." He moved a step toward Nannie. "Meanwhile, let's hear from you, Miss . . . Pritchard, right?" She nodded. "What happened?"

"I think he wanted to kill me," said Nannie earnestly, holding up her wrist, which had swollen like Popeye's. "His idea of love-making." Kerrigan looked at Joe and scratched his head.

"Listen," Joe protested. "This is insane. I may have been trying to kill her, but she was going to shoot me." Kerrigan's eyes popped. "No," Joe added quickly. "Let me rephrase that. I wasn't trying to kill her." His thoughts were swirling. "I was defending myself."

"Oh, Joe," said Nannie, as though he ought to be ashamed. "I *did* have his daughter here, Officer. But that was the arrangement Joe and I had. We agreed that he'd pick her up here. Please get me . . . to a doctor."

Joe fought to keep his voice down. "Are you suggesting that I —"

"Lemme get this straight," said Kerrigan impatiently. "Your ex-wife told us that you left a note saying you were going to the ATM. Then she sees you naked in the kitchen with Miss Pritchard and Miss Pritchard dressed . . . like this. Your ex-wife said she didn't know what the hell was up so she waited a few minutes 'cause she didn't see the gun at first. When she saw the gun, she freaked, rushed down here, you all had a fight for the gun, this guy gets shot, and you told your ex to get the kid out of here. That's what *she* told us."

"Mr. McBride was my lover and became increasingly jealous about my relationship with this man," Nannie said, indicating Dean. Dean was alarmingly quiet, listening closely, the throw pillow held to his thigh. "Joe and I had a fight about it this afternoon and he threatened to kill me. Tonight he saw me with Dean from his kitchen window, stormed in here with the gun, and just . . . went nuts. Dean got the gun away from him and I was holding it on Joe, that's true, but just to defend myself." She dissolved into sobs.

It was a strong performance, on a par with her latest. Joe imagined his life tied up in court forever.

The door swung open and an Emergency Medical team arrived. Kerrigan pointed at Nannie and Dean. The EMS guys moved to her and she screamed when one touched her wrist, but they quickly got her onto a stretcher.

"Where's the other stretcher?" Kerrigan asked impatiently.

"We only got a call for one," the EMS guy said.

"I can wait," Dean whispered. "Take her first."

"Are you allergic to any medications?" one of the EMS guys asked Nannie.

"No more questions," she said deliriously. "Not without a lawyer." Two cops helped the men move the stretcher through the front door.

"Joe?" she called feebly at the door while Riolo held it open for her. Joe looked up. She was pale, but beautiful. "I'll never stop loving you."

Kerrigan, Joe, and Dean sat silent for a moment while Kerrigan scribbled notes on his pad. Dean looked out the window, far away in thought.

"Miss . . . Pritchard and I didn't have a fight this afternoon," Joe said, breaking the silence. "I never saw her this afternoon. I was working."

"Doing what? Writing a review or something?"

"Exactly."

"Did you break Miss Pritchard's wrist?"

Joe thought about lying but had the distinct feeling it would come back to haunt him. "Yes," he admitted. "To get the gun out of her hand."

"It's your gun?"

"No. I don't own a gun."

Kerrigan made a note.

"May I call my wife?" Joe asked.

"You mean your ex?" Kerrigan corrected as though he'd caught Joe in a little lie. "Sure. G'head."

Joe called and spoke into the machine until Gayle picked up.

"Is Mollie asleep?" he asked.

"Yes. She's so out of it that I think I convinced her she just had a bad dream. I won't know till tomorrow. I hate you for this —"

"I have to answer some questions," Joe interrupted. "Go to sleep."

"You think *I* don't have questions?" said Gayle. "How do you expect me to sleep?"

"Please, Gayle. Try. Use my bed. I'll wake you when I get in."

"Joe, I really — "

He hung up.

"May I go now?" Joe asked.

The two other cops were waiting to talk to Kerrigan, who looked at Joe for a few seconds before answering.

"I may not have to hold you tonight," Kerrigan said.

"Hold me?" Joe shot back, flabbergasted. "What are you talking about?"

"Listen, guy," Kerrigan went on. "I'm kinda tired here from

combing this entire fucking borough for your daughter. Don't get me wrong. I'm happy she's okay. But we got a shooting here, I got only two possible suspects, and each of you says the other one did it. I also got an assault *and* a possible kidnapping. Not to mention I talked to Detective Goode in Queens, and she told me how you lied to her about your name — "

"I explained that to her — "

"Just a second!" Kerrigan said sharply. "You *seem* to be on the level, but Miss Pritchard's version isn't out of the realm of possibility. You were lovers, and listen — I don't want to analyze one more fucking thing here tonight. Nights like this make me wish I'd taken up my uncle's offer to become a sanitation worker." He looked down at Dean. "So let's hear from you, bucko. You've been awful quiet for somebody who just took a bullet. Who did it?"

Dean paused for what seemed like an hour. "I shot myself," he said calmly.

Kerrigan stuck his finger into his ear, as if to clear it. "What're you sayin'?"

Dean looked at Joe, who looked back at him. Something in Dean's eyes told Joe to keep his mouth shut.

"I'm saying . . . what I'm saying," said Dean.

"Why'd you wait till now to say it?" Kerrigan barked.

"I was scared." Dean spoke to Kerrigan but looked at Joe all the while. "Mr. McBride didn't shoot me. The gun went off by accident."

"Whose gun is it?" asked Kerrigan.

"Mine," said Dean.

"Is it registered?" said Kerrigan.

Dean shook his head. "No."

"Bingo," said Kerrigan. "The night isn't a total loss. Mr. McBride, you got anything to say?" Kerrigan asked.

Joe held Dean's look. He wasn't sure, but he felt that Dean was trying somehow to protect and hold onto a woman he hopelessly loved. Kerrigan got up and walked around a little.

"How'd she get her wrist cracked, guys?" he snapped. "And a lump on her head?"

"I tackled her," drawled Dean, "because for a second I was worried the gun she was holding might go off. She was mad at Mr. McBride and I didn't want something bad to happen, so I just went for her, you know, to disarm her. She landed on her wrist and her head hit the door frame going down." Dean pointed to a smudge of blood on the wall, and as Kerrigan walked closer to get a look, Dean turned to Joe and nodded, as if urging him to accept this version.

"So what are you sayin'?" asked Kerrigan. "I should go home and forget this? I can't do that. Nobody has to press charges, guys, but I gotta file reports."

Joe held Dean's gaze and imagined a lifetime in court trying to prove Nannie guilty of anything. He thought of Mollie being dragged up to testify and the damage it would cause, he thought of how effective Nannie would undoubtedly be in that particular forum, and visualized the media circus that would surely ensue.

"I think," Joe said, choosing his words carefully, "that you should get this man to a hospital and I should go to bed. In your report, you can say that I'm willing to consider . . . that my daughter wasn't abducted. I've been under a lot of pressure. I haven't been sure of anything lately." He hoped it was the last lie he'd ever have to tell.

Kerrigan looked at Dean. "I'm taking you in on an illegal weapons charge, Sunny Jim. Come on. We'll go to the hospital in the squad car. Who knows when the fucking EMS'll get here, pardon my French." He looked out the window. "You don't seem like a liar, Mr. McBride, but, hey, you lied to Amy Goode — "

"I was nervous. It was stupid, but I explained that to her — "

Kerrigan moved closer to Joe and spoke quietly. "Father to

father, I'd like to trust you. But I've been burned by people I trusted. I'm keeping a man downstairs. Don't leave the building — capisce? We'll talk in the morning."

Joe nodded reluctantly and started for the service door.

"Where you going?" asked Kerrigan.

"Her back door leads to my back door," Joe answered. "It's easier than going all the way down to the lobby."

"Convenient," Kerrigan observed drily, pushing Dean ahead of him.

Joe backed out toward the kitchen door watching them leave, then ran up the stairway, past his apartment to the roof. He walked around on the crunchy gravel, turned a corner, and found two planks that had been carefully set down — a perfect bridge from his building to the next.

So Dean had lied when he'd said somebody took the planks away.

Maybe, thought Joe gratefully as he ran down the stairs to his place, Dean *was* the remorseful type.

He opened his back door and walked through the kitchen to check on Gayle and Mollie.

No one was there.

CHAPTER 37

A POST-IT from Gayle was stuck to his answering machine. It said, "I left you a memo," and had an arrow pointing to the machine. Joe hit PLAY. Her voice was tight, almost out of breath.

"Listen. I'm not subjecting Mollie to any more of this. Or myself. Our agreement explicitly states that you provide 'a nurturing, safe, appropriate atmosphere' for our daughter on your visits. If you'd like to argue about this through lawyers, fine. I told Mollie you have a lot of work to do, and that she'd talk to you tomorrow. She's exhausted and it's the middle of the night so I'm sure she'll sleep in the car seat on the way home. But I want my daughter to wake up where I know she's safe."

Joe punched up Gayle's number. At this hour and with no traffic, he figured she might already be home. Her machine answered.

"It's me," Joe said after the beep. "Pick up. I need to talk to you."

"Go ahead," Gayle said, switching the machine off with a sharp squelch, "but if you ever want your daughter to spend another night with you as long as you live — this better be good."

Joe reminded himself that losing his temper with Gayle always made her dig in harder.

"You know, you saved my life tonight," he began. "And Mollie's."

"I should've called the police first, but when I saw that gun pointed at you, I was afraid there might not be time," she said.

There was a long silence.

"Thank you," whispered Joe, his voice about to break.

"It's not as if I don't love you, you know," she said quietly. When Joe didn't speak right away, she sniffed and jumped in. "What now?" she demanded. "How am I supposed to trust you with her after this? And what the hell *was* going on over there tonight? I'm tired and I'm so angry I can't talk. You talk."

Knowing his future with Mollie was riding on it, Joe told Gayle everything about the time since he'd moved in. It took close to half an hour. She railed and cried and told him she hated him, but she didn't hang up.

"Wait a second," she said suddenly. "I think I heard Mollie. Hang on." She put the phone down and Joe looked out the window at the dark kitchen one flight down. Gayle came back and picked up the phone.

"I have a minor emergency here," she said, hushed. "We were so crazed leaving that I just realized Mollie's bing is missing. It's not here. She's awake now and she's hysterical. She's *never* slept without it and I don't think I want tonight to be her first try. You wouldn't believe the explaining I've already had to do . . . never mind! Just find the damn blanket." She hung up.

Joe did a quick look through the apartment. Realizing it must be in Nannie's bedroom, he sank to a chair in despair. Then it occurred to him that her back door might still be unlocked. He jumped up and ran through his kitchen and down the stairs.

He turned the doorknob at 9B. It opened.

Moving through her apartment for what he felt sure would be the last time, he was headed toward the bedroom when a voice behind him spoke his name.

"M R. McBride," said a startled Detective Riolo. "What are you doing here?"

"Oh, my God, you scared me," said Joe, trying to catch his breath. "I'm sorry. I have a little emergency here and I was afraid if I called anybody, I might not be able to get it solved tonight."

"You shouldn't be here," Detective Riolo said.

"I know. But I think my daughter's security blanket is in the bedroom," Joe said plaintively. "Please. She's five and she's never once slept without it. I just have to know if it's lost. Could you take a look for me? It's about this big." He held up his hands to show the size. "And it's pink."

Riolo shook his head. "I should call somebody first. . . ."

"Please," Joe begged unabashedly. "My daughter can't stop crying."

Riolo exhaled sharply, went into the bedroom, and returned with Mollie's bing.

"I could catch hell for this," said Riolo. "But here." He handed the blanket to Joe.

"Thank you," Joe said, "with all my heart."

He hurried back to his apartment, grabbed his wallet, and started for the lobby. Remembering that there was a cop down there and that he was under a house arrest of sorts, he quietly took the fire stairs up to the roof. Dean's unused bridge was still in place. Terrified of heights, Joe took a deep breath and climbed up onto the planks on all fours. He stood up, his knees shaking and the planks wobbling. If I make it across, he told himself, the Mets will never lose another game — ever. He tried not to look down. Frozen in fear for a moment, he thought of Mollie crying and suddenly made a dash across, touching down on the other building's rooftop after three long strides. He caught his breath, found the door, and, just as Dean had planned, pushed it open, scampered down the small stairway to the elevator, and rode to the lobby. He exited the building feeling like a criminal, crossed the street to the Citibank ATM, withdrew a hundred dollars, and hailed a taxi on Madison.

It was a straight shot across Ninety-seventh Street and up the Henry Hudson Parkway to Hastings. When he got to Scenic Drive thirty-five minutes later, a light was on in an upstairs room. Gayle was apparently still awake.

Joe had the driver stop a short distance from the house. The night was clearing, a few stars were showing and the wind had died. He took Mollie's bing from his pocket, tiptoed to the front door, laid it on the doormat, rang the bell, and walked away.

Back in the cab, he watched until he saw Gayle open the door. She looked around quizzically in all directions, then down at her feet, finally noticing the tired little blanket. She put a hand to her face, bent down, and picked it up. She looked toward Joe's cab. He rolled down his window, put his arm out, waved, and told the driver to head back to the city. As they pulled away, Gayle waved back.

*　　*　　*

Nannie Pritchard's court-appointed lawyer advised her to go along with Dean's account of the shooting. As a result, no charges were brought against her and she apparently left town, because Joe never saw a light in her kitchen again. He soon found a notice under his door from the co-op board informing tenants that the apartment had been vacated and was about to be put on the market.

Dean copped a plea for illegal possession of a firearm and was sentenced to six months at Rikers Island.

The premiere of *Everybody's a Critic* was a media phenomenon as great as Brutus Clay could have hoped for. Clay replaced Joe with a actor who'd played a critic on *Murphy Brown*. Sandy Moss, an overnight sensation, was soon asked to appear on *Letterman*. To record-breaking catcalls, Sandy entered barefoot wearing a beach thong with a skimpy top. During their few minutes of banter, Dave kiddingly dared her to "chuck the T-shirt, woman, for goodness' sake." While Paul Shaffer and the band played *The Stripper*, Sandy took Dave up on his dare, flinging her top to the audience, and within weeks Brutus Clay's wildest ratings dreams came true. Twice weekly on *Everybody's a Critic*, Sandy managed tantalizing variations on her Letterman appearance and the Nielsens soared.

True to his word, Clay bought the *Dispatch* — but far from making Joe, or anyone else, its editor, he promptly closed the 120-year-old paper, sold its fine old building to developers for a hefty profit, and put Joe out of a job.

After a fling with Roger Shectman, Mary Beth Wise was fired from Paramount, made a lucrative deal at another studio to write, develop, and produce films — none of which, she confessed in a late-night phone attempt to get something going again with Joe, ever got made.

Joe sold his place and set about finding a modest apartment with a partial view of the Hudson River in Yonkers, about a mile from Gayle and Mollie. Gayle wasn't happy about it, so he kept as much distance as possible and contented himself with nightly phone calls and occasional weekends with Mollie. Gayle took Mollie to a therapist to work through the nightmares she was having about the blood in Nannie's apartment. Gradually, the dreams subsided.

Joe could see that the continued shuttling of Mollie back and forth between two residences was taking its toll. She told him fervently one Sunday that she wanted one room, one home, one closet, one toothbrush. She also wanted Joe and Gayle to get back together. Joe told her he couldn't give her that, but asked himself if he should force his kid to grow up in two places, with a mother who might always resent her father.

He gave up weekend custody, which pleased Gayle enough that she agreed to let him take Mollie to school and dinner several times a week. It turned out that he saw his daughter more than he had before.

Although he received an offer from the *New York Post* to be its second-string TV critic, Joe accepted a job writing for a Yonkers daily, the *Herald Statesman*. His new assignment was a Monday-Wednesday-Friday column called *P.S.*

Gayle broke up with her boyfriend, Brian. She was sure Joe would take up with some Hastings hussy or divorcee, but he didn't. In light of the Dean-Nannie potential disease chain, he got tested for HIV. The test was negative but his doctor said it would be six months before he could be absolutely sure and advised safe sex, which wasn't that tough for Joe since for once in his life he wasn't practicing any sex at all.

Gradually, he and Gayle became accustomed to seeing each other on school mornings. As Christmas approached, Joe suggested again that Gayle take Mollie to visit his mother, who was barely holding on and still refusing to check into a hospital. Unbeknownst to Mollie and Gayle, Joe followed by air the next day, and on Christmas Eve, he surprised them at his mother's house. In the spirit of the holidays, Gayle didn't throw him out.

They stayed for ten days, Joe at the Island Motel and they at the house. On New Year's Eve, they banged pots out the window at midnight, and Joe sat up with his mother after Mollie and Gayle had gone to sleep.

"Told you you should move," she said. She had a coughing attack.

"You're on a roll now, Ma," he said.

"Yeah," she agreed. "One in a row."

She stubbed out the cigarette, darkened, and endured another bout of hacking. Joe held the tissue box out for her, but she fell asleep. He adjusted her blankets to cover her chest and neck, tiptoed out of the creaky house, and drove back to the motel.

He didn't know till the next morning that he'd heard her last words.

Mollie met almost everyone on the Island at the funeral and to Joe's surprise asked if she could help scatter some of her grandmother's ashes over the snow that also covered Joe's father's grave. At the moment Mollie let the ashes fly, Gayle took Joe's hand. He figured it had been involuntary on her part, but he dropped to his knees and held on in the awful cold.

The three traveled back to New York together and Mollie invited Joe to join them for take-out pizza the night they got back. Gayle didn't overrule it and for the first time ever, he sat at her dinner table.

The three began having dinner together once a week after that, and Joe's old friend Buddy Monk came out for an occasional visit.

One night after Buddy, Joe, Gayle, and Mollie finished dinner at a little Chinese restaurant Mollie liked because they gave her extra fortune cookies, Mollie and Gayle excused themselves to use the bathroom. As she herded Mollie through the door, Gayle caught Joe's eye and smiled.

"Let's go bobbing for señoritas after the womenfolk depart," Buddy suggested.

"I'm gonna turn in," said Joe. "I'm taking Mol to school in the morning and I've been invited to talk to her first-grade class about writing. They're doing their own play."

The check arrived and Buddy reached for it halfheartedly, allowing Joe to do the honors. Gayle and Mollie returned and Mollie cracked open her fortune cookie. "What does it say, Daddy?" she asked, holding it out to him. Gayle took it from her, pretending to read it.

"You will have a small wedding in your own backyard," she intoned. Mollie made a face as Gayle handed the little slip of paper to Joe, who read the actual words to himself: "Forgiving is not forgetting." He slipped the fortune into his wallet as they got up. Gayle buttoned Mollie's jacket as Buddy moved in close to Joe.

"Have you, like, sworn off the ladies, Joseph?" Buddy asked, perplexed. "I don't get it. Aren't you and Gayle divorced?"

"It's not exactly my idea of family," Joe whispered, looking at his ex-wife and daughter. "But on a good day, that's what it feels like."

A FEW months later, Joe received a small box in the mail with a Montana postmark. It had been sent to him in care of what used to be the *Dispatch,* and David Teng, not knowing how to reach Joe, forwarded it to Ferdy Levin. Joe went to Ferdy's one night to pick it up and have dinner with his ex-editor. Caroline was in bed, her health having given out when the *Dispatch* had shut down.

"I like *P.S.,*" said Ferdy, who seemed frail himself. "Maybe Brutus Clay did you a favor."

He led Joe into the dining room where the package was waiting. Joe opened it to find a boxed jigsaw puzzle, which he and Ferdy began assembling as they listened to a Mets-Phillies game over a few nonalcoholic beers.

"If the Mets win tonight, they clinch the pennant, don't they?" asked Ferdy. Joe nodded and smiled, knowing the Mets owed it all to his not smoking.

"If we finish this puzzle before the game's over, the Mets will win," Joe predicted.

At ten o'clock, Ferdy decided to go to bed, asking Joe to let himself out when he left.

"Hey, Ferdy," Joe called out. "If the Mets take the pennant, I won't light up till they win the World Series."

Ferdy chuckled and waved good night.

Joe worked, growing increasingly uneasy, and placed the final piece into the middle of the puzzle with the game in the eighth inning and the Mets ahead, 1–0.

The finished puzzle was a photo of Nannie, dressed in Joe's *ER* T-shirt, smiling enchantingly with one hand hovering over a candle's flame while the other held a makeshift sign that read IF I WANT TO FIND YOU, YOU'LL NEVER KNOW IT'S ME.

Spooked and wanting to wake Ferdy, Joe disassembled the puzzle. He put it back into its box, grabbed a Winston and a pack of matches from Ferdy's bowl, and hit the street with the puzzle under his arm, feeling as though he was somehow holding Nannie's remains. Hopping a cab to Yonkers, he distractedly asked the driver to put the radio on. The Mets held on to win the game and their first playoff spot in years.

Joe started to light up. Just one drag, he told himself as his match flame was about to touch the tip of the Winston. But knowing how badly the Mets needed him, he crumbled the cigarette into the ashtray and watched the lights of Manhattan recede as the cab sped north.

After going through a tollbooth, they reached the far end of the bridge that separates the Bronx from Manhattan. Joe asked the driver to pull over to the right shoulder and stop. There was almost no traffic in either direction. Joe got out, stepped to the edge of a waist-high, rusted iron rail, and scattered the puzzle pieces over and down to the Hudson River, two hundred feet below. He watched the pieces wend their way to the smooth surface like falling leaves.

If I want to find you, you'll never know it's me.

"That's littering," the driver observed as Joe walked back to the cab.

"You're absolutely right," admitted Joe, as he plucked a twenty from his wallet and handed it to the guy. "I guess I'll just have to live with it."

"What's this?" the cabbie asked, holding up the crisp bill.

"I feel like walking," said Joe. "Keep the change."

"Yonkers has gotta be . . . five miles," said the driver, flabbergasted.

"Hey, the customer is always right," answered Joe, turning his back as the cabbie sighed, yanked the gearshift, and took off.

Joe went back to the rail and looked down again, as if he might see Annette Fontana in the river's reflection.

So wired that he felt he'd forever lost the desire to sleep, he turned and began to trudge toward Yonkers, ignoring the emerging pain of a blister opening on his right heel, his feet settling into a clip-clop rhythm. Like a song that wouldn't stop playing in his mind, the alternating voices of Amy Goode and Loree Battochi kept repeating in Joe's head. As if on autopilot, he continued along the parkway's shoulder, merging into North Broadway as he passed the Yonkers border, continuing another mile into the quiet Irish section where he lived. As he passed a commercial intersection, a solitary A&P truck interrupted the chatter of crickets as it backed up to make its late-night deliveries.

Joe continued up a steep hill, unable to shake the image of the puzzle, and kept going till he arrived, sweaty and wired, at the oak-lined side street that held the ten-unit post-war building he now called home. Not feeling even a trace of fatigue, he looked up to a sky swarming with stars and, wanting to avoid the solitude of his cramped apartment, he lay down in the deserted street. The pavement was still warm from the heat of a scorching late-summer day and the constellations above were almost as bright as when he'd sat on the dock with his mother. There was no danger of traffic; he could hear an approaching car a mile away. Sighting the Little Dipper, he found the North Star and let his mind drift to thoughts of how its twinkling light had left the star thousands of years before. It made him feel almost pleasantly insignificant and helped stave off both his loneliness and thoughts of the puzzle's message.

For someone who's made so many mistakes, he told himself, you should count your blessings. Then, remembering that a new *P.S.* was due that morning at eleven, he pulled himself to his feet and headed inside to meet his latest deadline, almost tripping in the tiny foyer over his only surviving TV set, still unplugged and unused since the day he'd moved in.